Jaishree Misra was born in Delhi and maintains an ambiguous relationship with the city. She has worked, variously and briefly, as a special needs teacher, social worker, journalist, broadcaster, writer. She is also a wife and mother. *Ancient Promises*, her first novel, garnered her wide readership. She lives in London.

JAISHREE MISRA

Accidents Like Love and Marriage

PENGUIN BOOKS

Penguin Books India (P) Ltd., 11 Community Centre, Panchsheel Park, New Delhi 110 017, India
Penguin Books Ltd., 80 Strand, London WC2R 0RL, UK
Penguin Putnam Inc., 375 Hudson Street, New York, NY 10014, USA
Penguin Books Australia Ltd., Ringwood, Victoria, Australia
Penguin Books Canada Ltd., 10 Alcorn Avenue, Suite 300, Toronto, Ontario, M4V 3B2, Canada
Penguin Books (NZ) Ltd., Cnr Rosedale and Airborne Roads, Albany, Auckland, New Zealand

First published by Penguin Books India 2001

Copyright © Jaishree Misra 2001

10 9 8 7 6 5 4 3 2 1

This is a work of fiction. Names, characters, places and incidents either are the product of
the author's imagination or are used fictitiously, and any resemblance to actual persons,
living or dead, events or locales is entirely coincidental.

For sale in the Indian Subcontinent and Singapore only.

Typeset in *PalmSprings* by SÜRYA, New Delhi
Printed at Chaman Offset Printers, New Delhi

With fondest gratitude to New Delhi for so exuberantly providing the creative fodder for this book and with many thanks to the person who insisted I send it for publication, one of Delhi's wisest, kindest, funniest, finest citizens, Khushwant Singh

1

Who are these Sachdevs anyway?

When it was all over, there were many who asked, 'Hai ji, how did this thing happen?' Tweezed eyebrows were raised in the hushed environs of the bridge room at the Delhi Gymkhana Club. Voices dropped to levels that indicated that the matter at hand was not quite a secret. (Such a thing simply did not exist in smart Delhi society, quite frankly.) This was more a kind of inexplicability, one of those unreal possibilities that life threw up sometimes. Delicious and thrilling when it happened to someone else, but filled with the terrifying prospect that it could some day, like the lottery advertisement with the spangly golden pointing finger, quite easily happen to you . . .

But here it was, happening (Thank God, said many) to the Sachdevs this time. Jagdish and Swarn Sachdev. Perfectly normal, law-abiding people by the looks of them. That was the frightening thing, they were like youji and me. Good family, quite well off, not rolling in it, mind, but comfortably off. Successful business, well-brought up children, excellent marriage of their older son to the daughter of Kammy and Manny Singh some years back. Two or three grandchildren probably by now. Time for retirement and time-share holidays, you would have thought. So why and how did this thing happen? Hoary heads shook dolefully, barely masking smirks. Men tch-tched, not forgetting to sip their single malts. Women sighed, vowing to be nicer to their husbands, because you never really knew when the tables could turn, did you? That poor Mrs Sachdev. What could have made things go so badly wrong?

There was, of course, the opposing school of thought that held that Swarn Sachdev was most deserving of it, most deserving! She did not have many friends, it had to be said. Never came to the club dinner dances, never threw lavish lunches. Of course, Swarn was perfectly capable of being nice whenever it was really required of her. But the truth was that, most of the time, she simply could not see the need for such an unnecessary and energy-consuming activity. She was, in fact, living proof of the theory that it was feasible to live an exceedingly comfortable life without having to bother being nice. Affability, she had discovered even as a young girl, was in direct proportion to effort, and effort was what Swarn did not like making. In the sapping heat of a Delhi summer, it was all 'just too, too much fuss and bother, ji'.

Her large, soft, perfumed person, usually draped in expensive chiffon saris, had a comfortable propensity for filling three-seater sofas in an unmoving, serene way. From various semireclining poses on one of her jacquard or silk surfaces, she would lazily raise an arm, the flesh hanging from its upper reaches jiggling gently, to beckon the cook, the gardener, the maid or the woman who came once a week to do her manicures and pedicures. She had great difficulty remembering their names and invariably mismatched them, calling the dhobi by the cook's name, the maid by the manicurist's and so on. They were all stupid, dumb creatures anyway who quaked and went goggle-eyed in her presence. She didn't see why she had to waste her vocal chords on them more than the bare minimum. So, once she had issued her orders—for the day's lunch, or for the flowerpots in the drawing room to be changed, or for her manicure to commence—she lapsed back into superior silence, lazily surveying her domain, which was Sachdev Mansion, 120 Main LM Road (opposite hole for cable connection), Maharaja Colony, New Delhi. This was the domain Swarn Sachdev ruled with a plump but iron fist, reluctantly relinquishing some control (but not all) of the first floor ever since her older son, Rohit, had got married and moved his wife, Neena, upstairs. Happily, Swarn still wielded considerable authority over her younger, unmarried son's apartment, the flat over the garage, Mecca to many a callow young lady who had ever suffered the misfortune of falling under Tarun's spell.

So that was the immediate world of Swarn Sachdev. Except, of course, there was also Jagdish.

Having to have a husband was one of life's cruel ironies for a woman like Swarn who did not especially enjoy male company—all that factory talk about weft and weave, and, even worse, cricket and politics. She had no particular desire for sex, and she knew that easy access to that messy, exhausting business was often the only reason for which men of her generation in India got married at all. To top it all, she did not especially want to have anything to do with dirty laundry and picking up after her man. Wifely jobs that some women, she thought scornfully, made careers out of, the silly fools. Swarn could, technically, have been a very good feminist had she lived in another place and time. But Delhi was where she had always lived and Delhi's rules were the ones by which she abided as best as she could.

Despite all that, it would have been difficult not to think of Swarn as a perfectly dutiful wife. Even though the thought of her husband's dirty laundry filled her with dread, she still endeavoured to have one of the maids pick up all the clothes he threw around when he returned from his factory at the end of the day. She supervised and sorted, albeit from a distance as she did not like any sort of assault on her delicate olfactory senses, and her husband's smells were no exception to this rule. She would then send those items that needed to be washed off to the dhobi. No loving hand washing of her husband's delicates, oh no ji! But she made sure the maid put the white leather slippers Jagdish favoured in the pull-out bottom shelf of his cupboard and hung his polyester safari suits on plastic hangers that would not stain them with rust. What did it matter that she had not (certainly in the last three decades) had a direct hand in any thoughtful little gesture towards old Jagdish? Supervision and delegation, that was the trick, she often liked to think.

Unfortunately delegation was not possible in the matter of sex, and so Swarn had succumbed on the odd occasion (albeit with eyes closed and lips tightly puckered) to having sex with her husband. Within the first four years of their marriage she had triumphantly borne him their two sons. Going by all the rules of the city and the society in which she lived, Swarn Sachdev was a very worthy wife indeed. There were few people who knew for certain that she wasn't really anything of the sort. The most obvious being Jagdish himself who had learnt (about ten days into their marriage) that he would always and only occupy a very small part of Swarn's heart. As long as no other man was the cause of this and as long as the rest of the world failed to notice that Swarn was an unloving wife, there seemed no reason for him to do anything drastic about this state of affairs. Except for gradually spending more and more time at his factory, making weft and weave the fabric of his life.

Oh, yes, Swarn was one of life's lucky ones. Fortunate things seemed to happen to her for no other reason than that she was Swarn, which could seem like an unfair state of affairs given how little she seemed to work at earning her good fortune. Not that she would agree with that assessment, of course. She would, in fact, have been genuinely surprised to hear her life described as charmed, widening those lovely eyes in disbelief. She would then proceed to remind you of the many reasons for which she believed life sometimes treated her quite unfairly. 'Varicose veins, my Tarun refusing to get married and always turning up with this girlfriend or that, a husband who is only interested in his factory and all that union-shooniun rubbish.' Then she would sigh heavily and say to whoever was listening, 'Life . . . life is not always easy, ji.'

Swarn was not to know, of course, that for the first time ever, life was actually going to deal her a dud hand, a turkey. Not just another varicose vein that would show up, shiny, plump and green, on her thigh. Not merely another litany of problems at the factory that would have Jagdish coming home at midnight, demanding to be fed parathas and dahi after the cook had turned in for the night. Not even her current favourite grouse—the various bits of giggly fluff that her errant younger son, Tarun, trailed around with, while showing no interest whatsoever in the business. No, this would be far, far worse. This was, whatever anyone said, the genuine article. For the first time Swarn would have a real problem to grapple with. For the first time ever her world would seem to be in the precarious position of shattering incontrovertibly into little bits.

To understand some of it, one must be reminded of one fact: All of Rohit and Tarun's bits of fluff had so far been home-grown (i.e., desi, Indian, the known and the familiar). Now something new and unusual was on the horizon. This was the first of the problems. A firangi, a white woman, was on her way into the Sachdevs' lives. A devil unfamiliar to Swarn. This pretty, curly-haired firangi was lurking in the wings of Swarn's languorous, enviable life, awaiting her entrance mere days away.

The irony of the situation would later strike everyone concerned (after it was all over, of course). For the first time it was not that Tarun wasn't showing any interest in getting married, but the reverse. It wasn't that Neena was going off and doing her own thing in her annoyingly modern daughter-in-law way. It wasn't even that the normally dependable Rohit was concentrating on his wife and children as usual, to the exclusion of his poor mother's needs. Everything, just about everything, was going to unhitch itself from its normal moorings and float off into unknown waters. What the Sachdevs were drifting so inexorably towards was uncharted territory, the foreign, the unfamiliar. The kind of things they knew about only from watching *The Bold and the Beautiful* every Thursday night. Now here they were, all those blonde, coiffed and lacquered Western problems, lining up, readying themselves to invade Swarn's home. Poor Swarn's domain was already, if you looked closely, starting to tilt gently to one side as if in terrified anticipation of what was to come.

Now, for the most part, the Sachdev boys had more or less toed the parental line, particularly Rohit. A rather less cavalier version of his brother, Rohit was no stranger to female charms, but he held an equally powerful regard for his vast inheritance and his father's proclivity for lifelong grudges. Without wishing to put either of these to the test, Rohit had, five years ago, meekly agreed without much preamble to an arranged marriage to Neena Singh, daughter of an equally wealthy Delhi business family. It did not matter that a certain comely young collegian had cried bitter tears into her pillow on the night of Rohit's engagement, tearing up letter after letter that he had written to her in the wooing months. 'I'm sorry, sweetie, but my father will kill you and me if we don't call it off now,' Rohit had said to the tearful young woman by way of explanation, looking for all his life as though he were indeed genuinely regretful. 'It's too, too dangerous to keep meeting you, sweetie,' he had added, 'except just maybe once in a while after I get this marriage out of the way.' To his dismay, this consolation had merely set off a fresh bout of weeping.

To his credit, Rohit never did see the young collegian again and was soon quite deeply in love with his wife, the fashionable, pretty, young Neena. Jagdish had stood back and eyed his handiwork with satisfaction. 'See, did I not tell you that Manny Singh's daughter would make a perfect match for our Rohit?' he had pronounced to his wife as they stood on their balcony, watching the younger Sachdev couple drive off in their brand new Tata Safari to a honeymoon cottage in Manali. Gifts, of course, from Manny Singh.

Swarn knew that Manny Singh's sugar mills and millions were the real reason for Jagdish's pleasure in this new alliance, but it would have been so much better if Neena's mother, Kammy, had been a little less à la mode and spent a little less time rushing around doing all that stupid social work. Wearing trousers at age forty-five and going into villages to teach village women how to divorce their men! Kammy, much to Swarn's barely masked disgust, had spent her entire first visit to the Sachdev household talking in a loud brassy voice about her work with some NGO that gave free legal advice to villagers. In Swarn's mind, work was only that activity (usually pursued by men, unless of course there was pressing monetary need) that paid back money in reasonable quantities. Not something that involved indulging in meaningless chitter-chatter with other women, all from supposedly decent homes, who were more interested in looking after other people than their own husbands and children. God knows what values the trouser-wearing Kammy might have passed on to her daughter. Swarn even suspected that her elder son's mother-in-law smoked ('Look at the colour of her lips, ji—purple!'). It also pained Swarn that the Singhs had mutilated perfectly reasonable names (Kamlesh and Manpreet) to the ridiculous Kammy and Manny, for heaven's sake! They had then given their children names that could have come from any old place in the world—Neena and Danny, ai hai!

Less than twenty-four hours after her son's marriage, Swarn had a premonition of doom about this new relationship and had retired to her room, complaining of a migraine. Jagdish knew better than to disturb his wife when she was having one of her migraines. He did not want to spoil the warm happy glow the recent nuptials had left him with. Everything had been done in exceedingly good style. He had known Manny Singh would spare no expense for his only daughter's wedding. The minister sahib must have been impressed. And the industries secretary too. All the trappings had been laid on, thank God, even some that Jagdish himself would never have thought of. Gifts of saris and suit lengths for all the boy's relatives—Manny had even remembered to buy a sari for the minister's wife and thrown in an expensive shawl for minister sahib himself, sensible man. Ice sculptures all over the place at the wedding buffet, a palanquin in plated gold to take the bride down the road to a waiting Mercedes—oh yes, Manny's daughter for Rohit had been a fine decision.

Swarn's feelings of doom took a while to dissipate but (pragmatic to the core) she took great pains to hide it from her new daughter-in-law, a subtlety she might not have vexed herself with if Neena had come from less desirable stock.

Neena had turned out to be an odd mix of her father and mother. From her father she had inherited a certain canny idea of what was wise to do and what wasn't. From her mother had come a strong notion of right and wrong. What had been confusing early on was that the two did not always match up. While she could see through her mother's eyes that certain things were just not acceptable, the Manny part of her would quickly take over, advising her to turn a blind eye because 'some things in life are just not worth bothering about, beti'. This is what Neena had more or less made the credo of her young life.

The prospect of married life in a joint family had not been entirely desirable as far as Neena was concerned, and Kammy had ranted briefly too about how old-fashioned the notion was. But Manny, just as keen as Jagdish not to lose the excellent proposed alliance between two such successful business families and already dreaming of joint ventures, had reminded his wife of how ill-equipped Neena was to run a house of her own. Neena, who had never even looked at a dhobi's account or been anywhere near a stove, had been persuaded to see the good sense in lazily occupying another woman's house in much the same way that she had occupied her mother's. She was certain that no one, not even a mother-in-law, would dare to make her work in a kitchen or do the housework. Besides, she knew the Sachdevs lived in a large house, and she had reasonably expected to occupy a whole wing of it with just her Rohit, whom she had now met a few times and was increasingly keen to marry. Kammy continued to rant for a while about the outrageousness of obsolete family structures, but Manny and his daughter had by this time quite firmly decided on the Sachdevs—Manny because of the business connections, and Neena because she wouldn't have to move out of Delhi and because Rohit had (if you ignored the nose) quite a thrilling resemblance to Imran Khan.

Life in Sachdev Mansion had turned out to be by and large peaceful. The senior and junior Sachdevs lived essentially separate lives, divided by a ground floor and a first floor. Tarun had moved enthusiastically into the flat constructed for him just before Rohit's wedding. The family met mainly at mealtimes, although Tarun was a welcome visitor to the upper floor and often used his sister-in-law as a sounding board in matters of the heart. Rohit drove his father to the factory every morning, but he returned in the early evening to take his pretty young wife shopping or to the cinema and ice cream parlour. The car and driver were sent back to the factory much later at night to fetch Jagdish, who had opted to take an unusually magnanimous view of his older son's sudden disinterest in the business. It was better, in the long run, he told himself, not to do or say anything to upset dear Manny's daughter. He, like Manny, nurtured dreams of a joint venture between the two businesses some day.

2

Ooffo, all these incompatibilities!

Five years of the junior Sachdev marriage had passed before both sets of fathers-in-law had come to terms with the fact that the only joint ventures likely to spring from the alliance were their grandchildren, Rinku and Ritik.

Certainly the occasional business idea had been mooted and bounced around briefly whenever the two men had met on social occasions in the Sachdev or Singh drawing rooms. Manny, whose energies had been taken up recently by his new sugar cubes venture, did not think much of Jagdish's idea of exporting drawstring trousers. ('Nothing better than bloody pyjamas,' he had thought.) And Jagdish had retreated hastily when Manny had talked about his next enterprise—something called marjipan that Jagdish had to assume was just another bit of sugary nonsense. In business terms, the two men found out, slowly and painfully, that they were completely and hopelessly incompatible. Fortunately their two offspring had found out little by little that they loved each other deeply and had embarked on a warm and meaningful marriage. The arrivals of Rinku and Ritik had added to that happy picture.

And that's where the story really begins.

Rohit and Neena have been married almost exactly five years. Their pretty little daughter, Rinku, is now four, and Ritik is a chubby ten-month old. The small family, unaware of impending doom swirling in from foreign shores, are at play in their upstairs living room. The windows are all closed, keeping out the summer glare and the noise of the traffic, while the air cooler hums and sends its pleasant khus-laden breeze through the house. Rinku is holding forth with a peculiar version of 'Humpty Dumpty' that she has learnt at playschool and that sounds strangely akin to Hindi. She is now using one of her grandmother's finest Kashmiri rugs as a stage to strut her stuff, perching her bottom coquettishly on a silken pouffe as she chants, 'Hunthy Dunthy sath on a wall . . .' Ritik is sitting up, surrounded by cushions and bolsters, watching WWF exploits on television with a goggle-eyed expression faintly reminiscent of his young paternal uncle. Every so often, at the execution of a particularly fine move on the programme, Ritik falls over with a delighted gurgle. He is then propped back up between his bolsters by his mother or father with a great deal of nuzzling and cuddling and baby talk. A happy scene, you would think.

So who had dared whisper something nasty about impending doom, you ask? How can that be! Can doom-ridden things happen to such seemingly blessed people? Can doom take the shape of a pert thirty-something Englishwoman at the moment completely unaware of these distant people as she sits in a Starbucks café on Shaftesbury Avenue, quaffing a large steaming mug of Kenyan roast, joshing with her companions?

But, back to the story . . .

■

'Oh, Rohit, look at him, he can't get his eyes off that woman's boobs! Gabloo-babloo, shtop looking at that aunty's bounchy-wounchies, you naughty little baba!' Neena whisks her baby son up in the air and nuzzles him in his small plump tummy. He screams with pleasure and pain and, as his mother lifts him mercilessly high into the air again, he lets a long line of dribble fall into her hair by way of revenge.

Rohit uses the ensuing chaos to get an eyeful of the aforementioned boobs, bronzed and glistening with sweat. 'Aaahhh!' he says by way of appreciation. For this he receives a whack across the top of his head by his magazine-wielding wife who has deposited the baby back among the bolsters.

'You're as bad as your brother, at least he's unmarried, you great big horny beast!' she cries indignantly, throwing herself on top of him in feeble attack. He, seeming not to mind this cuddly assault at all, proceeds to wrap his arms around her.

'Of course, I'm horny. I just don't get enough of it these days, you know.'

'Enough of what, Papa? Enough of what?!' Rinku shrieks, leaving her solitary strutting to join the melée among the cushions. 'What are you not getting enough of, Papa?'

'Nothing, Rinku,' Rohit replies, while his wife grins down at him from where she is balanced on his chest.

'Go on, tell her,' she eggs him on with a mischievous twinkle in her eye. 'Tell your darling daughter what you aren't getting enough of these days, considering it's bothering you that much, my sweet.'

Rohit rolls her off him and, sitting up, swings his little daughter on to his lap instead. 'Papa was just telling Mamma how she doesn't give him enough lunch these days, Rinku. See, look how thin I'm getting.'

Rinku bounces on his stomach, 'You're not thin, you're not thin, you're fat,' she cries.

'Yes, you tell him darling,' Neena says approvingly.

Rinku repeats, louder, encouraged by her mother's sanction, 'You're fat, you're fat, Papa, you great big horny beasth!'

'No!' Neena cries in consternation. 'You're not to say that!'

'What?' asks Rinku, large brown Swarn-eyes widening innocently.

Neena's voice drops to a whisper. 'Horny,' she hisses anxiously. 'You're not to say that, okay? It's rude!'

'You said it,' Rinku points out archly, 'to Papa.'

Rohit, tempted to pat his daughter on the back for the unknowing defence, decides to take the safer route of supporting his wife instead. 'Mamma's right, Rinku. It's very rude. It's one of those rude things that only mammas are allowed to say to papas.'

Neena gives him a grateful look. 'Yes, only grown-ups are allowed to use words like that one,' she trails off.

'But what does it mean?' Rinku demands.

'What?' Neena asks, hoping Rinku will have forgotten the offending word by now.

'Horny,' Rinku replies, also whispering.

Neena winces at the word issuing forth from her four-year-old's rosebud mouth. She throws a helpless look at the silent Rohit, who rises manfully to the rescue. 'Horny means a very ugly person with horns under his hair, Rinku,' he pronounces in an assured fatherly voice.

Rinku looks across at Moolchand who has just entered the room to clear the glasses away and announce lunch. 'Like Moolchand?' she asks, 'He's ugly. Is he a great big horny beast, Papa?' Neena giggles, and Rohit looks across at the dour old cook, trying to picture him with this new dimension added, but the thought is rather intolerable. Moolchand knows he is being discussed, although he cannot understand English. He mutters under his breath, balancing three glasses in one hand and wiping the table with a duster. He shuffles off, ignoring the stifled laughter behind him, unaware of how near the truth Rinku has arrived with regard to his secretly libidinous feelings for his memsahib.

The maid comes in with the post. Neena grabs the airmail envelope with the foreign postmark. 'This one looks interesting. Oh, look, it's from Gayatri. She hasn't written for ages.'

Rohit, going through his own mail, looks mildly interested, 'Your Ph.D. friend in Oxford? The one you've always said will sort Tarun out some day?'

'Oh, listen to this. She's coming back! "Completed my course ... not waiting for results ... June" ... She's mad! She's coming back in June. She hasn't been back to India in five years, and she chooses to come back in June!'

'So what?'

'So what! She'll die of the heat, that's what.'

'You don't get de-acclimatized as quickly as that. And she's a Southie, isn't she? Madrasis don't melt away as easily as that.'

'Don't ever say *Madrasi* to her! She hates it. She spent most of our college years telling everyone she was from Kerala, not Madras. And what she hated more than anything else was when people used to say, like a compliment, you know, that she was too pretty to be a Madrasi.'

Tarun, who has just come in and is twirling a gurgling Ritik in the air asks casually, 'Who's the pretty Madrasi?'

Neena throws her arms up in frustration, 'One is as bad as the other. Keralite, not Madrasi. Gayatri has a real chip on her shoulder about that, I warn you!'

Tarun brightens, 'Oh, Gayatri, that Southie friend of yours you keep promising to introduce me to?' His expression turns earnest as he remembers something important. 'You did say she was really pretty, didn't you?'

'Well, you can soon find out for yourself. She's finished her studies in England and is coming back in June.'

'June?' Tarun wrinkles his forehead, looking worried, 'that gives me roughly three weeks in which to have a haircut, spruce up my wardrobe and, oh, get a Ph.D.'

Neena laughs. 'You might find she's not in the least bit interested in haircuts and wardrobes. Yeah, and might turn up her nose at your piddling BCom pass too. That'll serve you right, Mr Oh-everyone-thinks-I'm-just-lovely Sachdev. Gayatri's really special, beautiful and brainy. You might as well count her out of your little schemes straightaway.'

'Schemes?' Tarun looks genuinely hurt. 'Would I ever scheme to do anything with a lovely girl, I ask you? Each of my relationships has been a new adventure for me. An adventure that just might lead to true love, who knows.' He trails off dramatically with one hand on his chest, the other still holding the baby, who is the only person in the room looking at him admiringly. Aware of how meagre an impression he is creating, he adds tamely, 'Anyway, I was sent to call you all for lunch.'

As the family clatter downstairs to the main dining room, a huge, dimly lit space occupying the centre of the ground floor, Rinku rushes up to Swarn, who is just starting to ladle out the dal. Without warning, she heaves herself on to her grandmother's lap, knocking the ladle out of her hand.

Rinku is perhaps the only person on the premises who does not feel obliged to don kid gloves when dealing with Swarn. Blessed with her grandmother's fair skin and light brown eyes, Rinku has the privilege to rush pell-mell into Swarn's presence and to throw her small person right into what she described as 'Dadima's softy parts'. A warm, puffy landing that Moolchand the cook had observed enviously, often wishing he could emulate it. Lately, he had even taken to shamelessly masturbating over this delicious, albeit remote, possibility in the privacy of his quarters. For fifteen long years he had watched his mistress's soft parts grow in direct proportion to her increasingly careless calorie intake, until they spilt deliciously out of this part of her sari or that, in pale wobbly mounds that sometimes drove old Moolchand (never married and now never likely to) into fits of utterly debilitating distraction, a condition that had, on many an occasion, completely ruined the dal.

Today the dal is well-cooked, though, whisked into a creamy yellow and dotted with finely chopped coriander leaves, a great dollop of which is now on Swarn's export-quality lace tablecloth.

'Ooffo, beta, gently, no!' Swarn always finds it difficult to be angry with her pretty granddaughter, not least because the little girl is like a pocket edition of Swarn herself. ('Hai Ram, the same eyes, the same complexion, even a smaller version of the same nose!' eagerly proclaimed the canny midwife in the nursing home four years ago, before gratefully pocketing a large tip.)

Rinku ignores her grandmother's admonition and stays on her well-upholstered perch, despite her mother's glare from across the table. Swarn carefully checks the state of her ribcage through its generous layers of adipose tissue with one pale and manicured hand. The smell of Pond's Dreamflower talc dissipates into the air before she has recovered enough to give the back of Rinku's curly head a distracted kiss. She now reaches around her to continue ladling out the dal into small steel bowls.

Rinku begins to hum loudly and pat time on the underside of her grandmother's upper arm, which is jiggling with the effort of ladling. Swarn doesn't seem to mind, smiling fondly as she passes the bowls around the table. Swarn Sachdev was a beauty in her time and rather liked the fact that, in Rinku, she could now watch that beauty propagate and blossom again, even as her own was fading. Her oval, gilt-edged mirror still showed traces of that beauty when she sat down to search for it. In the long lines of her nose, gently curving downwards at the tip and in large, still relatively lustrous brown eyes framed by lazy, long lashes. Those were the only features that had refused to be invaded and enveloped by the layers of fat that had taken over most of the rest of Swarn's face about ten years ago. Pink plumpness now masked those proud erstwhile cheekbones that had thrown a room of male classmates into complete chaos the year that Swarn (then Malhotra) had spent at Hindu College before giving up her education to get married.

But that was many years ago—when Swarn had been a beautiful blushing bride, nearly but not quite in love with her husband. Nearly, because he was young too and reasonably handsome (except for an unfortunately bulbous nose that the young Swarn had been willing to overlook then, but only because he had just been given sole charge of his father's thriving cloth mills). And not quite, because it was really genuinely difficult for Swarn to love anyone for any length of time apart from herself. Later she would, more or less, be able to add her two sons and grandchildren to that tiny list, but she was always her own favourite person. The faint twinklings of love (let's call it that for want of a less dramatic and more accurate word) that Swarn had felt for her new husband in 1969 had long since faded and died. Over the years (and partially because of the vast sums of money that the harassed Mr Sachdev continued to put her way), she had learnt to suffer him in the same way that she tolerated Moolchand's occasional eccentricities, the searing heat of Delhi's summers and her granddaughter's exuberant leaps into her soft parts.

Her granddaughter is at the moment exuberantly testing her lunchtime boundaries by singing 'Humpty Dumpty' very loudly and bouncing on Swarn's lap. Swarn grumbles half-heartedly as it is now time for her own lunch, 'Okay, beti, Rinku, now go sit like a good girl on your chair, so Dadima can eat her food, na?'

Rinku makes a pretty little moue to indicate she has no intention of moving from her commodious seat. Swarn tries another tack. 'Which pyaari little baby is going to get a big-big piece of Toblerone chocolate after lunch, Rinku or Ritik?'

'Rinku, Rinku, Rinku,' Rinku cries, using her endearing voice. Suddenly, halfway through a particularly big bounce, she is whisked upwards by an irate Neena and plonked very hard on to a high chair. 'Owww!' she yells in surprise and briefly contemplates embarking on a long moan, but the look on Neena's face indicates that it will probably be a waste of time today. Rinku has no intention of eating lunch with her baby brother and his maid in the smoky kitchen again. Instead, she smiles sweetly at her grandmother and lisps, 'Pleathe can I have my dal in a bowl too, Dadima?'

As Neena reoccupies her place, a thought occurs to Tarun. 'Neena, you did say June, didn't you?'

Neena nods, helping herself to a chapatti. She knows that even as he goes through the motions of lunch, her irrepressible brother-in-law is already making plans to gently disengage himself from his current girlfriend in time for Gayatri's imminent visit.

'What is happening in June?' Swarn coos, trying to sound friendly, because she dislikes it intensely when Neena shares any secrets with either of her sons.

'Nothing,' Neena says sweetly. Which, as it turns out, will be very far from the truth.

■

It was eight years ago that Neena and Gayatri met as expectant undergraduates in the hallowed, ivy-clad portals of that venerable institute, Lady Shantibai Women's College. Long queues of eighteen-year-old school-leavers clutching certificates and accompanied by anxious parents had formed at the entrance to the college even before eight o'clock. Neena, escorted by a determined Kammy, had squeezed herself into a tiny space behind a pretty girl in a salwar kameez. The girl smiled at Neena as she moved along, making room for them. With her was a tiny fussed-looking woman (another anxious mother, Neena guessed) wearing her sari an inelegant two inches above her ankles. Neena, while trying not to stare rudely, observed her in amazement out of the corner of her eye. She did not normally meet unfashionable people, and this was about the most unfashionable person she had seen in a long time. The sticky-backed bindi on the woman's forehead was askew, dangling precariously over one eyebrow. She wore her hair in an antiquated jooda, scraped back so severely that bits of her scalp were shining triumphantly through. If all that wasn't enough, her spectacles seemed to be waging a constant battle against gravity, sliding down her nose before they would fussily be pushed back, only to come sliding slowly down the sweaty nose again. She talked nonstop, in a marked south Indian accent, throwing the pallu of her sari over her shoulder every few minutes as though it were a terrible inconvenience that she had to wear clothes at all.

Nonetheless, they all got talking and discovered to their mutual delight that both girls were hoping to get into the B.A. course in English literature. Neena was looking for a stop-gap arrangement while her father looked for Delhi's most eligible bachelor for her to marry, and Gayatri had wanted to study English since she was six. Kammy, less prone to judging people on the basis of the latest fashion stakes than her daughter, was impressed that Raji Menon, Gayatri's mother, was a senior professor in botany at the Indian Institute of Science, presently researching the marrow family for a book she was writing called *Cucurbits*. Her husband worked for the Indian Standards Institute, an organization that Neena had only an indeterminate idea about. The Menons lived in Saket, a crowded, bustling housing estate that the Singhs sometimes visited from their nearby sprawling Sainik Farms residence, but only when they had fruit to buy and wanted to choose personally their mangoes and lychees.

It was suggested that the girls could travel to college together if they got into the same course. It would be a crying shame for Neena to be travelling in their chauffeur-driven Esteem all the way on her own, Kammy insisted. Despite Raji's obvious embarrassment, it was agreed that it would only be reasonable and most practical, and telephone numbers were duly exchanged.

By the end of the month, both girls had been granted admission to the B.A. course in English—Gayatri sailing in with ease on the basis of the 88 per cent she had received for English in the school-leaving exams, and Neena just about scraping in on the basis of Kammy's vehement assertions that a certain sum of money would be put towards the college fund to ensure completion of long-delayed repairs to the canteen.

Despite their obvious differences, a tentative friendship was struck up, which gained strength in the first few weeks of the term as both girls were mercilessly ragged by manic college seniors, inducing a certain defenceless togetherness.

On the day that Gayatri had to dance on top of a canteen table while Neena was told to wail like a musical banshee, they bonded firmly. It was an accidental friendship as the two girls had in fact precious little in common (save for a shared passing interest in Mel Gibson), but it went in an odd sort of way from strength to strength. At last their classmates stopped noticing that Gayatri was wearing Neena's clothes again. Or that Neena was mysteriously missing the week that Gayatri went down with a viral flu. It was a friendship that not only survived its incompatibilities but seemed to thrive on them.

■

'Ma, did I tell you Gayatri's coming back from England in June? I had a letter yesterday.'

Kammy looks up over stylishly retro spectacles. She has always liked Gayatri. Early on she had hoped the Menon girl would be a good influence on her Neena, creating a genuine interest in scholastic pursuits and inducing her perhaps to go on and do an M.A. Goodness knows, even a Ph.D.! Neena had it in her surely, however deeply it lurked.

But it was not to be so. When Gayatri got the gold medal at the end of the first year exams, Neena rejoiced for her but showed no shame over her own lower second-class grade. When Gayatri started applying to American and British universities for her M.A. a year later, Neena accompanied her to the British Council and the USIS but clearly had no intention of leaving her own cosy Delhi life. Sometime after their B.A. was complete and long after Gayatri had left for Oxford, having won a prestigious scholarship, Rohit had breezed into Neena's life, making it incumbent upon her to get married and have children rather than concern herself anymore with the literature of Pope and Dryden. Kammy firmly put the blame for her daughter's disinterest in academics on the genes she had acquired from the Manny part of her, of course.

'Old Gayatri returning home.' Kammy looks pleased.

'How long has she been away?'

'Five years—she's never met Rohit, remember, and we'll have been married five years this year.'

'Oh, yes, she left just a couple of months before your wedding was fixed. Strange that she's never been back, though.'

'Her excuse was that her grant left her with no extra money. I think she just liked England too much.'

Kammy turns back to her newspaper, 'Well, she was always a bit of a fish out of water here in Delhi, wasn't she?'

Sultan, the old family boxer, wanders lugubriously into the room. With a huge sigh he flops down at Kammy's feet, emanating a distinctly doggy aroma. Neena is patting him cursorily when a thought suddenly occurs to her. 'I wonder whether Gayatri's got a boyfriend now! Her letters never give any real gossip—just boring descriptions of dreamy spires and whatnot.'

She curls up against her mother's ample hip on the divan and puts her head on her lap. Kammy strokes her hair absently, still perusing her paper, while Neena slips effortlessly into baby mode. She clutches the fold of fat her mother carries around her waist and says something puerile and unintelligible by way of affection. Her mother pats her head again. She is accustomed to Neena's occasional descents into childishness and is neither impressed nor embarrassed. Once her immediate duties as a mother had been done with (which was when Neena was about seven and Danny five), Kammy had turned her attentions to the more important things in life with a sense of overwhelming relief. Floods in Orissa, earthquakes in Gujarat, all those ghastly events so specific to India, these were what really moved Kammy. Those parched helpless faces on television—those were the people that really needed her. Husbands had businesses and children had ... what did her children have? Kammy sometimes asked herself. Neena ... well, Neena had Rohit and the children. And Danny? Danny, as far as Kammy could see, just had a jolly good time. For long Kammy had attempted to alter this state of affairs, but, faced with the combined force of husband and two children, had long since admitted defeat. Kammy was a firm believer in the theory of nature invariably triumphing over nurture—and, in the case of her children, it was definitely Manny's genes that were to blame.

A few seconds later, there is a happy humming sound as Manny enters the room.

'Daddy!' Neena squeals, still retaining the lisping tone she had adopted for the earlier communication with her mother.

Manny responds in similar vein. 'Beti! My choti-choti little Neenabeti! When did you come?'

Neena, who visits her parents at least once a day, rushes into her father's embrace as though she has not seen him in months. 'You're late!' she says, pretending to be cross.

'Where are my grandchildren?' Manny demands.

'Oh, I left them behind today. They were getting on my nerves. Rinku especially.'

Manny looks cross. 'You know the rules. We must see our grandchildren at least once a day, Neena!'

Kammy, less inclined to dandling grandchildren on her knee, contributes to the conversation lazily from behind her newspaper, 'So what if you don't see them every day, Manny? Some grandparents don't see their children for months at a time.'

Neena interjects sulkily, putting her father in his place as is her custom, 'Oh, Dad, don't be such a fusspot! You can have them over to spend the night if you like. I'll send the driver back to pick up them and the maid.' Always prone to look on the bright side, she adds, 'Maybe Rohit and I could go to the disco.'

It's Kammy's turn to look concerned, 'Oh, beti, I can't have the children tonight,' she says. 'I have my Seva AGM taking place here. The children will disturb us, darling. There'll be lots of women attending tonight's meeting who will not be in a good frame of mind, shall we say.'

Neena considers going into another pout but is feeling generally too cheerful to care very much. In any case, her father is taking up cudgels on her behalf as usual. His shrill voice goes up a gear. 'What do you mean, Kammy! We hardly ever get Neena asking to leave the children here, and you say she can't. You know sometimes this Seva-sheva stuff becomes just too much. Who are more important—us or them?' Manny's English, despite all of Kammy's early tutoring, has a tendency to go awry whenever he is agitated. It has also been an observation of Kammy's that her husband's agitation coincides unerringly with the meetings of Seva, the non-governmental organization Kammy set up twelve years ago. Nonetheless Manny has managed to throw Kammy into temporary throes of guilt. She looks beseechingly at Neena who is clearly not in dire need of her parents' babysitting services.

'Oh, never mind, Dad!' she interjects, 'Ma's work is important too, whatever you might think.'

'I don't know,' Manny mutters ungracefully. 'On the first of every month I have to vacate my drawing room to accommodate all these women who come here, chittering and chattering away about how awful we men are. I put up with that silently, don't I?'

'Well, it is a feminist organization, isn't it? Isn't that what they're supposed to do?' Neena queries doubtfully. She has never completely understood the philosophy of her mother's organization, even though Kammy has often tried to explain it to her. Feminism for Neena is still a bit of a scary word, conjuring up images of hatchet-faced women who walk out of perfectly reasonable marriages. Yet marriage to young Neena is pretty much sacrosanct. Why, it has been the very reason for her existence until now. The message was dinned into her head as a child as she was jounced on her father's knee, when he would tell her of his intention of combing the far reaches of the country to find the 'bestest, handsomest bridegroom' for his darling daughter. She has also seen her parents stay together despite what must be one of the most incompatible marriages in Delhi. It would be very odd indeed if she did not respect the institution with the fervour that she does.

'Oh, come on, Manny,' Kammy says crossly. 'Our meetings are only once a month, and we do have better things to do than sit and tear men apart, you know.'

'Achcha! Tell me what else you discuss then, hanh?' Manny is clearly itching for a fight.

'I do believe I've told you that a few times already,' Kammy replies in her frostiest tone. 'Must I keep repeating myself?'

'And also how much of my hard-earned money is poured into this Seva-sheva thing, I just don't know.'

'Money—don't talk to me about money, Manny!' Kammy growls menacingly. 'Go look on the sideboard, there is an aerogramme from your darling son asking for more dollars, if you please. He's already spent double the recommended amount for living expenses stated in the university pamphlet. Double.'

'That pamphlet was outdated, I already told you . . .'

'By a year, Manny! I've heard of inflation, but don't even try telling me it's doubled!'

Neena, who has very little idea of the intricacies of inflation, makes a feeble defence of her distant brother. 'Don't they say, though, that everything is more expensive for foreign students over there?'

Kammy returns to a furious perusal of her newspaper, continuing to mutter, 'All those poor people in Gujarat, needing tents and medicines, and what does Manny do? Send his good-for-nothing son off to some third-rate university in the US just to waste some more money.'

Neena, who has heard this argument a few times before, has no intention of sitting around watching while her parents slug it out again. 'Oho,' she says irritably, 'do stop bickering. I have to be off, or I'll be late for my appointment at the beauty parlour. Must have my arms waxed before Rohit calls me cuddly bear again.'

Manny, who can never resist the opportunity to thump his chest and be a protective father, inquires with exaggerated concern, 'I hope he's looking after you well, that son-in-law of mine?'

'Of course he is!' Kammy snaps. 'Credit Neena with being able to look after herself, Manny, for heaven's sake!'

'I was asking Neena, not you,' Manny whines, not enjoying having the wind taken out of his paternal sail.

Neena waltzes over to her father and plants a big kiss on his shiny bald pate. 'Oh, come on, Ma, these are just the questions my darling sweetie-pie Daddy can't help asking me! And I can't say I don't like it!' Manny beams, the monetary woes visited on him by his son temporarily forgotten as Neena kootchie-kootchies with him. Whatever Kammy may say, spending money on one's children always pays off, he thinks happily.

Kammy tries not to grimace and tickles a grateful Sultan's ear with a weary, resigned air. 'You'll be late for your waxing appointment, darling,' she reminds her daughter dryly. Neena squeals, making Sultan jump in fright. As Neena rushes out, Sultan mournfully rearranges himself and presents Kammy with his other ear.

■

The question Manny had earlier asked his wife is one that Swarn has frequently asked of Kammy too, but only in her head. In many a happy daydream, she has strolled up to her son's mother-in-law to ask her exactly the same question—politely, in tones of genuine curiosity and without an ounce of snideness—'Tell me, Kammyji, what to you is more important—looking after your husband and children or doing this voluntary-work thing?' Not that she has ever received a satisfactory reply or one that would ever convince her of the necessity for such tedious do-gooding nonsense. But, for some reason it always gives Swarn immense satisfaction to merely be able to ask the question, even if only in her dreams. She has often hoped that some day, somehow, real life would present her with the opportunity. To score one over the annoyingly competent Kammy. To see those purple lips part when she finally reveals how little Swarn thinks of her stupid, pointless, showing-off volunteer work. Ah, what sweet release that would be. Until that happens, she has to receive her son's mother-in-law in the ornate Sachdev drawing room with warm namastes as though she were indeed her favourite relative. Serve her tea and paneer pakoras as though she really wanted to put more food into that already well-fed frame. Listen wearily to all her talk of volunteers and villages, as though she cared a whit about these depressing rural types. Oh, what a pain life sometimes was, ji.

Swarn and Kammy's incompatibility (like that of their respective spouses) was not a matter of much concern to anyone. Relatives have to be suffered, like illnesses, disease and death. 'You unfortunately cannot choose-shoose them,' Jagdish often said.

But Manny and Kammy's incompatibility was another matter altogether. As husband and wife for nearly twenty-eight years, the Singhs were an odd couple. The top of Manny's head, once resplendent in a sardarji's turban but now bald and shiny as a polished nut, hovered just below Kammy's imposing eyebrow when they stood close to each other—an act they were inclined to perform with less and less frequency since they were newly-weds in the sixties.

Their romance then had been as sudden and unexpected as a summer shower, passing with the same rapidity. It was a matter of youthful recklessness that had led to their getting married before that shower had passed—in a moment of extreme ardour under a bougainvillea bush one warm summer evening at Lodhi Gardens. The young Manny, his forearm a considerable distance up the folds of Kammy's sari, had heard his disembodied voice passionately croak a proposal of marriage. The horizontal Kammy, looking up at the young man's expression of unabashed fervour framed by scarlet bougainvillea blooms, fully forgot that (vertically) she towered two whole inches above him, and said yes.

The following day they had decamped on a bus to Vaishno Devi, armed with a pair of gold rings and two flower garlands. Kammy's father, the late Lt. Gen. Sodhi MC had plucked his double barrelled 12-bore off the drawing room wall and waved it about briefly, threatening death and destruction on a mass scale until restrained by two orderlies and a weeping wife. By the time he had decided to come to terms with the fact that his adored daughter had gone and married a useless, good-for-nothing, unemployed, uneducated scoundrel, the young Kammy, ardour having cooled, had come to more or less the same conclusion. She still liked Manny—his impulsiveness, his generosity, his irrepressible optimism—but often wondered what life would have held in store had she married that Major Balasubramaniam who made eyes at her every time she visited Central Vista Library. At least he visited libraries.

As for Manny, having dropped out of college before completing his B.A., he had spent many a happy afternoon in the tea shops in and around the university area, exchanging political views and dirty jokes with his fellow drop-out cronies. It was from this vantage position that he had first spotted the young Kammy as she languidly strolled past with her girlfriends. How beautifully her long plait had swayed over a pert derrière! Had Manny been able to look beyond that derrière, both into its own burgeoning future and into the speed with which it would cause his jolly tea-shop life to come to an end, it is debatable whether he would have pursued and then married the luscious Kammy in such haste.

Once he had, however, he was bright enough to recognize that his tea-shop roosting days were truly over. He had married an expensive woman; he would now have to find himself a job—anything to prevent his father-in-law from turning up every week at their one-room barsati to dramatically hand over an envelope of money to Kammy. The old general never had anything to say to his new son-in-law on these occasions, sending in his direction only a series of meaningful bristles through angry moustaches.

Poor Manny had to act fast, which, to his credit, he did. It all started with the old tea-shop owner suggesting that Manny collect the supplies of sugar from the wholesaler in Old Delhi for a fee. The fee would not have been enough to buy even a week's supply of provisions for the young Singhs, but the sugar wholesaler took a shine to the cheerful Manny, who always had a dirty joke to swap.

When his main delivery man drank two glasses of frothing sugar-cane juice that summer, succumbing to a ferocious case of hepatitis C, Manny was given his job. Soon he was not just delivering sugar but also collecting it for the wholesaler from a factory in Haryana. For this he was given use of a three-wheeler tempo truck, which he drove home every night to take Kammy out for a spin. Now there was enough money for not just the provisions but also the vegetables and the occasional extravagance of the season's fruit. There was, of course, no problem at all with the sugar stocks in the Singh household, which would thenceforth always be plentiful.

In less than two years time, Manny had inveigled himself into the factory owner's good books. When this venerable old gentleman's only daughter got married and was sent off to her new home in Toronto, he decided to sell the old mill and retire to his village in the Punjab. Manny bought the mill for a song, because the old man liked him and his enthusiasm for the commodity that had given him such a good, prosperous life. He had seen in the young Manny's eyes the kind of wonder he knew few others shared when they beheld a mountain of the pale white crystal substance, which in his opinion shone like tiny diamonds on certain days. He knew his factory would be in excellent hands and laid only one condition: that it retain its name, Ahluwalia Sugar Mills. Manny, aware of some sort of propitious hand at work, carried the Ahluwalia name, only succumbing to one little change over the years: to rename it Ahluwalia Export House in the late eighties, despite the fact that he was only allowed to export sugar by-products, which were admittedly not terribly lucrative. But it was the eighties, *export* was the golden word and virtually every member of Manny's Rotary Club of South Delhi was getting himself a license. 'Much catchier name,' he had said to Kammy, who had merely looked heavenwards, accustomed as she had become by then to occupying a completely separate world from her husband's.

It was sad, though, that despite Manny's success, Kammy's father could never quite bring himself to congratulate his son-in-law. Whenever any of his old Army acquaintances asked what Kammy's husband did, he would reply brusquely, 'Scoundrel doesn't really do anything proper, you know, old chap.' At this his voice would drop a level and grow gruff and scornful. 'Has some sort of business, I believe. Wish he'd get himself a job.'

3

The making of a businessman

Tarun is creeping into the living room. He looks like he may be stalking something, but it is hard to tell what this might be until he arrives at his target and straightens up with a look of relief on his face. For many days now he has been trying to get his parents to get him a separate telephone line in his flat, but this is where even his mother seems most determined to draw the line. 'Oho, beta, then I think I will never see you again. Whenever you want to call anyone, even if they are girls, you just come in here. I will make sure your father never says anything, hanh?'

Tarun's father's disapproval has long since ceased to matter much to Tarun—since he was roughly four. About this time he realized that he would always have a staunch, if ineffective, protector in his mother. His father, he had figured by then, was a generally bad-tempered person who appeared at odd intervals to chastise him for some misdemeanour or the other. He had a vague memory of having been occasionally bounced on the paternal knee when he was younger but, once he had outgrown the baby years, his father had seemed to retreat to a lofty distance from where he descended at regular intervals to issue reproach. Initially he remonstrated him for offences like making too much noise banging his new toy truck about and later for a whole catalogue of crimes—taking the BMW without permission, locking himself up with some girl in his bedroom for a whole afternoon of God-knows-what, showing absolutely no interest in the family business. Tarun was, it is sad to say, not a devoted son by Jagdish's standards.

He was handsome and charming, though, possessing an ebullient personality and a boyish smile that was irresistible to most people (except his father). Thanks in part to a lock of hair that flopped appealingly over his forehead, girls found him terribly hard to resist. Even men found him hard to resist sometimes. Tarun was still fond of recounting the time he was taken to the health club at the Hyatt by a young man he'd met at a party. 'Bastard thought that by enticing me into the pool he could get his hands on me,' he'd said, clearly more flattered than agitated at the thought of near molestation by a member of his own sex.

Despite an inability to remain unflattered by any sort of attention, Tarun himself was firmly and avowedly heterosexual, a discovery he had joyfully made after a short period of confusion at the age of twelve that had involved a school senior and a fumbled encounter behind the basketball court. Tarun sometimes looked back at that incident with the shuddering realization that it could have become the catalyst to tip his budding sexuality over to the other side. But, fortunately for him, a few months afterwards, Mrs Duggal, his friend Robby's mother, had lain provocatively across her bed one afternoon, flaunting a magnificent cleavage that loomed unabashedly out of her sari blouse while talking to the two boys. Tarun had felt an unfamiliar stirring in his half-pants and had to be excused to the bathroom to examine his suddenly errant privates. That night he had dreamt a wondrous dream in which Mrs Duggal's breasts figured prominently, causing him to come suddenly awake in delicious agony among a certain wetness in the sheets, much to his brother Rohit's disgust. Although Rohit proceeded to make much of the night's happenings for long after, cackling maniacally at the memory of it, Tarun could hardly have minded. He had exuberantly and ecstatically discovered his sexuality and discovered the delights of the female form. From this point on there was to be no looking back in this gloriously heterosexual sex life.

■

Tarun picks up the phone, looking over his shoulder first to make sure there is no one else around. He consults a small diary he is carrying before swiftly punching a number. As the ringing tone begins, he bends his head low, keeping his face to the wall. As it clicks and a female voice answers it, he breathes in his sexiest voice, 'Hello, sweetie'.

He starts as the reply is not the honeyed one he is expecting. 'Who is that?' the female voice replies sharply.

'Erm … erm … is that 6239875?' Tarun asks, losing confidence.

'Yes,' comes the reply, not giving anything else away.

Tarun begins again, 'Erm … is that … Suneeta Kohli's number?'

'Yes,' the voice is starting to sound more and more curt and less and less like the lovely Suneeta Kohli. 'Who is that?' it barks again.

Tarun contemplates giving his name and then decides pragmatically that it is unlikely to open any magic doors. Swiftly, before walking into any traps, he hangs up. He consults his small diary and dials again. This time he is more circumspect, 'Hello,' he says, trying to sound officious, businesslike, 'may I speak to Pramila Lal please?'

'Tarun!' comes the excited reply. 'I never thought you'd call, yaar!'

It's obviously safe to trot out the endearments now. 'Hi, sweetie!' Tarun replies, beaming.

It is worth the effort. The reply he receives is fervently enquiring. 'Haven't seen you for absolutely ages! Where have you been?'

'Oh, busy helping my Dad in his business. I've just managed to get an evening off after many days and was wondering what you're doing tonight, babe.'

'Nothing,' is the prompt reply.

'Care to come boogeying then?'

'Ya, where?'

'Club 21.'

'Ya, great!'

'That's settled then. Pick you up at nine.' When everything is going smoothly, there's no need for a flood of words. Tarun hangs up the telephone and then rubs his hands together gleefully. Turning around to leave the room, he walks right into a large, kurta-clad frame.

'Oh!' he says, taken aback.

'So!' is his father's curt reply.

'Hi, Pops,' Tarun pretends cheerfulness as he tries to dodge around him. But Jagdish has grabbed him firmly by the collar. Tarun yelps in disbelief, but Jagdish only tightens his grip on the bright yellow Benetton sweatshirt and twists it slightly, temporarily cutting off his younger son's air supply.

'Where do you think you are going?' he asks.

Tarun tries to reply, but only a few breathless squeaks emerge. His father loosens his grip slightly, but only enough to allow for a few strangulated attempts at explanation. Jagdish repeats his question. 'Just where do you think you are going, hanh?!' The 'wh' of his 'where' blows a breeze through Tarun's charming floppy lock.

Tarun manages a weak, 'Out, Papa.'

Jagdish ignores the meagre explanation and shouts, 'Club 21, hanh? Club 21!' With each *hanh*, he shakes Tarun's collar from side to side. Tarun cannot help thinking that if his father knew the name of his destination, he really had no reason to ask. But, prudently, he decides against pointing out this fact and nods desperately. The collar-jerking, however, doesn't stop. Jagdish has today reached the end of his not too extensive tether. Still holding on to his son's collar, he bellows, 'I have had enough of all this to-ing and fro-ing of yours, you hear! This coming and going, hither and thither, this chitter-chatter with stupid girls, not taking any interest in the business when there is such problems with the unions, not taking life seriously! You are wasting your life, hear? Wasting your life!'

Tarun, aware that he is in real trouble, uses his father's apoplectic fit to wriggle out of his grasp, but he does not make good his escape. Instead, he stands before him, looks down at his involuntarily shuffling feet and mutters, 'Yes, Papa.'

Jagdish is not easily taken in. He has seen this expression on Tarun's face before. Various versions of it since his younger son was a tiny four-year-old. Many years ago, he taught himself (with great difficulty) to resist that hurt expression in those brown eyes. That look of helpless little-boyness. That maddeningly heart-melting look. Jagdish does not like being reminded that he has a heart, let alone feel it melt into terrifying gooeyness at times like this. He is not normally an unkind man but, as far as Tarun is concerned, he feels obliged (nay, compelled) to be so. He shakes his head sadly and sits down on the sofa, making room for Tarun next to him. 'Sit here, son,' he says.

Tarun can feel familiar waves of panic rise within him as he anticipates a lecture that will traverse the old familiar territory of 'This is going to hurt me more than it will hurt you, beta'. Gingerly, he occupies the proffered space on the sofa, sitting on its edge as if hoping for a miraculous escape.

'Look, son,' his father says earnestly, 'I am having so many problems in the factory, I need your help, your assistance, your support. You are now nearly thirty. It's time you started to think seriously about what you want to do in the business.'

Tarun feels inclined to tell his father that he is a mere stripling at twenty-eight and that thirty is a long way away. But even Tarun knows this is not a propitious time for hair-splitting. He remains silent.

Jagdish continues to speak. 'As you know, I need your brother's help in this new export venture of ours. He might be travelling abroad frequently. I'm not getting any younger. Isn't it time you took some interest? Took over the Noida operations maybe? Hanh? Beta?'

The specificity of the request, combined with the rare endearment, goads Tarun into a reply. 'Take over Noida?' he croaks disbelievingly. The disbelief is not mingled with particular delight at the rather generous offer of a 20,000-square-foot factory with imported machinery and a new elastic-tape-making facility. Noida is a thirty-seven-mile round trip from Maharaja Colony, through traffic that would make the driver of a juggernaut blanch. It also employs twenty factory hands in constant need of supervision, all members of an active union sometimes known to turn ugly. Tarun is not enthused. 'But Papa . . .' he entreats, unsure of being able to wriggle out of it this time. He is right. There is to be no wriggling out of it this time. Jagdish is quietly determined. He has not lived sixty-three years for nothing, he will triumphantly say later to his wife. He has not been blessed with a fine brain for nothing, he will also say. Cannily, he recognizes that if he continues to rant and rave while shaking his son by the collar, he will only give him sanction to rebel, to go off somewhere and be an angry young man. Jagdish is determined not to allow him this luxury. He keeps his voice low, his tone soft.

'My dear son,' he says, inwardly cringing almost as much as his son is, 'I need your help. I am now an old man. Why I have worked so hard all my life? Only for you. For you and Rohit to have a good life. Don't throw all that away, beta.'

Tarun is not quite the analysing type, but he will actually spend a few minutes afterwards trying to work out whether Jagdish's words truly issue forth from the heart or if they are an elaborate ploy to get him to join the business finally. Has Jagdish really worked hard to give his two sons a handsome inheritance? Or has he merely been another victim of businessman's disease, must-expanditis? It is hard to tell. But the upshot of the conversation is that Tarun will from henceforth spend from 9 a.m. to 6 p.m. in the Noida factory, leaving Rohit free to conduct the export negotiations. In return, Jagdish will not question Tarun's movements in the evening hours. He will be free to dilly-dally (Jagdish's choice of words) with whomsoever he pleases.

The making of Tarun the Businessman is, if you look at it later, really the first step in our drama, the chapter without which we might not have had this story at all. When Swarn later looks back at the series of events that are soon to engulf her life, submerging it completely in hitherto unknown horrors, she will actually lament the making of Tarun the Businessman. She will accost her husband with it down a tinny telephone line, as he listens silently, surrounded by grimy walls in a motel room. 'If it wasn't for you, ji,' she will spit bitterly, 'if it wasn't for you and your wanting only to expand your business, all this would never have happened. My Rohit and my Tarun were just two innocent boys, wanting to enjoy life. But you ... you ... only wanted to make businessmen out of them. That is all you have wanted from them. To become businessmen.' She emits this word with particular venom and now starts to wail, 'Now are you happy, ji? Happy that now that you have got your two businessmen and I ... I have lost my sons!'

■

Lunch is being served in the Sachdev dining room. Slats of fuzzy sunlight pattern the wall across from the window, which is closed and tightly covered with cane blinds to keep the fierce afternoon sun out. It is Sunday, and the whole family is present. Swarn is presiding, buttering the rotis before passing them around, fluttering her lashes now and making a little moue when Rohit says he'll go for the rice instead; Neena is trying not to notice her mother-in-law's coquettish expression as she smacks Rinku's arm because she is trying to stuff a bit of roti into her baby brother's ear; Tarun, still smarting from the rumpus with his father yesterday, is not his usual ebullient self; Jagdish is eating swiftly and silently at the head of the table, thoughts miles away, in Sweden and Italy, chasing elusive buyers as ever.

'No, Mummy, no more rotis, thanks.'

'Have one more, beta, you only had two, na?'

God, she's counting, thinks Neena disgustedly.

'No, Mum, I'll have some rice instead.'

'Okay, you have this roti, Tarun beta, look I've put lots of butter on it, just the way you like it.'

Tarun, preoccupied, mumbles, 'No thanks. I've finished.'

Swarn does a little pout. 'Nobody wants my roti. Here, Neena, you have it.'

Afterthought as usual, Neena thinks, beginning her usual lunchtime simmer. She decides to get one up on Swarn. She takes the roti and, turning to Jagdish, sweetly bats her eyelids at him. 'Papa, you have this roti. You must be so tired after such a long day yesterday at the factory.'

Jagdish flies in from Sweden with a start. 'Oh, thank you, Neena beti,' he says, taking the roti from her. He tears a large piece off it, dips it into his dal and stuffs it into his mouth with scant elegance. With his mouth still full of masticated roti, he makes his announcement: 'Tarun has offered to take over the Noida operations to give you more time to go and meet A&G Group this month, Rohit.'

Rohit, startled, looks across at his younger brother for some clues, but Tarun keeps his eyes fixed on his plate. Rohit turns back to look at his father. 'Do you mean go to England to meet them?' he asks.

'Yes, there is no point trying to send faxes-shaxes and all sorts of messages. You have to go to see them now. Maybe you can meet those Svenskys people in Sweden while you are there. Take a suitcase of samples with you. Only then will they get interested.'

'Well, not that I mind, Papa, but will Tarun be able to handle everything at Noida? I mean, with training the fellows to use the new machinery and things this month ...'

'Yes, Tarun will manage it fine,' Jagdish says brightly.

Even Swarn looks surprised at Jagdish's new-found

confidence in their younger son. She pinches Tarun's cheek between thumb and forefinger and shakes his head slightly, 'Mela pyala pyala beta, my wittle, wittle son has become a bijnichman?'

Tarun knows this is only a hypothetical question and smiles weakly. Neena looks at him sympathetically and passes him the bottle of his favourite pickle. He throws her a grateful look but does not take his customary large helping of pickled green chillies. Apparently nothing will lift him from his misery today. Even his floppy lock is drooping sadly.

But Jagdish, seemingly unaware of the high emotions pulsing around the table, has a hearty meal, finishing off with a large bowl of mangoes chopped into yogurt. Scraping back his chair, he gets up without looking around to see if the others at the table have finished eating too. This is not unusual, and the rest of the family continue their meal unperturbed. They know that Jagdish has genuine trouble stopping himself from mentally chasing his foreign buyers, even when he is eating, sleeping or sitting in the company of other people. Swarn gets up and follows him into the bedroom.

Neena turns to Rohit after they have left the room, 'Does this mean you'll have to travel a lot?'

Rohit counters with a question to Tarun, 'When did all this happen? How come I wasn't told?'

Tarun, deeply unhappy, looks out of the window where the BMW awaits, newly washed and gleaming, ready to be driven off to distant pleasures. 'I have no choice any more.'

'What do you mean?' Rohit asks.

'You should know better than anyone else how good he is at putting pressure on people to get them to do what he wants,' Tarun says bitterly.

Rohit has never told Neena of the time his own arm was twisted to drop his young collegian and marry her. 'Yes, yes,' he says hastily.

Neena's question has still not been answered, 'Tell me,

will you be travelling a lot?'

Rohit is vague. 'Travelling, yes, I suppose so.'

'Where? When? Will I be able to come too?'

Tarun cuts in, 'You know what a scrooge the old man is. Can't see him letting you go along too often.'

A Manny look passes across Neena's face. She sticks her lower jaw out and mutters determinedly, 'Let him try to stop me.'

Gloom seems to have settled firmly across the table now. 'It won't be the money stopping him from sending you along. It'll be just to make sure I don't get to mix even an ounce of pleasure with business,' Rohit predicts darkly.

'God, how I hate him and his bloody business,' Tarun adds.

It is blazing hot outside and cyclists are labouring their way to shelter on LM Road. In the main bedroom of the Sachdev household, Jagdish is getting ready for an afternoon siesta on his Extrafoam divan bed. In a rare show of affection, Swarn sits down next to him. Filled with renewed confidence, Jagdish puts his arm around his wife while telling her of how he brought Tarun around to agreeing to join the business finally. Her look of open-mouthed wonder is most gratifying, and Jagdish remembers suddenly that it has been a very long time since he last dared to even contemplate the business of conjugal rights. He pulls Swarn closer to him, wondering tentatively if there might just be some scope in this for a bit of long denied hanky-panky. Gingerly he swings his leg over her vast hip.

In the dining room, the air conditioner continues to chug its cool air over the three youngsters who are seated on soft upholstered dining chairs, leaning their elbows on perfectly polished mahogany, still continuing to bemoan the business that has brought them these comforts.

■

A week later, Tarun is a businessman. He has been waking up at seven and having a bath before wearing smart clothes—

not Benetton sweatshirts, but clothes more befitting a managing partner of Sachdev Textiles and Exports. He has supervised, negotiated, planned and held conference. He has stayed within view of his father and followed him on occasion like a faithful puppy. As for Jagdish's side of the bargain, he has kept his word and not questioned his son's movements after 6 p.m., simply because he has no need. Tarun has been so exhausted by the day's events that he has asked for an early dinner and retired to bed by ten. Once again, five years after arranging Rohit's wedding, Jagdish pats himself more than a few times on the back, reminding his wife of what a wise and insightful head he has.

4

An ill wind (from London) blows in.

On the other side of Delhi (in the vast housing estate of Saket to be precise) another cast of characters is getting ready to drift into our frame. Neena's old classmate, Gayatri, has returned home. She and Keshava, her father, are pulling into the drive of their home in his dusty, clanging Standard Herald that has miraculously managed to survive the thirty-mile round trip to the international airport.

'Isn't it time for a new car, Appa?' Gayatri sighs as the car stalls again while trying to negotiate a speed breaker outside the gate.

'Nothing wrong with this one, moley. Just a little trouble with the carburettor sometimes.' With a great deal of crunching and scraping, he finally manages to get the car over the hump and into the gate. After parking it, he pats the dashboard and gets out with a loud groan. 'It's not the car but my knees that are packing up on me. Unless I shout, they just won't swing into action.'

'Oh, come, Appa, you look in the pink of health and haven't changed a bit since I last saw you. Now let me get the suitcase out.'

They open the boot of the car and together pull a large

suitcase out. 'You really should have come to see us at least once in these past five years, moley,' Keshava chides gently.

Gayatri is about to give him her stock excuses, but stops short as a tiny figure bustles out of the front door, sari flapping delightedly around her ankles. Gayatri bounds up two small stairs to give her mother an enormous hug. Raji emits a little shriek as she is lifted into the air. She flaps her blue-slippered feet in alarm, shrieking, 'Aiyyo, put me down you silly girl. I'm much heavier than when you last tried this.'

Gayatri, who is a good head taller than her mother, disregards the order completely, swinging her mother around effortlessly a few more times before finally putting her down. Raji, feet back on terra firma, clings dizzily to her daughter, looking her up and down through thick bifocals. 'You've become scrawny,' she says disapprovingly.

Gayatri, who is as lovely as Neena had described, has no reason to be concerned with her mother's critical appraisal. Fully aware of her own good looks, Gayatri figured out, even as a canny seven-year-old, the reason for which her mother seemed to be the only person loath to appreciate her loveliness. There was nothing malicious or envious about this. Raji would, given a choice, have spent her entire life with nose buried between the pages of an academic book. Instead, she had been married off as soon as she completed her two master's degrees and, ten months later, had found herself faced with the terrifying task of bringing up a baby girl. Completely unprepared for domesticity and parenthood, Raji had retreated into a state of disarming confusion that had caused her mild-mannered young husband to step manfully to the rescue. So when Gayatri, as a baby, needed lullabies and cuddles, it was Keshava who provided them. When she had to be admitted to school, again it was Keshava who did the rounds with his infant daughter in tow, and Keshava who attended PTA meetings, unravelled the mysteries of multiplication tables and applauded and wiped away fatherly tears at school concerts. Raji flapped helplessly around the fringes of this picture, able to cope marginally better as her daughter grew into a young woman.

At this point she started to notice, with some alarm, that Gayatri was blossoming into a beautiful young girl. Once again, Keshava took this in his usual placid manner, complimenting his daughter when deserved or banning the halter-neck she had once attempted wearing to a teenage party. Raji's method of coping with her daughter's good looks, however, was to surface every so often with a critical remark. This, Gayatri and Keshava both knew, was merely an occasional and absent-minded exercise in ensuring that she make some kind of contribution to the all-round development of her only child. Having never been a beauty herself and having produced by a quirk of fate a daughter who was, Raji felt it her duty to ensure that her daughter did not become arrogant. So Gayatri's second incisor was definitely crooked and looked terrible when she smiled, and her forehead was positively growing upwards because of Gayatri's bad habit of always running her hand through her hair, and wasn't that a great big pimple appearing on her left cheek—so big it was bound to leave a permanent mark. In all those remarks of Raji's were a strange combination of parental insecurity and overwhelming pride.

Gayatri helps Keshava bring her suitcase into the house. 'Do I still have my old room?' she asks.

'Exactly the way you left it,' her father replies, 'including the poster of Sting above your desk.'

'Sting! I'm impressed you remember the name, Appa.'

'Your Appa used to talk about you every day. Ev-very-day!' Raji says, as though surprised that a parent should remember his only child on such a regular basis.

Gayatri emits a cry as she enters the room. 'Goodness me! It is exactly the way I left it! Heavens, even those old slippers under the bed! Amma, you're sure this place has been cleaned since I left?'

'Every little thing cleaned and replaced every week,' Raji replies, even though it is Keshava who has religiously performed this task every Sunday. He hauls Gayatri's suitcase on to a tin trunk covered daintily by a Jaipuri sheet.

'Oh, God, we don't still have all our old trunks thinly camouflaged by bedcovers, do we?'

'What's wrong with them? They look perfectly nice to me,' Raji defends her decor hotly.

Gayatri replies with a laugh, 'Well, we've always hoped someone will be taken in by their masquerading as divans, but I'm not sure we ever succeeded.'

'Now, now, five years in England aren't going to make you turn your pretty nose up at everything you see here, I hope!'

Gayatri smiles apologetically at Keshava's admonition and gives him a warm hug, 'Oh, Appa, it's just great to see you both again. And I love your luxury divans, I wouldn't have them any other way, whatever I might say so cruelly about them sometimes.'

She goes to her suitcase and fiddles with the locks. 'Pressie time!' she cries happily, throwing open the lid and rummaging around among the T-shirts and jeans. She pulls out a polo neck jumper and hands it to her father. 'Pour vous, mon papa!'

Keshava takes it from her, laughing. 'I thought we sent you to England to learn English!'

'In England, Appa, you have to be able to throw the odd French word around with panache if you really want to sound English. Believe me, there's no snob like an English snob. But, tell me, how do you like your new jumper?'

'Very good. Wasn't expensive I hope?'

'Nah,' Gayatri replies, diving back into her suitcase, 'and this is for my Amma—a lovely scent for my lovely Amma.' She hands her mother a large bottle of perfume.

Raji takes it from her and sniffs at it worriedly. 'This must have been expensive,' she says. 'Why have you spent all this money, moley? Your grant couldn't have afforded you very much.'

'The grant was reasonably generous actually. I always

had a bit left over, and I worked during the holidays in a bar, don't forget. The money from that always came in handy for the odd bit of luxury.'

'We were so worried that you were struggling financially and kept wishing that we had money to send to tide you over. But the exchange rate is always so hopeless, they tell me. It was about a year after you left that we found we were really missing you. Your father especially. He would come and sit here in your room for hours sometimes.'

Gayatri is silent. She cannot bring herself to say that money had never been what had held her back. A face drifts through her mind briefly, a face she has tried very hard to forget these past few weeks—angular, grey eyed, loved. Well, loved once, she reminds herself swiftly.

She quickly brings her mind back to the present. To this little home in Delhi that has waited, filled with real love and longing, all the years that she has been away. Suddenly guilty at how often she has allowed herself to forget this fact, she sits next to her father on the bed and gives him another hug. 'Oh, Appa,' she says tenderly, 'I missed you too. But you two worry too much about me, really. I was fine there. And I'm glad that I'm back.' Her voice is emphatic and her father looks at her profile, sensing she is speaking more to herself than to either of her parents. He feels a sudden clutch of fear on behalf of his lovely daughter. Protecting her was so easy when she was a little girl.

Raji says briskly, 'Do the rest of your unpacking after lunch, moley. Can you smell the sambar bubbling away?'

Gayatri smiles at her mother. 'Sambar! Haven't had sambar in absolutely ages! There was a place near the institute that did dosas. Run by Bangladeshis, would you believe it! And you'd get about one thimble-full of sambar if you ordered the special dosa. Perfectly ghastly sambar too. Some sort of Bangladeshi version of it.'

'Well, give me another five minutes, and then lunch will be ready. The geyser's on. Do you want your bath now or after lunch?'

'Oh, lunch first, please, if it's your sambar and rice, Amma.'

■

Neena is going through her wardrobe in a state of some distress. 'Nothing fits!' she wails to no one in particular. She pulls out a voluminous dress and holds it against herself, looking at her reflection critically in the mirror. She is not pleased with what she sees and stuffs it angrily back on to the shelf. She turns to Rohit, who is just coming into the room. 'I've got nothing to wear, Rohit!' she cries.

'The universal cry of female despair,' Rohit says absently, really not too worried about his wife's grave lack of apparel.

'I hadn't realized how much weight I'd put on, Rohit, with the two pregnancies. Damn those kids. Look at my bum!'

'I know, darling. Never mind.'

'Oh, and don't give me that the-more-there-is-of-you-the-better sanctimonious shit. I know you don't mean a word of it. Don't think I don't notice you staring at some of these slim beauty types.'

Rohit looks confused, throws his hands upwards in exasperation but says nothing.

Neena continues to rant, turning back to her wardrobe, 'I bet she'll be all slim and svelte and lovely as ever!' She is referring, of course, to Gayatri, whom she is due to meet at six.

Neena is still more or less the pretty young girl Rohit had married, perhaps veering closer now to more rather than to less. It is certainly true that she has expanded in all directions in her contented years of marriage and childbearing. 'Pleasantly plump' is how one would describe her, if one were of a kind and gentle disposition. 'Really getting rather fat' would be the somewhat more honest description, particularly if one were to be given the benefit of Neena's ample derrière stuffed recklessly into a pair of jeans.

She now takes such a reckless decision, plunging back

into her extensive wardrobe, emerging with a pair of jeans in her hands. With a look of determination on her face (and it is at these moments that she most resembles her father), she puts her feet into the legs and, taking the stance of a sumo wrestler, proceeds to haul them over her hips and buttocks. First stage complete, she takes a deep breath and yanks the metal zip upwards. The zip, out of approximately three years of disuse and unaccustomed to its passage obstructed by a fold of overhanging adipose tissue, refuses to budge. Neena sticks out her chin again and makes a few more unsuccessful attempts.

Many a weaker woman would, by this point, have given in gracefully and reverted to Plan 1, voluminous dress with vertical stripes, but Neena is not Manny Singh's daughter for nothing. She throws herself on to the bed and focusses her gaze on the lazily swirling ceiling fan. Once she has reached the point of complete concentration, she makes one more attempt. Cellulite, obeying the laws of gravity, slides back, occupying handy spaces between liver and stomach, this time allowing the zip to make an unsafe and laboured journey towards the fastening button. Button is to be the next contest, but fortunately it goes into its receiving hole, with the only casualty a broken nail. This is but a small price to pay for zip and button to have occupied their rightful places.

Neena, pleased, now hauls herself to her feet, staggering only slightly as her ample tissue returns to its normal position, straining against zip and seams. She totters back to the mirror and examines herself. She puts her feet into a pair of stiletto-heeled sandals to make the picture look better. She looks distastefully at the tyre of fat that is overhanging the waist of her jeans, obscuring the button completely. Loose top, she thinks. Lunging back into the wardrobe, she pulls out a large T-shirt with vertical stripes and yanks it on over her arms. She looks at herself again. Hmmmm, she thinks. She sticks her hands on her waist, elbows akimbo, and strikes a model-like pose. Not bad, she mulls, not bad at all. She turns around to look over her shoulder to get a rear view. Almost slim. She then reaches out for her make-up kit.

Rohit, who has been watching the battle with amazement, wisely does not comment. Neena's gaze is now squinting and focussing fiercely on her left eyebrow as her tweezers are poised for attack. Rohit takes advantage of his wife's concentration to slink unnoticed out of the room.

Once ready and looking really rather presentable (almost the girl she once was), Neena totters carefully down the stairs to check that Nek Singh, the driver, is free to take her to visit her friend in Saket, on the other side of town. She finds him sitting on the steps of the kitchen, exchanging beedis and gossip with Moolchand.

'Ready to leave?' she asks him as he scrambles to his feet hiding the beedi, but not its smoke, behind his back. He would really rather have the glass of tea Moolchand is making first, but he nods.

Neena trips back into the house. Already she is feeling out of breath. With her tight jeans and high heels, she knows she is best advised to stay in either a vertical or horizontal position, but she knows that she and Gayatri are unlikely to be slipping upstairs to lie on her bed and chat as they used to all those years ago. As college friends, they had come to treat each other's houses with the familiarity of their own, often sleeping over at one place or the other, giggling and talking into the night under cover of the blankets. Boys, elections to the drama society, clothes—these had been their concerns. For Neena, visits to Gayatri's house were an eye-opener because the Menon family were her only insight into ordinary middle-class life. Through them she had learnt, inadvertently, that the price of rice had gone up again or that bedrooms were not always air-conditioned spaces. To her credit, she had taken on this learning exercise with a sense of wonder and humility, never slipping into snobbish comparisons to the luxuries of her own home.

Gayatri, on the other hand, had never allowed herself to be overawed by the plush Singh residence at Sainik Farms, with its five cars (among four people), dogs so lazy that they seem not to have bothered to even master the art of barking and, of course, a battery of servants. Gayatri's obvious advantages, both academically and in terms of natural grace and charm, made it easier for her to accept that there were certain things she was not born to have. There was no cause for worry because she knew that her intelligence and charm would help her to acquire all those other things some day.

Neena's plan today is to drop her two children off at her parents' house at Sainik Farms before going to Gayatri's. There the maid will find it easier to keep them amused because of the sprawling garden and the swing that has been tied for them under the mango tree. Being evening, it will also give Manny the opportunity to perform some grandfatherly dandling and coddling. She now calls out to her mother-in-law to tell her that they are about to leave.

Swarn has roused herself from an extended afternoon nap but is still lying in bed, reading the latest *Good Housekeeping* and wondering why Moolchand is taking so long with the tea. She does not know that the tea has been made a while ago, and that the delay is because Moolchand is plucking up all his measly courage to perform this daily task, one that has become truly unbearable for him. Age seems only to make it worse. Weakened sphincter muscles are not as obedient as young ones, he has discovered to his mortified cost.

Finally, gathering all his wits about him, he enters Swarn's chambers. It is just as he has thought. The half-darkness created by the drawn curtains, a lilting raga playing on the stereo and the soft body of the memsahib, lying prone and still half-drugged by sleep, is all it takes. Suddenly Moolchand has lost his composure again. He can feel the palpitations begin, his hands start to tremble as he puts the tray of tinkling tea things on her bedside table. He can smell her from here—a whiff of stale talcum powder, a bit of afternoon sweat, remnants of some perfume from her morning card session. It takes all of Moolchand's self-control to prevent himself from launching his bony brown frame on to Swarn's pliant person. Conversation is too risky. He leaves the room hurriedly, intending to take his wayward penis off to the servants' bathroom.

Swarns wonders what Moolchand is sulking about now as she drags her plump self up, rearranging the cushions behind her. She can hear Neena hollering for her from somewhere outside. What does the silly girl want now, she thinks irritatedly. Let her wait, she mutters as she stirs two large spoonfuls of sugar into her cup. But Neena, never the shy, retiring type, knocks briefly on her mother-in-law's door before barging straight in. She comes straight to the point: 'Mamma, I'm going to visit my old college friend who has come from abroad. I'm taking Rinku and Ritik over to Sainik Farms to Mummy's. We should be back for dinner.'

Swarn doesn't think any of this really warrants either a reply or the generous bestowal of permission. Modern-day daughters-in-law, she has realized, do not hang around waiting for permission or blessings as they did in her day. Now one just has to accept, she thinks wearily. Accept, adjust, accommodate—the mantra for today's mother-in-law. She nods weakly and takes a deep breath as Neena sweeps out of the room in a flurry of some expensive perfume.

Through her sleep-addled brain, Swarn later wonders why Neena is wearing something so strange and tight, but it is too late to ask. And it isn't as if she would have dared to ask, anyway. You could never predict how these modern-day daughters-in-law would react to the most innocent of queries. And who was this friend from abroad? Surely she was entitled to know more about her daughter-in-law's movements! That's how it used to be anyway. Daughters-in-law did not just announce their departures and up and leave like that, moreover wearing such strange, tight clothes! These days men were such idiots, allowing their wives to wear stupid clothes and go off wherever they wanted with no questions asked. Poor Rohit, so innocent, so much in love with that girl that he had lost all sense of what was right and wrong. Swarn sighs deeply before taking another long sip of sugary tea. Through the window, she can hear Neena's high-pitched voice as the car starts up and pulls out of the drive on to LM Road.

■

Mrs Menon is trying to make her drawing room look plush. It is a room overwhelmed by hundreds of books. Even the sofa, except for a corner that someone has cleared to make room to sit, has not been spared this deluge of printed material. Raji fusses around, picking up papers from one area and putting them down willy-nilly in another. She finally gives upon this futile exercise, sticks a money plant into an old brass urn and plonks it on top of a pile of papers and files. Not that she would normally bother with such earthly details, but even she is conscious that her daughter's old friend is visiting after so many years.

She had last seen Neena at her lavish wedding over at the Sooraj Intercontinental. Even though Gayatri had already left for England, Neena and her mother had come over to invite the Menons, insisting they attend. Mrs Menon did not usually have much truck with these moneyed Punjabi types, but she had grown fond of Neena over the years and rather liked her mother too ... what was her name now? ... something sort of modern and Punjabi rolled into one. Puppies, Mr Menon called people like them ... Punjabi Upcoming Professionals. Kammy's name was still eluding Raji. All she could remember at the moment was that she did some sort of social work, despite all her money.

The Menons had gone for the Singh-Sachdev wedding in the end, taking a small Kerala lamp as a gift, and had felt considerably out of place among the Jamawar shawls and diamonds. Their old Herald chugged its way up the steep drive to the hotel portico, coughing and wheezing and finally stalling in front of the surprised commissionaire, a large dignified Sikh more accustomed to seeing Mercedes sweeping grandly towards him. Unused to hobnobbing with the likes of secretaries and ministers, the Menons had eaten a hasty dinner huddled together in a corner of the plush Raj Pavilion, crowded with ice sculptures and chandeliers. They had managed to hand over their gift to Neena, battling their way through the glittering crowd to meet her and her sweet-faced new husband, and had then left without sampling even one of the twelve sweets on offer, much to Keshava's disappointment.

Raji wasn't usually a competitive type, but today, partially for Gayatri's sake, she wanted to create a good impression with Neena Singh . . . Neena Sachdev, she corrected herself. She wondered whether marriage and children would have changed her much, as she dusted around the piles of books littering coffee tables, window sills, arms of chairs, even the floor. Not that she thought it was a good thing that Neena had gone and got married so soon after graduation. But then she had plenty of money, her parents' money, to fall back on, unlike Gayatri, for whom education was the only gift her parents could confer. Maybe now was the time to start thinking about marriage for Gayatri too. There were, even for the best-educated women, certain comforts only marriage could bring. Raji in particular knew how poorly she would have managed in life without the gentle support of the kindly Keshava. She had tentatively broached the subject of marriage with Gayatri last night and had been surprised at the vehemence of her response.

'Never, Amma!' her daughter had said.

'Never, moley?' Raji had been genuinely startled.

'Never. Couldn't be bothered with all that.' Gayatri tossed her head, looking mutinous.

'No, I don't mean you should necessarily marry a Malayali boy. If there is someone you are interested in . . .'

But, contrary to her parents' wishes, Gayatri is clearly not interested in anybody. Her face has worn a distant look whenever marriage had been mentioned these past two days. Her parent will never know that marriage is an institution she has grown scornful of during her years in England. She knows, better than most, how easily those ties can be betrayed. She has returned to India with marriage furthest from her mind. In fact, she has no particular plans at all. As soon as she had completed her Ph.D., she booked her ticket and flew back to India with her parents' faces floating in front of her eyes. It was one of those rare occasions when Gayatri did something impulsively, without weighing the pros and cons, without planning for it months, even years, in advance. She had just wanted to see her parents, suddenly, and with the kind of longing she had never felt before.

She comes into the room just as Raji is trying to stick some fern leaves among the yellow plastic blooms in a vase on top of the TV. 'What on earth are you doing that for, Amma?' she asks.

'Maybe these will look like real flowers, moley, if I put these leaves in the middle of them.' She steps back and surveys her handiwork. 'No, they still look like plastic flowers, no?'

Gayatri, who has not taken the kind of trouble Neena has in choosing her apparel for this visit, does not feel the need to relieve her mother of her stress nor get the house in sudden shape. Her self-assurance has often been mistaken for arrogance, but she has never tried to correct people in this misconception. She now flops down on the brown Rexine sofa, miraculously cleared of its cargo of books, and asks, 'Where's Appa?'

'Market,' her mother replies, 'to get some samosas and sweets for Neena.'

'Oh, Amma, he shouldn't have bothered! It's only Neena, and she's probably on a diet anyway.' Gayatri smiles fondly as she remembers, 'One of life's eternal dieters, old Neena.'

'I know, but he felt we should have something nice to offer her. She is your oldest friend after all. And married to such a rich businessman now!'

'As if that should make a difference at all, Amma!'

'No, no. No difference, but you don't want her coming here and thinking we don't know how to do things nicely, do you?'

'To be honest, Amma, I don't really care if she thinks things like that.'

'But she's your friend. Used to be your best friend in fact!'

'Friend or no friend, it's what I think about me that counts, Amma.'

Raji wonders from where her daughter could have picked up such a lofty attitude. Sometimes she has felt a little guilty about having been too busy in her own academic pursuits to have bothered much with her only child's upbringing, although she had tried to make amends once Gayatri had grown up a bit, taking an interest in her college admissions and later her search for scholarships. But, in a sense, it was by then too late. Not that Gayatri was a bad girl, in fact, quite the reverse. It was merely that Keshava's bringing up of her had left her with too great a sense of her own importance, Raji believed. Sometimes she even felt strongly enough about it to accuse him of having spoilt their daughter shamelessly. But the truth was that Raji herself sometimes observed her self-possessed, confident daughter with a twinge of envy. Girls in her time, and in the small town of Varkala where she had grown up, had never been encouraged to think too hard for themselves. The fact that Raji had actually managed to get an education was purely a function of her not being good-looking enough to have made an early marriage like most of her cousins. In that respect, she knew that she had merely got lucky.

She sits down next to her daughter on the sofa and gives her a hug. 'Just a few years away from home and now you are teaching your mother some lessons in life, eh?' Before Gayatri can reply, the doorbell clamours. Raji flies up in a state of agitation, trilling, 'Oh, that must be your Neena. Get the door, straighten the cushion, I'll put the water for tea.'

Gayatri throws the front door open, and there are loud, shrieking noises for a few minutes as the two girls throw themselves into each other's arms. Even the tranquil Gayatri has temporarily lost her composure in her excitement at seeing her old friend again. They part for a few minutes, take an arm's length look at each other before throwing themselves at each other again, loudly jabbering all sorts of unintelligible things. Finally, peace prevails as, giggling and wiping away tears, they unclasp themselves from each other and make their way indoors. Neena, following Gayatri into the room, spots her friend's mother smiling unsurely from the kitchen door and runs to give her a warm hug. She wonders vaguely why Mrs Menon is greeting her with a ragged duster clutched tightly in one hand, but she remembers that Gayatri's mum has always been a little peculiar.

The girls sit down together on the sofa. 'Oh, it's so marvellous to see you!' Gayatri cries again. She never made any proper friends in England and knows that the old bond she shares with Neena is terribly special.

Neena looks enviously at Gayatri, languidly occupying a loose pair of jeans. Her own are cutting terribly into her waist and crotch. 'Hey yaar, just look at you, as slim as ever! I do love my kids dearly, but I hate them for having done this to my figure.'

Gayatri laughs. 'You should have brought your kids. I'd love to have seen them,' she says.

'The kids? Heavens, no! There's no chance of decent conversation with those two around.'

'How old are they?' Raji asks.

'Oh, four and ten months. Rinku and Ritik.'

Puppie names, Raji thinks, but she smiles and says, 'You should bring them over sometime. We never saw you again after your wedding.'

'Oh, you know what it's like, Aunty, with kids and all. Never a moment for the things one wants to do.'

Raji, fairly certain her experience of marriage and childbirth has been very different from Neena's, gets up saying, 'I'll leave you two girls to catch up and go and make the tea.'

Neena puts on her charming voice. 'Oh, Aunty, can I have your coffee, please? I do so love your south Indian coffee.'

Raji is not sure whether Keshava has put coffee powder into the percolator this morning, but she nods obligingly as she makes her way to the kitchen. She opens up the old steel percolator, inherited from Keshava's mother, and peers into it. Bless him, a bit of black liquid gleams up at her. It is a universally acknowledged fact that Keshava makes a far superior cup of coffee than she does, but she takes to her task with enthusiasm, opening up an old biscuit tin to arrange a few murukkus on a plate. She remembers that Neena used to love these crunchy snacks, purchased by Keshava from the south Indian stores at R.K. Puram. By the time Raji has returned to the living room, the two girls are engaged in animated chatter and are completely oblivious to her. She leaves the coffees and snacks on the table and tactfully leaves the room.

'No, yaar, it's not too bad really. We have our separate lives upstairs. She doesn't ever come up to our floor. The stairs make her asthmatic, fortunately.' The person whose asthma Neena is referring to with such a marked lack of sympathy is her mother-in-law, Swarn.

Gayatri giggles. She is still curious about Neena's living arrangements. 'Yes, but don't you all eat together? I mean, who chooses the menus?'

'Oh, she does, of course,' Neena replies matter of factly.

'But what if you don't like what she's chosen?'

'Oh, I don't mind that because it makes me eat less,' Neena replies patting her belly. 'I could do with losing some weight, no?'

'You're okay, sweetie,' Gayatri says, contemplating the value of truth within a friendship. 'Well, maybe just a weenie bit around the hips, perhaps.'

'It's terrible, isn't it—the price one has to pay for having kids. But look at you! Still so gorgeous and trim.'

'Yes, but I haven't got a little four-year-old, nor a cute ten-month-old, don't forget. I'm sure I've lost out on a great deal too.' She smiles ruefully at her friend. 'The price to pay for slim hips, eh?'

'But, surely you don't plan to carry on like this. You must want kids some day?' Neena notices the shadow that passes over Gayatri's face. 'What's up?' she asks. 'You are happy, aren't you?'

'Of course, I'm happy,' Gayatri replies quickly. 'Why shouldn't I be? It's just so great being back.'

'Well, you must have liked being there, looking at the frequency with which you kept coming back!'

'Sarcasm has never suited you, love. Your face is far too sweet to carry it off.'

'Well, tell me then, what was it that kept you from coming home to visit us all?'

Gaytri looks for a minute as though she is tempted to open up her heart to her old friend. Then she shrugs her shoulders and says, laughingly, 'Oh, this and that.'

'This and that! What sort of a reply is that? Surely you owe us all a better explanation!'

Gayatri takes a deep breath. Her years amongst the English have left her unused to such an openly curious and affectionate barrage. She speaks gently to her friend, weighing her words carefully, 'Well, there was my Ph.D., of course. I couldn't leave without completing that. Then, money wasn't exactly in plenty. And then, I'd wanted to use my stint abroad to travel a bit . . . Europe, particularly.'

'Oh, how exciting, where did you travel?'

'Mmm, let's see . . . France, Germany, Austria.'

'You lucky thing! I haven't been abroad since that trip to the US with my parents when I was in school. How I'd love to bum around Europe!'

'Rohit too busy with work?'

'God, yes. And his father's a bit of a miser too. Just because they never seem to want to go anywhere together, they happily assume that we'll be the same.'

'Well, I suppose, the kids being so small doesn't really help either.'

'Yeah, there's that too. Although I could always leave them and the maid with my mum. Things could be looking up soon. Rohit might have to travel abroad quite frequently soon on business—and guess who'll be tagging along!'

Gayatri laughs, 'It won't be quite the same thing, trying to squeeze in some fun in between Rohit's appointments. Now, if you'd only thought of doing that when I was there, we could have taken off and had some fun, you and I.'

'Oh, that would have been just too good to be true!' Neena sighs longingly at the thought.

They are interrupted by the arrival of Keshava, who shouts a loud hello on spotting Neena. He rescues the oil-stained paper bag he is carrying by holding it high above his head as Neena jumps up to envelop him in a bear hug. He notices that she feels distinctly podgier than she did before, but he smiles down at the young woman affectionately, 'How are you, Neena? Now you have to give me some very good explanation for why you never came to see us while Gayatri was away.'

'Oh, Uncle, busy, busy, busy. What more can I say? Two kids, you know.'

Keshava nods forgivingly. It had only been a hypothetical question anyway. Many years of living in Delhi have taught him too to utter these meaningless things that have to be said. 'First let me give you these lovely samosas I have just got from the market, hot-hot.'

'Oh, Uncle, you shouldn't have!' Neena exclaims after Keshava as he goes into the kitchen to arrange the samosas on a plate. In a few minutes he emerges with the snack. 'I'm really trying to lose some weight,' she adds unconvincingly as she helps herself to a large samosa, dribbling the accompanying tamarind sauce liberally over it. Keshava assesses the change in Neena's appearance in the years since they have met and wisely refrains from comment. Gayatri smiles at him gratefully and, like Raji, he too makes only a little small talk before mumbling some excuse and vanishing indoors.

The two girls carry on talking long into the evening, their conversation spanning all manner of things from mothers-in-law to leg wax to the relative merits of Indian and Englishmen.

'Englishmen make far better husbands, believe me,' Gayatri expounds knowledgeably to her open-mouthed friend. 'They're not doing you a favour if they happen to do the hoovering or the dishes. You don't even have to thank them.'

Neena is suitably impressed, 'What! All Englishmen?' Gayatri is, of course, making her sweeping remark on the basis of a mere handful of men she had made acquaintance with during her years in England, but she nods authoritatively. Neena gasps delightedly, 'Oh, what a little heaven England must be then!'

It will take another few meetings and a session of sprawling together on an old teenage bed, looking up at the whirling ceiling fan and the deepening shadows on the ceiling, before Gayatri will find herself able to tell Neena about the one Englishman she did get to know particularly well. Of the only man who ever had the nerve to reduce the otherwise proud, vain young woman to a trembling, pleading state merely three months ago. It is a memory that still makes her want to shudder, that can still, in an unguarded moment, make her stop short and relive, horribly, the breathless whirling state of confusion and pain she had found herself in so unexpectedly.

Michael . . . Michael, whose dark grey eyes had seemed so intriguing once. Eyes that had once seemed so fascinatingly to reflect the brooding uncertainty of English skies. How Gayatri had come to love them. Making him close them by stroking her forefinger gently up his chin and nose and over his eyes. First closing one and then the other. Just to see him open them again to smile up at her as she lay over him. It was with those same eyes that he had later looked at her so coldly, when she had begged and pleaded, hating herself for doing so. She remembers, despite the state of bewilderment she found herself in that awful day, how like cold, dirty ice they had looked, sharp and jagged and merciless.

But today, as Neena leaves Gayatri's house after her visit, she is completely unaware of the travails her friend has suffered while abroad. All she has seen is an old friend who has acquired a Ph.D. and stayed annoyingly slim hipped in the process. She gets into her car and, as the driver turns on to Mehrauli Road, finds herself thinking, for the first time ever, of the way her own life has turned out. This is a line of thought quite new to her. She has enjoyed making Rohit and the children the centre of her life, she tells herself irritatedly. Achieving one's own potential (a favourite Kammy phrase) is a highly overrated thing. What is important is love . . . and marriage . . . and, of course, physical comforts and good health and money and so on and so forth, she adds hastily. Her life has been a comfortable one, why, an enviable one by most people's standards, she reminds herself, feeling cross that she has to do so.

Another thought occurs to Neena: not having had the freedom Gayatri enjoyed abroad has actually cocooned her away from many of life's stresses. For all her slimness, Gayatri's eyes seemed listless and dull, with little shadows under them. Life's stresses—she wonders what those might be. But she is smart enough to know that, alongside those stresses, she has probably missed out on some of life's thrills too. Ups were sort of always accompanied by downs, weren't they?

Neena is no great philosopher, and all this uncustomary thinking is wearing her out. She feels exhausted suddenly and just wants to scoop her kids up in her arms and give them a great big hug. She doesn't notice the lights of passing cars that are illuminating her face. The traffic is heavy as office-goers return home, and even her driver does not notice the passing shadows on Neena's chubby, normally pleasant face.

5

A love game

Tarun, the businessman, is hard at work. He has spent the entire morning with Mr Iyyengar, the chartered accountant, a dour and humourless man even at the best of times. Now, even though it is lunchtime, he is going through the files again to check some of the queries that have been put to him by the nit-picking accountant. The transformation in Tarun has been amazing. Even Jagdish, watching through the glass of his nearby cabin, cannot quite believe how neatly he has managed to pull off this seemingly improbable stunt.

Admittedly it has only been two weeks, and it is still perfectly possible that Tarun will tire of this newly acquired persona, that the call of the Float, Delhi's newest nightclub, will resound too heavily in his ears one evening until his feet take him there unbidden. He will then be far too bleary-eyed and wretched the next morning to go into the office with his father, and, in the space of a few hours, Tarun the Businessman could very easily be back to being just cheerful, irrepressible Tarun again. But what is happening, in fact, is that the Fates are conspiring against young Tarun, completely unbeknown to him. Now they are setting about, creating a storm on his horizon that will seal his life in that direction forever. The mischief was started on the afternoon that Jagdish finally reached the end of his famously short tether. Poor, poor Tarun.

Roughly, what is to happen is this: Love, in all its glory and splendour, is coming Tarun's way. It is gathering its wiliest, canniest tools together, placing them in the hands of a small, plump, determined woman, to ensure that this young man will be caught and condemned inevitably to its powers. For Tarun there is to be no escape. Not that he will seem particularly keen to escape its clutches when it does come. As with most people who fall in love for the first time, Tarun will feel more agreeable about his state of mind than he has ever done before. Of course, he has briefly felt love on other occasions. Very briefly. When he first slipped his hot palm up sixteen-year-old Pamela Kochar's blouse, for instance, feeling her peanut-like nipples and his penis spring simultaneously and painfully to attention. Or when, on a balmy autumn evening, the Dusshera bonfires had suffused the face of his visiting young cousin Aruna Sachdev with a soft, glowing pink. Tarun can still recall the stirrings that broke out (within and without) as she had looked breathlessly up at him with a thin film of sweat breaking out on her upper lip.

Was any of that love, one may ask cynically, uncaringly? The important thing is that to Tarun (at that precise moment in time), it was. He would have been truly horrified if, on any of those sweetly wretched moments, anyone had been unkind enough to point out that love was not merely a breathless, gasping quality that stirred so riotously at the private parts. That there were far better things to come— companionship and conversation too, surprisingly. Those new pleasures Tarun will discover very soon.

But we get too far ahead. Many new things await Tarun, but he needs to be warned that his joy will not be met with any enthusiasm by any of his immediate family. A common enough scenario, one might say. But, wait, there's worse to come. Sadly, Tarun's joy will not be met with much enthusiasm by the very subject of his emotions. That, most would agree, is more than just a small inconvenience in the matter of love.

■

Swarn is preparing for a visit from her samdhin. When the children of two women marry, they are bonded together by this word that indicates, all at once, the jealousies, the comparisons, the careful calculations of their children's time spent at one place or the other. It is generally not a happy relationship. In Swarn's case, it is exacerbated by the fact that she has absolutely nothing in common with her only samdhin, Kammy.

But these are the motions one must go through once one's children are married. Kammy feels obliged to make that once a month visit, gritting her teeth, preparing herself for Swarn's litany of complaints about life in general while she dolefully passes around her greasy cheese pakoras. Swarn, on her part, is girding her loins to receive more boring news of Kammy's social work with those dreary village types. It is a monthly ritual that both women have come to dread but have learnt to put up with because it just has to be done, ji. Only for the sake of one's children, ji.

Swarn picks up her cut-glass vase and places it prominently on the coffee table. She knows it is one of the few pieces she has that Kammy secretly covets, and it gives her great pleasure to watch Kammy's eyes slide lovingly towards it all through the conversation. She then sits heavily on her sofa, her soft flesh oozing out of the folds of her chiffon sari, and calls out to the maid to bring in the flowers. Orange gladioli, to draw attention to the lovely, tall vase. She then starts to arrange the flowers, while the maid runs between the sitting room and the kitchen with jugs of water, pairs of scissors and bunches of ferns. Surveying the arrangement critically and making sure the leaves do not obscure the vase, Swarn pushes it to the centre of the glass table and orders the maid to mop up the water she has spilt on its surface.

Her eyes flick over the rest of the room. The gilded, carved chairs are perfectly aligned, their maroon cushions glinting and velvety. The Rubens look-alike paintings glisten darkly in the dim light filtering through the thick, drawn curtains. Swarn bought these paintings of bathing nudes at the Pragati Maidan exhibition last winter, after some hesitation over the possibility that they might make Tarun even more libidinal. The pair she had finally chosen were of two fat women sitting half-submerged in a stream flowing through dark woodlands. She felt that English paintings like these would make her drawing room look sophisticated. She had no time for all that ethnic art rubbish that Kammy crammed her own living room with. Terracotta Ganeshas and brass bells everywhere—hai, who wants to see Indian things in India anyway!

The doorbell is bonging gently. Oh, dear, she's here. 'Moolchand!' Swarn cries out before she sees the tall shambling figure of the cook emerge from the kitchen and make his slow, grumbling way to the front door. What is his problem now? Just as Kammy appears at the front door, Neena comes rushing down the steps with the baby in her arms. Rinku is trailing after her, dragging a doll by its hair.

Always she does this, Swarn thinks to herself, always coming down to see her own mother. The amount of time that Neena spends in her upstairs quarters has been another of Swarn's secret bugbears. She carefully calculates every day the amount of time that Neena spends downstairs, taking out the time for eating meals and the fifteen minutes when Rohit comes in from work and has a cup of tea before going up to change. It is an average of less than half an hour. Unless Rohit is around, of course, as on Sundays or holidays. He, good son that he is, makes it a point to spend time with his father and his mother, and then, of course, Neena hangs around as well. Swarn thinks she ought to tell Neena some day that it is not that she doesn't notice any of these things. She is just too decent to say anything and make a great big fuss. She now hoists herself up laboriously from the sofa, wincing a little with the pain in her knees, and hobbles her way cheerlessly to the front lobby.

'Oh, Mummy!' Neena is saying. 'You shouldn't have!' Kammy is carrying a large bunch of flowers.

Doesn't look like they are from a shop, Swarn thinks (noticing that they are wrapped in household cling film), must be just from her own garden. But she goes up to Kammy to give her a fumbled sideways hug, their cheeks barely touching, and says with as much warmth as she can muster, 'Helloji, Kammyji. How nice to see you.' She raises her voice a pitch. 'Oh, what beautiful flowers!'

Kammy is looking resplendent in a cream Dhaka cotton, worn with the kind of easy panache that Swarn has struggled all her life to acquire. Swarn is much the better looking woman, of course, except for the layers of fat now enveloping her beautiful chiseled features. But what Kammy has is a certain indescribable quality that can still make men eye her appreciatively. Perhaps it is the warm rumbling voice. Perhaps it is her husky smoker's laugh. Maybe (although Swarn would never ever be able to comprehend this) it is her easy familiarity with India's villages and villagers that makes her somehow different from other Delhiwallahs. A difference she flaunts in the knick-knacks she has unique access to— wooden beads and terracotta bangles, custom-made for her by grateful village women, all of which she wears with style and confidence. But there is something earthy and musky and distinct about Kammy that sometimes makes even Swarn's husband feel weak at the knees. Not that Swarn doesn't notice, but it is one of her pet theories (and another secret one) that men have a certain uncontrollable liking for women of the soil, women who are dark-skinned and look dirty. Those tribal types, with their unkempt hair and wide hips. It makes Swarn shudder, but she knows it is this unwashed, tribal look of Kammy's that gives Jagdish that faraway look in his eyes after a visit from the Singhs.

They all go into the drawing room, and Moolchand is dispatched to get the tea things. As they seat themselves,

Neena holds forth, treating her mother and mother-in-law to a litany of complaints about her two children. The two older women listen with fond smiles on their faces, the grandchildren being about the only thing they have in common. Even reproaches about those two small individuals are pleasing to listen to somehow. Neena, aware of this, is careful to maintain this as the primary subject of conversation whenever they are together as a threesome. There is little point in allowing Kammy to embark on her favourite subject of Seva, as this will only bring about a glazed look on Swarn's face. It will be even worse if Neena allows Swarn to indulge in her favourite grouses about the difficulty in finding good domestic staff and the rising price of meat, as this will only make Kammy shift about in her chair, heedless of concealing her boredom. So Neena prattles on, beginning to feel increasingly sorry for herself as she notices that she has much more than she had realized to complain about. 'They are taking up all of my time, those two, Mamma. Even Rohit is not helping as much as she used to.'

'He must be busy with work, beta,' Kammy puts in soothingly. In polite society, a woman never complains overtly about her son-in-law, nor does she openly protect her son, so Swarn remains silent.

'But, Mamma, he used to spend at least the evenings with them before. Now he is too busy for anything. He comes home so late from the factory. Every day.'

By now Swarn is cut to the quick to hear her beloved older son being defamed so wildly. 'You see, they are expanding the business, Kammyji,' she says, trying not to sound defensive. She continues, this time addressing her daughter-in-law, 'This is nothing, Neena. When I was your age, your father-in-law hardly came home at all. Always bijness, bijness, bijness. That is all he would ever think about. I had to bring up my two boys completely on my own.'

Neena knows this is untrue but holds her tongue. She is hardly ever rude to Rohit's parents, despite the occasional temptation. On the other hand, she is not given to being particularly cordial to them. Neena has, over the years, found what she feels is a good balance in her relationship with her in-laws. She is still deeply enamoured of her husband and does not want to do anything that might displease him, but her upbringing (both the Kammy and the Manny elements) will always ensure, much to Swarn's displeasure, that she will never stray into the realm of the doormat daughter-in-law. She looks at her feet, examining her new pink nail polish, managing not to convey how much she disagrees with Swarn. Wriggling her toes and admiring the little pink squares, she changes the subject, 'How's Danny, Mamma?'

Danny, Neena's younger brother, is at the moment studying for a degree in business administration at an American university. If any of Danny's professors back in his college at Delhi University had ever heard the words *study* and *Danny Singh* used in conjunction with each other, there would have followed an astounded raising of eyebrows. Danny spent most of his recent three years at Bhagat Singh College roaring in and out of its portals on his Kawasaki Bajaj motorcycle, and study was very far from his mind at the time. Not that it is greatly on his mind at the moment in faraway Reno, but he is vaguely conscious of the fact that his father has paid vast quantities of money to send him to the US for further studies. He is also particularly keen to impress a certain female classmate who wears shorts so tiny they only half cover her plump bottom, a feature that has, on perusal, nearly made a sweaty Danny all but pass out.

'He is fine, Neena, as far as we know. He never writes, you know, Swarnji, but once in a while he calls. Collect, of course.'

Swarn nods mournfully. She knows of the heartache young sons visit on their parents. But then she thinks of Tarun and his new businessman avatar and perks up slightly. 'Yes, Kammyji, these boys do not know how much their parents struggle to bring them up. To give them the best of everything. But when they are in trouble who do they come back to? Of course, the parents.'

This is a faint sideswipe at Neena, who so airily coasted in a mere five years ago and promptly relieved Swarn of the affections of her son. Every so often Swarn likes to remind Neena, ever so subtly, that the mother-son relationship is one that cannot be broken, unlike the husband-wife one. Blood, you see, is much, much thicker than water, ji. Having made her point and suddenly conscious that she is neglecting the comfort of her guest, she bellows out in the direction of the kitchen, 'Moolchand! Paani lao!'

Moolchand comes shuffling in, carrying a brass tray on which three tinkling glasses of iced water are condensing rapidly. 'Oh, so hot it is,' Swarn says, fanning her face with the tasselled end of her sari pallu. 'Moolchand, woh air conditioner lagana.' Once again, Moolchand follows his orders obediently, shuffling across to the wall to turn on the air conditioner. A cool shaft of breeze wafts into the room. Swarn could have had the air conditioner turned on before Kammy had arrived, but doing it this way makes it more obvious to Kammy that the Sachdevs have acquired a new split-level unit this summer—the most expensive in the market, with imported parts, only assembled in India, ji. She notices, with satisfaction, that Kammy's eyes flick towards the large unit framed on the wall. Aha, she has seen it! It is fifteen-love to Swarn, and the game has only just begun.

But now it is Kammy's turn. Picking up Ritik, who has crawled up to her, she asks 'Neens, darling, how are his teeth coming along? Any sign at all?' She proceeds to push the baby's lips apart to examine a pair of pristine pink, completely toothless jaws. 'Oho, still no sign of them?' she says in mock dismay. Then to a baffled Ritik, accusingly, and a bit unfairly, she adds, 'You little devil, hanging on to all those lovely big-big teeth, are you?' This is her moment to strike. She turns to Swarn and says in a voice rumbling deeply with warm reassurance, 'Never mind, Swarnji, it has always been like this in my family. Neena and Danny took forever to start teething, you know, until I almost thought they would have to go through life toothless.' She reserves the cruellest cut for the last. The one she knows will fly straight through Swarn's well-padded ribcage to embed itself in her heart. 'This thing, this late arrival of the teeth, I believe it comes from Manny's side of the family.'

Swarn remembers, with a sudden shudder, the night Ritik was born. The rain, the deafening thunderclaps, the night the monsoons had broken, with nocturnal sound and fury, over a sleeping, unprepared Delhi. That phone call from the Singhs (to whose house Neena had moved a week earlier) to say that Neena's pains had started at midnight, rousing the Sachdev household and throwing it into a state of complete panic. It was a night of whirling, swirling confusions to say the least.

But most of all (and worst of all) she remembers her first glimpse of her first, her only grandson. Neena had finally delivered the baby at 5 a.m. The doctor had hurried out to give them the good tidings. 'A boy! It is a boy, ji. Healthy and smart and fit.' She remembers how they all rushed in to see him. Jagdish had looked into the crib first and, stepping back, had allowed her to take her turn.

She still remembers that first glimpse. Through the murky half-light of dawn breaking through the nursing room window. She had strained to look again. It could not be true! When Rinku had been born, it had been like looking into a mirror (the same eyes, the same complexion, even a smaller version of the same nose, ji). But what was this! There was Swarn's first grandson, her only grandson, swaddled against the cold of the rain now beating furiously against the windowpane, tiny hands clutching at nothing, sightless eyes looking around, not seeing the shocked expression on his new grandmother's face, tiny and perfectly formed fingers and toes and nails and eyelashes, but there it was, there for all to see, undeniable, unerring, inescapable fact—almost as if Nature knew there were certain imbalances that had to be redressed. No, this baby was certainly not Swarn Sachdev's grandson. One would struggle even to think of him as Rohit

Sachdev's son. Not a trace of that Sachdev aquiline sweep to the bridge of the nose. Not a single eyelash to compare with the lustrous Sachdev ones. No, this particular union between the Sachdev and Singh families has resulted in a child undeniably of the lowly Singh variety. This baby was, without a doubt, Manny Singh's grandson. The same round, bald head, the same plump cheeks, even the same button nose, *ji*. In fact, if he weren't so tiny and swaddled and only a few hours old, that person in the crib was Manny Singh!

It took many days for Swarn to get over the shock. She did not say anything to anyone, of course, but inwardly she blamed many people. Rohit, for marrying a girl who (though reasonably pretty) did not have anything like the Sachdev looks. Jagdish, whose idea it had all been in the first place. Manny Singh, quite simply, for looking like he did—all small and round with a little head framed by its crescent of brown hair. That was the only feature of Manny's that the baby did not have (but might well develop later), Swarn thought bitterly. That fuzzy horseshoe-shaped piece of grey hair that Manny wore so inelegantly from earlobe to earlobe over the back of his neck. The joy that Swarn could have derived from having a grandson had been cruelly, cruelly dimmed.

Later, after Neena and the baby had been brought home, it did not get much better. The baby, features fast developing, was looking more and more the spitting image of his maternal grandfather. Swarn could see where the term *spitting image* came from now—it was a resemblance that made poor Swarn want to spit. Even when the eunuchs came to dance in celebration of the male heir to the Sachdev fortune, Swarn could only muster up a weak smile and a few thousand rupees.

In the months since he had been born, however, the shock had worn off slightly, especially as Ritik grew into as fine a ten-month old as one could expect, grunting, dribbling, rolling over and up into a sitting position. But Kammy, who hadn't taken long to work out what was eating Swarn this time, never missed an opportunity to rub it in. Not that she had ever been of the opinion that Manny had desirable looks. Even when he had been an ardent young lover with his hand exploring the mysteries lurking beneath the folds of her sari, she had not been able to think of him as handsome. But, oh, how she loved the look on Swarn's face every time Manny carried Ritik on his shoulder—and the horrified way in which her eyes darted from Manny's round features to the baby's tiny, identical ones, as though still trying to work out why it was that those stupid genes hadn't known which pool to emerge from. Swarn's prejudice was one that was hard to rise above, even though Kammy had tried. Her social work with the poor usually helped to elevate her beyond most pettinesses, but every time she was back in Swarn's presence, those claws seemed to emerge unsheathed from somewhere.

As they all look at Ritik's toothless jaws again, he obligingly smiles around at them, pinkly, blankly. Neena lunges for him and whips him off her mother's lap, gurgling some maternal nonsense. Swarn calls out for the tea to be brought in, and a temporary truce is called.

■

On this occasion Gayatri wants to make sure she is dressed well. Not that she is any more concerned than normal about how she looks, but she knows how much it means to Neena. In fact Neena has already called twice today to remind her to look her best. 'My in-laws notice that kind of thing, you know' has been the explanation offered. This, as we know, is only half true. Jagdish, ever busy mentally chasing potential buyers in Sweden and England, is hardly likely to notice that Gayatri is wearing trousers and not a salwar kameez. Swarn, while noticing and judging things like that, will not spot that the trousers are by Peter Goldstein, beautifully cut around the hips and flaring flatteringly down from the knee. But Neena knows that her brother-in-law, Tarun, will notice all this and more, and that, for her, is the important thing. She has wisely refrained from telling Gayatri her motives, of course. It is too complicated to explain at the moment.

Neena figured out a while ago that it is only a matter of time before which Tarun will get married and she will have either a companion or an enemy in the house. Naturally her preference is for the former to be the case, and who better a life companion for Tarun (and, consequently for her) but her best friend. The fact that Tarun and Gayatri are probably terribly incompatible is not a detail with which Neena wants to be vexed at the moment. While Gayatri is putting the finishing touches to her ensemble in front of her bedroom mirror, Neena is preparing to be a conniving and determined Cupid.

The Sachdev car is being sent to pick Gayatri up. She protested that she is perfectly capable of making her own way to LM Road, but Neena cannot bear the thought that Gayatri will hail an autorickshaw in some ridiculous bid to save money, arriving at the Sachdev residence with her hair all tangled, her make-up blown away. She knows Tarun likes his women sleek and well groomed. None of this *au naturel* tangled hair and shiny skin rubbish for him.

So it is that Gayatri is stepping into a gleaming black BMW, looking quite the picture of perfection, unaware, of course, of how important it is for her to be looking quite the picture of perfection. Her long hair has been neatly brushed, all tangles taken out, lying in a rippling black mirror down to her waist. Her face is matte and quite beautifully made up with a touch of Number 7 Honeyed Almonds, lifted over the cheekbones by Dusky Rose powder blush. Along the rim of her upper eyelid she has carefully drawn a thin black line, accentuating the brown depths of her eyes. On her lips she has daubed a tiny amount of lipgloss (Maybelline's Sunset Peach, to be precise).

The finishing touch is a dab of Anais Anais on her slim wrists and behind her delicate earlobes. It is later this (this whiff of summer flowers and the delicate shell-like earlobe from behind which it seems to emanate) that will ingrain itself into Tarun's consciousness. With a ferocity that will frighten even him. He will, on later occasions, attempt to exorcise the tiny haunting perfumed image away, shaking his head like a man possessed, hitting his crazed forehead against a wall, rubbing his hands over burning, sleepless eyes. But we move ahead too fast . . .

For now, Gayatri is walking through the heavy wooden, ornately carved Sachdev front door, unaware that her left earlobe (behind which a strand of her hair is charmingly tucked) is about to shortly begin to play its part in poor Tarun's fate. She gives Neena a hug, smiles and murmurs greetings to the older Sachdev couple to whom she is being introduced, folding her hands in traditional greeting. Then Rohit arrives down the stairs, shakes her hand warmly and says something cheerful about how much his wife has told him about her lovely absent friend. They all go into the drawing room and take their seats, awaiting the arrival of the doomed, unsuspecting Tarun.

It is about seven, and Tarun is only just returning from the factory. He pulls his car in behind the BMW and enters the house. From the lobby he can hear voices emanating from the drawing room, some familiar, some not. He vaguely remembers Neena saying something about a visitor and asking him not to be late, only half hearing that breakfast conversation because he had been preoccupied with the missed deadline on the delivery to A-One Stores. Neena's friend from England, of course. It comes to him just as he enters the drawing room and sees her.

She is a vision in black and white, illuminating his mother's drab brown velvet sofa. Had Tarun been a poet, he would have likened the image to that of a newly awakened water lily floating serenely on a muddy pond, but Tarun is not a poet, only a reluctant businessman and now completely overwhelmed by this new event he is hurtling so uncontrollably towards. Through a blur of voices and faces, he shakes the hand of this beautiful water lily and mumbles something. He takes a seat on the sofa next to her, trying not to faint. As she laughs softly at something Neena has just said, he knows it is safe to turn and look at her. He sees a laughing profile, a creamy brown neck and that tiny earlobe. Anais Anais has never smelt so heavenly before, transforming this ornate and really rather garish drawing room (fake Rubens and all) into a perfumed bower. A place reserved only for sudden brilliant events, for celestial happenings, for the making and breaking of hearts, for the whole sorry business of falling in love.

'Have another pakora, beti,' Swarn coos to Gayatri as Neena passes the plate around.

'So, tell me,' Jagdish says, turning to Gayatri, 'did you live in London?'

'Well, Oxford at first and then later, for a short while, London.'

'Ah, London!' Jagdish is wearing a faraway, nostalgic look. He is not thinking of double-decker buses and flower-laden pubs and the sweep of an old grey river. In fact he is not thinking at all of the brief trip he had made to London in 1971 with Swarn in tow. All she had done, he sometimes recalled, was complain about the cold, the rain, her Indian footwear and the fact that he was only doing business and not taking her to see Big Ben. He is, on the other hand, thinking of the many buyers who must be thronging London's streets. 'Tell me, erm . . . erm . . .'

'Gayatri,' Neena puts in.

'Yes, yes, Gayatri. Tell me, what sort of clothes are the youngsters in London wearing these days?'

Gayatri, not getting the point straightaway, is a bit nonplussed. 'Clothes? Well, embroidered jeans seemed very popular just before I left.'

'Embroidered jeans?' Jagdish is not impressed. 'Any drawstring trousers?'

'No, I think those are probably considered passé now. Pashmina shawls were all the rage last winter, though.'

Jagdish looks even more unhappy. His new line of drawstring trousers are not doing well at all, and pashminas are not in his line of trade, but Neena perks up at this bit of information. 'Pashminas? Do they wear them like we do here?'

'I think the ones sent abroad are a bit smaller. People seems to wear them as mufflers or scarves over their coats.'

'Embroidered borders?' Neena asks.

'No, not usually embroidered. But they do seem to like them in bright colours. Colours that you would think of as Indian. Magentas and crimsons and the like. Though, of course, they'd give them names like fuchsia and vermilion.'

'Fuchsia, vermilion,' Jagdish mutters softly and absent-mindedly to himself as he helps himself to the cup of tea Swarn is passing to him. Perhaps the mistake had been to do the drawstring trousers in light colours. The conversation rolls on around him as he sips his tea contemplatively.

Across from him, on the sofa next to Gayatri, his younger son also sits silently, thinking less about the future of fuchsia drawstring trousers than his father is. He cannot understand it, but he is suddenly ecstatic and miserable all at once. He has also temporarily lost the use of his tongue. He nods whenever he is asked anything. He smiles witlessly at all the jokes. The only noises he makes are occasional vapid whispers, such as 'Yes, yes' and 'No, thank you'. From across the room Neena can see that her plan has started to work, but she feels an overwhelming desire to kick her brother-in-law very hard. 'Say something to her, you idjit,' she hisses into her teacup, but the unfortunate young man continues to throw sidelong glances at his companion on the sofa with silent devotion. Words are destined to elude him completely today.

An hour later, Gayatri leaves the Sachdev residence, carrying with her a largely favourable impression of Neena's new family. That Rohit's quite a sweetie, she decides, completely besotted with Neena. Mother-in-law seems a bit of a battleaxe; father-in-law a bit distant and vague but nice enough in an eccentric sort of way. Ghastly house, especially those awful paintings. And Tarun? Gayatri considers the young man who had sat so silently next to her on the sofa. Quiet sort of chap, she thinks, seemed nice enough. Certainly quite nice looking, in a foppish sort of way. Supposed to be running a great big factory, if what Neena says is true, but had strangely little to say for himself. In fact, Gayatri cannot recall now whether he had anything at all to say for himself. He's probably a bit of a dimwit, she decides, and, with that unfortunate conclusion, Gayatri dismisses him completely from her mind.

Neena's job as Cupid is only half done.

6

Love is a many splendoured thing.

Tarun is at his sister-in-law's feet. Literally and metaphorically. She grins triumphantly down at him from her perch on her cane hammock chair. 'See, didn't I tell you she was lovely?'

'Perfectly, perfectly lovely!' Tarun wails. 'Just tell me what I can do to impress her, Neena!'

'Well, you should have thought of preparing something in advance of her arrival, sonny. I think you might already have blown it.'

'But I didn't know it would be like that. For one, I didn't know she would be that lovely. And who would have thought that I'd go and lose it so completely, Neena! Tell me what to do! Surely all is not completely lost?'

'Hmmm, let's see now,' Neena furrows her brow and taps a contemplative foot on the floor. Tarun has his eyes glued eagerly to her face as she starts to speak again. Even she cannot keep the excitement out of her voice as inspiration strikes. 'Tell you what, Tarun,' she says, 'why don't I arrange for you to bump into her somewhere.'

'Bump into her?' Tarun likes the sound of *bump*, as it conjures up images of being able to bounce his person off that rather comely, curvaceous one clad in black and white yesterday, a day that now feels as if it were aeons ago.

'Yes, yes. I could always find out very casually what her plans are for any given day. And then you could just arrange to be there too. And then get chatting or something. And for God's sake, prepare something to say this time. She's really big on conversation and things like that.'

'Like what? What should I talk to her about? She seems so bloody intelligent,' Tarun says this as though it were a dirty word.

Neena sighs tolerantly, 'Well, it depends on where you are, Tarun. If, for instance, you bump into each other at the British Council library, you'd just talk about books or favourite writers or something.

Tarun pales visibly. 'Books?' he croaks as though he is hearing the word for the first time.

'Oh, don't worry, I can prepare you for all that, give you the names of writers and things.' A naughty expression comes over her face. 'You might even be able to learn up a few lines of a poem or a sonnet or something to quote to her over the Shakespeare shelf.'

'I don't know. I've never had a head for remembering things like poems.'

'Oh, don't be silly, Tarun. If you really want something, you'll do anything to get it.' Tarun's expression does not mirror Neena's determined one because he does not share her Manny gene, but under these circumstances, he is willing to take any instructions, suggestions and advice. He nods obediently, awaiting them, although he is fairly certain that the mastery of poetry will probably be even more arduous than becoming a businessman. For now, though, he is content to be led to the slaughter by his sister-in-law.

She picks up the telephone while Tarun watches anxiously, even ignoring his nephew who is plucking at his trousers asking to be picked up. He starts as, after a few seconds, Neena trills, 'Hi, Gayatri.' She's there! She is sitting (or maybe standing) at the other end of that telephone line, indubitably looking a vision in white or pink or whatever colour it is that dreams are usually cast in. It takes all of Tarun's self-control to stop himself from snatching the telephone receiver from Neena's hands; to clutch it to his ear; to hear, just once, that mellifluous voice again; to whisper his desires to her and to have his voice commingle and conjoin magically with hers on the humming, thrumming lines of Mahanagar Telephone Nigam Ltd.

To his credit, he merely stands leaning on the wall, listening to Neena's end of the conversation, wearing a fervent expression on his face. Neena seems to take forever to get to the point, going on about yesterday's meeting. 'My Rohit thought you were absolutely wonderful, of course,' she says, giving Tarun a broad wink. After a few seconds, she giggles and says, 'Yes, I know, he's lovely isn't he?' Tarun has an instinctive feeling that they aren't talking about him. Neena's eyes glaze over at this point, and she will graciously not tell Tarun later that Gayatri had, after complimenting Rohit, added that his younger brother seemed a far cry from him. ('He seems awfully quiet. Just doesn't have his brother's personality, does he?' being her exact choice of words.) Now Neena is laughing very hard, snorting ungracefully, and Tarun guesses from her discreet effort not to mention any names that the person being commented on now is his mother.

She's still not getting to the point, Tarun thinks desperately, just as Neena does get to the point. 'So what are your plans for the day, Gayatri, anything interesting?' she asks casually. Tarun leans forward, trying to hear the thin crackle that is the honeyed tone of his prospective lover. Neena is only nodding, not giving anything away. Tarun counts twenty-seven nods and a few *hmms* and the odd *maybe* and *yah* until, finally, Neena bids her friend goodbye and puts the telephone receiver down. Turning to Tarun, she says in a business-like voice, 'Aerobics. She's joining up today. Come on, sunshine, get your trainers on.'

■

Gayatri has decided to cycle out to the DDA Sports Club, which is only around the block from where she lives. Pulling out her old cycle from the shed, she gets down on her knees to examine the condition of its chain.

'I've been keeping that clean too!' Keshava calls out from the kitchen window.

'You're a darling,' Gayatri replies. 'Where would we all be without you, Appa?'

'Well, I've been using it too,' Keshava says, strolling up to Gayatri as she continues to tinker, getting her hands greasy.

'Aha, you never told me that! Where do you go on it?'

'Oh, just nearby places—to Khoka Market if your mother needs some vegetables, the library, that kind of thing.'

'I don't know if you should be attempting that kind of thing, Appa. I mean, weren't you complaining about your knees the other day? Cycling won't help that, surely. And the traffic has got so bad around the market area. It's suicidal trying to drive through that melée.'

Keshava ruffles her hair, smiling fondly down at her. She now has hands covered in grease, and a large black smut is smeared across her nose. Tarun would no doubt still find this picture of her, breathless and sweating, absolutely irresistible, but Keshava reminds her to clean up before she goes out for her classes. A few minutes later, a spruced up Gayatri is wobbling off on her cycle, trying to remember the best route to the sports complex that will avoid the roadside Romeos who throng the market area in the evenings. She smiles in surprise at the easy familiarity with which the old term she and Neena had used in their college days has returned. She is, Neena will be pleased to note, looking exceedingly fetching in a white T-shirt and grey cycling shorts, her hair tied back in a bouncy ponytail.

At about the same time, at LM Road five miles away, Neena and Tarun are getting into their car. Neena is reminding a sheepish Tarun of all that he owes her for this latest favour. 'You'd better not forget this, sonny,' she says with mock sternness. 'I mean, come on, do I look like the type who'll enjoy aerobics three times a week? The things one has to do for a brother-in-law these days!' Despite the fact that she could well do with a session or two of aerobics, she sighs self-pityingly as she reties the laces of her trainers.

By now Gayatri has reached the DDA Complex and has registered herself for the evening classes. She is pleased to see that the trees and plants at the complex have been well tended over the years and that the whole place is now lush with huge green ferns and great white bunches of bougainvillea. There is even a fountain tinkling prettily in the centre of the garden, throwing a fine mist over delightedly blooming beds of crimson portulaca. She sits on the grass awaiting Neena, who has told her that she is enrolling too as this is her own best chance to lose some weight. Neena also said something about being accompanied by her brother-in-law, that strangely silent young man, who is also keen to tone up his hamstrings for some odd reason. Gayatri casts about in her head, but cannot for the life of her now remember his name. Ten minutes later, she sees them walking down the gravel path towards her.

'Hiya!' she calls out.

'Hello, sweetie,' Neena trills.

For one terrifying moment, Tarun imagines he has lost his tongue all over again. He finds it, fortunately in the nick of time, and adds his own mumbled greeting to the two girls' effusive ones. He cannot bear to see how fetching Gayatri is looking in her sportswear. Tempted as he is to examine the shape of her legs, he refrains from taking a second look. Neena has carefully tutored him.

Neena and Tarun sit next to Gayatri on the grass as she informs them they have another fifteen minutes before the classes begin. A few other girls and a couple of young men gather under the shade of a gulmohar tree. Tarun can see that one or two of the girls are quite pretty, but, amazingly, he finds that he suddenly has no desire at all to ogle. He is mulling over the strangeness of this phenomenon when he realizes that Gayatri has just asked him something and is looking at him with large expectant eyes, waiting for a reply. As he can feel himself begin to slowly drown in those liquid orbs, he can feel, from behind Gayatri, his sister-in-law's eyes boring into him unsympathetically.

'Hanh?' he says, blowing his second chance at impressing Gayatri with his so-far-latent gift for scintillating repartee. He notices Neena throwing her eyes heavenwards. Gayatri only looks faintly amused and repeats her question with the patient air of one who is having to make conversation with a four-year-old, and a rather stupid one at that.

'Have you done aerobics before?' she asks again, slowly.

While Neena is nodding frantically from behind Gayatri, Tarun manages, finally, to connect a few words together to form a whole sentence. 'Erm, yes, many years ago, while I was in college, I tried a few classes then.' Having got this out, he and his sister-in-law heave twin sighs of relief.

'And you enjoyed it?'

'Yes, I suppose so,' Tarun replies, adding disarmingly, 'although it is seen as a bit of a girlie thing, isn't it?'

Gayatri tosses her head, 'All the more reason to break that myth then. I don't believe there should be anything seen as either girlie or not girlie. Do you Neens?'

Neena, who is, of course, not intent on ensnaring Gayatri's affections, feels free to disagree. 'But I think there will always be things that will be easier for women to do and vice versa,' she declares.

'Like what?' Gayatri challenges.

'Childbirth?' Tarun offers tentatively.

This has perhaps not been a wise interjection. Neena throws her eyes heavenwards again while Gayatri looks at him scornfully. 'Apart from the obvious, of course,' she sneers in a voice dripping with sarcasm. Tarun retreats into mortified silence, while the two girls carry on the discussion, arguing with good-natured vehemence about the injustice of women players at Wimbledon being paid less prize money than the men. Neena knows tennis is a subject on which Tarun can hold forth with some acumen and throws him a few encouraging glances. At one point she even attempts a more direct rescue by throwing him a line. 'Isn't that so, Tarun?' she queries loudly, but Tarun has sunk back into miserable silence, perplexed and humiliated by Gayatri's apparent coldness. Ten minutes later they are summoned for their class.

Tarun takes a safe place at the back of the room, and Gayatri and Neena occupy determined positions in the first row. From his lonely spot, Tarun can now observe Gayatri's anterior and charming posterior in the mirrored wall in front of them. It is this mirrored wall that also makes it impossible for his actions to remain unseen by the two girls, and it becomes obvious very soon that it is, as he has told Gayatri, a very long time since he has attempted aerobics. He has some vague memory of it being, even on that occasion, a bid to win over some particularly sporty lass, but the details are now fuzzy.

Poor Tarun is feeling deeply unhappy as cheery music strikes up on the system, and the whole group begins to march to a speeded-up version of the theme from *Flashdance*. Dolefully, Tarun tries to focus on the sprightly young instructor who is getting rather quickly into the swing of things, bouncing around and shouting strange commands such as 'Grapevine!' and 'Jazzwalk!' Even he has to stop thinking about the gorgeous Gayatri in an effort to keep up as the pace quickens. In front of him, the group is seeming to maintain an effortless synchrony, fifteen pairs of arms and legs travelling in more or less the right directions at the shouts of the instructor. 'Grapevine,' he mutters as he tries in vain to master the looping step. 'Vee! Ah that's an easy one. Step, touch! Bloody hell, got that one wrong. Jazzwalk! What the fuck!' Tarun stops as he becomes aware that the music has stopped and the whole class is observing him with amusement, some in the mirrors and others turning right around to laugh and stare. In a corner, Gayatri and Neena are clinging to each other, convulsed in hysterical laughter.

'You are doing everything the exact opposite of the rest

of the group,' the instructor complains, bearing down on a sweating Tarun.

'I . . . I'm just following your movements,' Tarun protests.

'Well, when everyone is moving to the right, you are going to the left, and when everyone has hands down, yours are up. Please concentrate!'

Tarun thinks how like a weasel she looks as she frowns furiously, returning to the music system in the corner. He notices Neena has wiped her eyes and is smiling at him encouragingly. He waves sheepishly at her. She waves back as the music cranks up again and, before his astonished eyes, Tarun sees the lovely Gayatri give him a thumbs-up and blow him an encouraging kiss across the room. His head is swimming, and his concentration is suffering yet another lapse, but he could not care about that now. Gayatri has smiled warmly at him! She has even blown him a kiss! He does not know that, by tying his legs up in knots, he has made her shake with laughter for this first time in a very long time. He does not know either of the old adage, repeated down the centuries between women of sense and discernment. It has been whispered in far corners of the world, from Jordanian souks to Alaskan wastes, in many different tongues and languages that it is far, far better to fall in love with a man who can make you laugh than make the mistake of giving your heart away to someone tall and handsome and grey eyed, who will think nothing of breaking it in two.

∎

A sweating Gayatri comes up to Tarun at the end of the class. 'Well, you certainly picked up the steps as we went along,' she says.

'I try, I try,' Tarun replies, attempting a touch of modesty.

Neena walks up to them, panting furiously, 'If there's . . . one thing . . . you can't accuse . . . Tarun of . . . it is that he . . . doesn't bring great . . . enthusiasm . . . to everything he takes on.'

Tarun grins at her. 'I thought you looked pretty determined yourself, Neena! Are you okay?'

The podgy Neena grabs him by the arm as she takes another few deep breaths shakily. 'Oh, I'll survive . . . I think.'

They stagger out of the room, walking slowly down to the car park, discussing the wisdom of attending these classes every day.

'Oh, alternate days should do,' Gayatri says.

'Yeah . . . I agree . . . alternate days,' Neena agrees, still gasping.

Tarun is outvoted but pleased nevertheless that he will be seeing Gayatri on a regular basis. He offers to drop Gayatri home, but she is already unlocking her cycle, smiling and waving at them as they get into their car and Neena reaches hastily for the air-conditioning switch. Tarun watches Gayatri as she wobbles off ungracefully, thinking how wonderfully agile she looks. Turning to Neena, who is still faintly purple in the face, he grabs her hand and shakes it furiously, 'Thank you, thank you, thank you, Sis. Ask any favour now, and you shall get it!'

Neena flops heavily back on the car seat. 'She's lovely . . . Tarun. All I ask is that . . . you don't go and . . . blow it. As for doing me a favour . . . I'll certainly hold you to that some day! Now . . . please . . . get me home.'

7

But love (for parents) is a many dreaded thing.

Tarun has, for a few days now, been wandering around wearing a strange beatific expression on his face. Rohit, who has been put in the picture by his wife, is not puzzled. Jagdish has not noticed because there has been no glitch in Tarun's attendance of the factory at Noida. As the Gayatri rendezvous are still confined to the alternate evenings at the sports complex, there has been no necessity yet for Tarun to play hooky from work. If anything, Tarun finds it helpful to be busy at work in the hours before his aerobics sessions; this keeps his mind from getting too fevered. But Tarun's new persona, resembling at times the silent, distant demeanour of a Buddhist monk, has not escaped the canny Swarn's notice.

'What hash happened to my widdle widdle bijnichman, beta?' she asks her younger son one evening as they lounge in front of the television. Tarun's mind is precisely seven miles away, in Saket. He does not hear her, and so she makes sure he does by pinching his cheek hard.

'Oww!' he responds angrily, clutching his cheek.

'So what's happened to my bijnichman beta, hanh?' she repeats, undeterred. 'Is your Papa working you too, too hard

in the bijnich, hanh? Tell your mamma. I will tell your papa
to give you a break. I think you should go away on holiday
for a few days. Go to visit Aunty Sheelu in Shimla, maybe.'

'No!' Tarun cries in alarm.

Swarn is now genuinely puzzled. Tarun usually likes
visiting Aunty Sheelu in Shimla—not least because of the
comely presence of his young cousin, Aruna. He is evidently
not dating anyone, considering the amount of time he is
spending at home. He goes only to the factory, where he is
accompanied by his father. In the evenings, he is generally at
home, unless he is accompanying his sister-in-law to the
exercise classes three times a week.

So what is this new expression on his face, Swarn
wonders? This air of satisfaction almost. As though some
distant dream has been finally realized. Surely it could not
be that he has finally come to terms with being a full-time
businessman! Much as she would like this to be the case,
Swarn accepts mournfully that it is an unlikely explanation.
She resolves to do some sleuthing. Tarun is, after all, her
younger son and her last chance at ensuring she gets the
right kind of girl for the Sachdev household, a proper
daughter-in-law this time (demure, homely and not very
fashionable). Some investigation is definitely called for,
she decides.

As usual, her approach is one that calls for the least
energy output. 'Beti, Neena,' she begins later that evening,
hoisting her ample bottom on to a chair next to her daughter-
in-law at the dining table. Casually sprinkling some jasmines
brought in by the maid into a brass bowl of water, she starts
again, trying to instil friendly curiosity into her voice, 'Tell
me, beti, is our Tarun going steady-sheddy with anybody
these days?' She has chosen her moment well, for there is no
one in the room but Neena, the baby and herself. (One has
to be careful what one says in front of Rinku these days,
everything she repeats, ji.) The baby jumps up and down,
cheerfully full of food, leaning over his mother's forearm,
grinning toothlessly—Mannyishly, Swarn thinks, turning

away with a shudder. Neena, who is trying to get Ritik's bib off, does not look at her mother-in-law and merely shakes her head with a terse 'No'.

Stymied, Swarn contemplates her next move. In a few minutes, it comes to her. 'These exercise classes, they must be very good, hanh? I must say, you are looking as if you are losing a lot of weight in these past two weeks.'

She has prudently pressed the right button with Neena, who brightens and looks up. 'Really?' the young woman asks a touch eagerly, Swarn notes with satisfaction.

Swarn warms to her theme. 'Yes, really, Neena beti. See, there, around the hips? Last week they were huge. Now see, it's all gone—almost,' she adds quickly so as not to overdo it.

Neena looks dubiously down at her hips, thinking dolefully that they do not really look much smaller than before. Swarn's own hips, which should be pictured as permanent and terrifying warning on all boxes of halwa sold in Delhi, are rippling over the edge of her woefully inadequate dining chair, warning Neena of what may lie ahead in years to come. Lately, Neena has started to get increasingly depressed at the sight of her burgeoning hips in the mirror. It hasn't helped, of course, that Gayatri has returned after five years abroad, looking the picture of perfection. Neena has, of late, even taken to pestering the tolerant Rohit with her angst, sitting him down in front of the mirror, asking him if she has put on weight. It has been a thankless task for Rohit so far—answering in the negative has had him accused of lying and offering a tentative affirmative has resulted in some of the worst tiffs in their marriage. Swarn has watched all this with silent interest. Swarn likes keeping tabs on people's weaknesses. You never know when the information will come in handy, you see.

It is certainly coming in handy now as Neena smiles at her, rubbing one hand over her thighs saying shyly, 'Well, maybe I have lost just a little bit. These jeans were really tight last week.'

Having softened her up, Swarn now asks casually, 'Do

lots of people come to these aerobics classes then?'

'Oh, about fifteen,' Neena replies, struggling to contain the writhing Ritik who is attempting to annihilate an ant dragging a grain of sugar slowly across the table.

'Boys and girls separate?'

'No, we're all together. The boys tend to fool around at the back, though. The girls are a lot more committed. Gayatri makes sure we always get a place right in the front row.'

'Gayatri? Achcha, that friend of yours from London? She is also attending these classes?' The picture is starting to get clearer to Swarn, and she is not very pleased to see it.

'Yeah, that's why I go all the way to Saket to attend classes. There's no one like Gayatri to keep me motivated.'

■

Swarn waits for an opportune moment to confirm her suspicions that Gayatri is motivating not just Neena but (in some cheap little way, ji) her dear Tarun as well. Once again, the scene is the dining room, and Swarn is seated this time next to him supervising his dinner. There is no one else around as Tarun has asked for an early meal to recover from an especially tiring day at the factory. Swarn, preparing the ground, has asked for his favourite mutton chops to be made. Tarun's preference, unlike Rohit's, has always been for English food. (Eenglees phood, to old Moolchand, who has always imagined this to be some sort of strange and suicidal art involving hazardous use of the cavernous, temperamental old oven in the kitchen.) Swarn now calls out to him to tell him to check the state of the chaamps as they sizzle in the frying pan.

Moolchand, who has been bending over to get a look at the bhaked bhegetable bubbling away in the oven, straightens up with a groan and tosses the two chops over in the pan. Once they are nicely browned, the onions melting softly around them, he puts them on a plate. Then, grumbling loudly to himself, he gingerly opens the door to the oven, jumping back in fright as the hot air hits his face. 'Ooffo!

Bekaar ki machine!' he exclaims angrily, fanning the air around his singed face with a dirty tea cloth. To Moolchand this firangi contraption, the memsahib's oh-bhen, is frighteningly reminiscent of that new-fangled machine that incinerated his dear father's body at the electric crematorium ten years ago. He has often had premonitions that Swarn's old Belling will one day be the death of him, swallowing him up whole and turning him out, baked to a crisp stiff. He now carefully removes the bubbling tray of vegetables and clatters it down hastily on the kitchen surface. Placing a large dollop of the baked vegetables next to the chops, he squirts a generous pool of ketchup over them and then picks up the plate. Balancing a smaller plate of buttered bread in the other hand, he shuffles his way to the dining room. The memsahib and Tarun are sitting next to each other at the table. 'Mother and son doing their usual git-pit in Eenglees,' he thinks sullenly, 'always, always this git-pit talk in Eenglees, just to make sure I can't understand what they are saying about me.' Muttering under his breath, he returns to the kitchen where the temperature is now boiling relentlessly upwards into the forties.

Mother and son are, however, not discussing Moolchand at all, as we well know. Swarn has managed to steer the subject discreetly around to Neena and her friends. Just as Tarun tucks into the first of his chops with an appreciative 'Mmmyumm', Swarn strikes. 'You know, Tarun beta, Neena was telling me the other day that her friend Gayatri might be getting married soon. Nice girl . . .' She is interrupted by the sound of Tarun choking terribly on the chop. As she thumps him vigorously on the back, solicitously offering him the choice of water, Pepsi or Sprite, she has already started to plan the expert removal of Gayatri from her son's life. 'Chudail!' she thinks furiously to herself, tenderly mopping up Tarun's tears with a paper napkin as he continues to cough and retch.

Now, one may wonder why Swarn has chosen this terribly rude epithet to use on the luckless, unknowing

Gayatri. There are many reasons, of which we shall list just a few ...

1. Gayatri is quite obviously the current love of Tarun's life.

2. She is not a Sachdev. Not even a Punjabi. She is (horror of horrors!) a Madrasi.

3. She is not demure, homely and not very fashionable. She, in fact, is very beautiful.

4. She is probably not very well off. (Swarn does not know any Madrasis who are.)

5. She is (Hai Ram!) foreign returned, returned with probably all sorts of godforsaken foreign ideas.

6. She is Neena's friend and Swarn's idea in acquiring a second daughter-in-law has been to leave Neena out in the cold.

The last point is perhaps the one most infuriating Swarn. Not only has Jagdish seemingly effortlessly transformed Tarun, her baby, into a big businessman, but her daughter-in-law may successfully hand-pick her next daughter-in-law. How can that be, ji?! As if she, Swarn Sachdev, was not able to find the most suitable girl for her own son. And why on earth should she allow him now to be jhapoed by some useless Madrasi-shadrasi type, ji? Perhaps we can forgive Swarn for believing Gayatri to be a foul and loathsome witch.

But what of the luckless Tarun? He is at the moment collapsed in his chair, shocked beyond belief by the ghastly news of Gayatri's nuptials and is now probably dying of a broken heart and a piece of half-chewed chop. In one fell swoop Tarun has been transformed from a carefree, jolly young man, teetering on the threshold of true love, into a broken, choking, gasping wreck, tears streaming down his purple face, hands clutching at his throat. Swarn, irate at the confirmation of her suspicion, gives him a hard thump on his back, dislodging the offending piece of meat from Tarun's gullet. It ejects itself on to his lap, a small regurgitated piece of meat not looking half as appetizing as when covered in onion marinade. Tarun looks at it for a few uncomprehending moments before picking it up gingerly with his fingers and putting it back on his plate. With a scraping back of the chair, he gets up and staggers off, whispering a feeble 'Not hungry any more' to his mother's plaintive request to finish lunch.

It will, unfortunately, be another four hours before he will be able to speak to his sister-in-law and find out that none of it is true. Neena has gone with her mother for a play and a meal at Bali Hai. She is so enjoying tucking into her meal that she has forgotten to turn her mobile phone back on. She will wonder why a desperate Tarun is coming stumbling out at her from his bedroom at midnight when she returns. He will tell her. She will laugh and say it is all nonsense. But Tarun will still sleep only fitfully the rest of the night. He will, as he watches the sun's rays begin to creep over the satellite dishes of Chic TV next door, resolve to declare his undying devotion for Gayatri without further delay. Later Neena will ask her mother-in-law why she had told Tarun that Gayatri was getting married. Swarn will only look at her vaguely and drawl in a voice full of surprise, 'Oh, isn't she? I thought you said . . . oh, maybe I was thinking of someone else.'

■

Tarun sets out for his aerobics session the following evening with his jaw set in a certain unusual way. Even the cheery Neena senses something new and strange is about to happen. So far the aerobics rendezvous have followed a certain set routine. After Neena and Tarun arrive, they walk to the fountain, where Gayatri has usually already seated herself, watching the spray dry up on the hot concrete edge. After the customary chit-chat, they move to the aerobics room where Gayatri and Neena take up determined position in the first row, three feet in front of the mirror. Tarun, along with the small scattering of other men, lurks unsurely at the back. So far he has only worshipped from afar.

In the strange manner in which these things have been known to happen, it has been a happy accident that Tarun has felt too overwhelmed by Gayatri to make any of his normal moves yet. By this time, he will usually have inveigled the subject of his affections to give him her telephone number, called her a few times, addressed her as *babe* and, no doubt, persuaded her to go with him to the nightclub a few times. Fortunately he has felt far too bashful to perform any of these moves with Gayatri. Consequently, Gayatri has gradually formed a false but rather good impression of young Tarun in the space of the past few weeks.

'What a pleasant young chap,' she thought to herself after their last meeting, having observed him sympathetically hold the car door open for his sister-in-law. 'Doesn't speak very much, but what a refreshing change from these run-of-the-mill Delhi types who are always shooting off their mouths about something or the other. Pushy geezers always trying to impress and never really succeeding.'

And so, when that summer afternoon Tarun resolves to ask Gayatri out, she is more than ready to be asked out. It has been over four months since she has allowed herself the attentions of a man. And nearly four years since she has been with anyone but Michael. Michael, who took her heart (despite having a wife, by the way) and thought nothing of breaking it in two. When, after the aerobics session that day, the red-faced shambling Tarun tentatively asks if she would like to go out for d..d..dinner with him, the feeling for Gayatri is akin to rain falling on parched earth. And, like the baking hot concrete that gratefully receives and swiftly swallows up falling drops from the DDA Sports Complex fountain, Gayatri simply, but resoundingly, says, 'Yes.'

■

'Aha, a date, is it? Anyone we know?' Keshava asks as his daughter emerges from her bedroom, looking more dressed up than she has bothered to get since her arrival in India.

'Well, I suppose you could call it a date, Appa. But only because he's a young man. He's only Neena's brother-in-law.'

'And what does Neena's brother-in-law do?'

'Oh, Appa! As if it matters. I'm not about to marry him or anything.'

'But these are the things one always asks—even of people who are not about to marry one's daughter, I believe,'

'Oh, I don't know what he does, business or something,' Gayatri replies crossly.

'But what business? And, if it's not business but something, then what thing?'

'Is it really that important, Appa?' Gayatri wails.

'But, of course it is, moley, seeing that he is your date.'

'But it's not a date, I just told you!'

'How can it not be a date if a young man is taking you out, eh?'

'Well, would you describe it as a date if Neena and I were going out? Or if Neena and I and her brother-in-law were going out? Or if Neena and her husband and I were going out?' Gayatri takes a deep breath and glares at her grinning father.

Keshava contemplates her tirade for a few seconds and then tries another tack. 'Okay then, I accept he's not a date. But I hope I'm allowed to ask very simply—what is his name and where does he live?'

'Tarun,' Gayatri mutters, 'Maharaja Colony. Same house as Neena.'

'Tarun,' Keshava pronounces the name slowly, as though this might help him decide whether his daughter is going out with someone worthy of her lovely company. Just as he is about to open his mouth and ask another question, the doorbell rings. Gayatri gets up in a flash, shouting a loud 'Bye!' to her parents before rushing to the door and bundling a baffled Tarun out. All Keshava can get is a fleeting glimpse of a pleasant young face behind a floppy lock before Gayatri is in Tarun's car, and they are a cloud of dust on the horizon.

Turning back from the window, he addresses his wife, who has been sitting at her desk, oblivious to the earlier conversation, pencil scribbling busily in her voluminous manuscript. 'Raji,' he says, wearing a worried expression on his face, 'I think our Gayatri is falling in love. With some Tarun fellow, I believe.'

■

Neena and Rohit lie on their king-sized bed, looking up at the plastic chandelier that Swarn had got for them (specially from Kathmandu, ji) as one of their wedding gifts. In this half-light it looks rather nice, tinkling away gently, catching a bit of light from the streetlight outside the window. It is nearly midnight and, indoors, only the night light is burning as, after a protracted struggle, Neena has only just managed to put her two children to sleep. They now lie on the bed, in between their two parents, looking, in sleep, very unlike the devils they have been all evening. Neena yawns and whispers sleepily, 'Tarun's not back yet, is he? You don't think he'll actually manage to charm old Gayatri, do you? She's always been so bloody snooty about the kind of men she'll even deign to talk to.'

Rohit, whose mind is on other pressing concerns, does not respond. Instead, he turns on to his side and reaches his arm out over the two small bodies barricading his wife away from him to tweak her left nipple. 'Ouch,' she says, slapping his hand away.

'Come over here,' he orders.

'You must be joking,' Neena responds.

'Whatever happened to the meek Indian wife who would come scurrying if her husband even twitched his eyebrow at her?'

'I hate to tell you, but she became extinct sometime in circa 1800, O lord and master,' Neena retorts cheekily.

'Come here, na?' Rohit switches to a more pleading tone.

'Rohit, careful! You'll wake the kids up. It was such a nightmare trying to put them to sleep tonight. Gosh, I thought for a moment you'd woken him up there.' They both look down at Ritik who, unwittingly jogged by his lustful father, is fortunately still asleep but now furiously sucking on his thumb.

Rohit laughs at the wet, slurping sounds emanating from between thumb and mouth. 'God, what a racket he makes doing that!' he whispers with paternal pride.

'Your mum says you were a great thumbsucker too.'

'Yeah, he's my son all right,' Rohit says proudly, magnanimously overlooking all the little Manny features that are in blissful repose at the moment. He then looks at his sleeping daughter, who, lying in this half-light and clad in a white flowered nightie, looks like a tiny slumbering angel. 'And this is just the most beautiful girl in the world, isn't she?' he states to no one in particular, leaning down to give her a gentle kiss. Reaching out to ruffle the top of his wife's head, he seems to have forgotten his earlier libidinal feelings as he then turns over, bidding her goodnight.

Neena mumbles back, but even through her sleep-addled, exhausted brain, she is still thinking about Tarun and Gayatri. 'Wouldn't it have been marvellous if I could have been a fly on their table tonight' is her final thought, before she is enveloped in sleep.

8

So what is this thing called love?

And so it transpires that Tarun and Gayatri have a very pleasant meal at the Imperial Hotel on Janpath. Tarun has chosen this venue for many different reasons, the first of them being that it is miles away from the Menon household in Saket, which translates into more time spent with the lovely Gayatri by his side, especially if he takes care not to drive at his usual breakneck speed. They do not speak very much during the drive because Tarun is still trying to calm his nerves, and Gayatri imagines that he is trying to concentrate on the traffic. On the one or two occasions that she looks at his profile as she asks him something, he seems to frown terribly before replying. She decides it is the traffic, although we know that Tarun is merely trying to concentrate desperately on getting it right. The fact that he does get it right (well, most of the time anyway) is down to a happy blend of instinct, accident and plain good luck. By the time they are nearing the Imperial, Tarun's nerves have stopped jangling, although one would hesitate before describing them as being anywhere near a state of tranquillity.

The noise of the chaotic traffic, trying desperately either to get into or depart from Connaught Place, recedes as they coast up the old palm-fringed drive and park in front of the hotel. After Tarun has locked the car, Gayatri takes him by the arm, mainly to ensure that she does not totter in her high-heeled sandals. To Tarun this is, of course, the sweetest start to the evening, and he knows that from here on it will be plain sailing.

Inside, everything is encased in expensive silence broken only by the muted tinkling of nondescript music and tiny marble fountains. Gayatri has not seen this hotel—not because (as Swarn has already gloomily predicted) she has very little money, but because it has only just been renovated. Tarun, on the other hand, knows the place well and is now eagerly showing her around.

'Apparently they sent a team out to the Raffles in Singapore to try to recreate its atmosphere,' he says.

'Really?' Gayatri looks around appreciatively. It is truly beautiful, and her spirits lift a little more.

'Let me show you around before we go and claim our table. That, over there, is a pub, supposedly designed to look like one of your English pubs, but you'll be able to tell me if it's anything like the pubs over there.'

Gayatri looks into the crowded darkened interior with interest. There is a long counter behind which bottles have been upended and a barman is pulling expertly at the draught beer. She is reminded suddenly of her first job back in Oxford and the ache in her arm by pub-closing time at eleven, as she pulled her thousandth pint of the night. She smiles at the bartender sympathetically. And remembers suddenly that that was exactly how she first met Michael, four years ago, handing him his Guinness (with a huge smile) over the bar counter at the Coach and Horses. She was new to the job then and still smiled when she served the customers, however raucously they were behaving. Professors came in there rarely and only when they wanted to socialize with the students. Michael soon became a regular, however, and she hadn't realized at first that she was the reason for his daily appearances. Later she was flattered that someone so learned and so much older seemed so fascinated by her.

They got talking one night as she was clearing away, and he walked her back to her digs. It was only a matter of days before she started visiting him in his rooms. She questioned her haste, she really did, but he seemed so perfect then—erudite, brilliant, liberal, persuasive, nothing like any of the raw, unworldly men she had met back in India. Or the Pakistani chap (medical student, she guessed, from the thickness of his bifocals) who had gawkily and relentlessly pursued her since the day she had arrived in England. The very fact that Michael wasn't an acne-faced student seemed the biggest boon initially. And the fact that he was married, strangely irrelevant.

Afterwards, when his wife found out and he told Gayatri that she would have to leave his life, she longed for the carefree company of those fellow students she had spurned once. But it was much too late by then, of course. She'd already cut herself off from student life for four whole years, and she was considered by a lot of people to be a bit of an oddball by then. In her final weeks, she took to standing alone at her window, feeling the swirling icy winds cut into the tears on her face as she watched coat-clad figures returning from their pub crawls, laughing, huddling together, seeming to have no cares at all. It'll get better when summer comes, she thought, but the desolation only got worse and worse. Finally, her GP pleaded with her to take a holiday, and she simply left for India, for her Appa and her Amma, and for some kind of comfort that she knew she would never ever find in the cold land that she had once been so sure she could make her home.

She shudders at the memory, and Tarun puts his arm around her and asks her if she is cold. She looks up at him, and even he is taken aback to see the warmth in their soft brown depths—as though he were suddenly her best friend. Not that he minds at all. Amiable, easy-going Tarun has learnt, even while still a half-pant-wearing schoolboy, that opportunities to win over girls are meant to be grabbed. He is not the most introspective of young men, but he can sense a certain yearning in Gayatri tonight. He is not always a shameless opportunist, but all this is too jolly good to resist. He takes his chance, *carpe diem*, and the gods appear to smile from somewhere among the chandeliers above (big, abundant, expensive chandeliers, these—not from Kathmandu, but the real thing, ji). He bends over and, tightening his grasp around Gayatri's waist, kisses her gently on the lips. He almost cannot believe his own audacity and, even better (Hai Ram! Jai Jai Krishan ji ki!), that she does not smack him away. A passing group of plump Punjabi matrons nudge elbows and roll their eyes—but who can really mind when young love is unfurling its wings, tentatively, sweetly shaking them out before attempting to take flight.

They walk arm in arm to the Spice Route restaurant. With stunning walls painted over in terracotta, ochre and gold ('All done in vegetable dyes, sir,' says the maître d', puffing out his chest as though he had personally carried out this task). They sink into sofas, deep and warm and welcoming. Waiters hover, discreetly obsequious, and stringed music wafts around them. The food is simply splendid. Could there be a setting more suited to romance?

Probably not. But romance, depending on the subject and the circumstance, can either be shallow and short-lived or deepen into something less exciting, more lasting. Love, let's call it love, even though weary cynics among us may cringe. So, do Gayatri and Tarun fall in love, I hear you ask pleadingly ...

Well, the upshot of the matter is this: by the end of the evening, as Tarun drops Gayatri at her gate, giving her another chaste kiss, he is a man deeply in love. He simply cannot, will not, be able to comprehend life minus Gayatri any more. (Even though, as we all know, he has lived a perfectly happy one until now and really might have been better off merely maintaining that particular status.) And what of Gayatri, you ask next. Will this rather young woman find love at last?

■

Gayatri lets herself silently into the house, breathing a sigh of relief that her parents have turned in for the night. She kicks off her shoes and pads her way to her bedroom, closing the door gently behind her. Wetting a bit of cotton wool under the bathroom tap, she wipes her lips and eyes with it. Unlike Neena, she has never bothered too much with expensive lotions and cleansers. Then she peels off her clothes, seeming to watch herself contemplatively in the small bathroom mirror while pulling on her nightshirt, her mind, in fact, miles away. Turning off the lights, she walks to her bed and sinks into it, pulling the sheet up, tucking it under her chin. Is she thinking of Tarun as she closes her eyes and covers them with her forearm—as though trying to blot something out? Yes, she is. But no, not in the way we might want.

She still thinks he's a nice chap. ('*Nice* chap? Nice *chap*?' Tarun would have echoed hollowly, disbelievingly.) But she is an intelligent girl and given to far more introspection than the straightforward Tarun. She now feels herself grow perturbed that she has allowed herself to get drawn into the shallow pleasures of being with a man so clearly smitten by her. The evening has left her feeling confident again in her ability to attract men. She had clearly enjoyed the look in Tarun's eyes tonight. She has revelled in the knowledge that she holds the easy ability in her hands to hurt a man, rather than have him hurt her. To her discomfiture, she rather likes the feeling. But love? Even though the evening has left a warm glow somewhere in her innards, love is not what she would call it at all. Oh, dear.

■

Neena is quizzing Tarun excitedly with a plethora of breathless 'And thens?' He is lapping up every bit of it— telling her some, not telling her some, letting her know, nastily, that he is only telling her some. She is furious with him and delighted with him and really rather amazed that he has managed to pull the stunt off.

'You mean she allowed you to kiss her again?' Neena is clearly impressed.

Tarun nods and shrugs as though it were the easiest thing in the world.

'And she said she had no intention at all of ever returning to England?'

Tarun nods again, proudly, as though he were the sole reason for this decision of Gayatri's.

'Have you planned to meet again?'

For a moment, Tarun loses his composure. He knew he had forgotten something.

'Never mind, you'll see her at aerobics this evening, you can sort it out then,' Neena says kindly. She is still filled with admiration for her brother-in-law's astonishing feat. Old Tarun, who would've thought, eh?

But at aerobics, later that evening, will begin the first of Tarun's myriad confusions. Being in love is a confused enough state, without adding to it a potential lover who does not know at all what she wants or where she is going. Gayatri recognized last night that she has the potential to hurt Tarun grievously, which she does not want to do at all. It is easier and kinder, she decides, to let him off the hook gently. She will not confuse him by being friendly, as she was last night. In fact, she is feeling jolly silly about having been overly friendly with him, a relative stranger. She will, instead, be polite and distant and cool. It will not be possible, of course, to avoid him completely because of Neena. So she will meet him, but only when there are others around, and then she will be pleasant enough, but certainly not encourage any more advances.

But the hapless Tarun does not have the benefit of this information and is completely confounded as to why, having glowed at him so warmly last night, Gayatri is today all bunched up and quiet. She has barely three words to exchange with him at the fountain but seems normal enough with Neena. He tries to rekindle yesterday's spark a few times and then lapses back into disconsolate silence. He goes through the paces of the aerobics session half-heartedly. He is now pretty much an expert at Grapevine and Jazzwalk and can go through the motions without having to concentrate too hard. His mind is wandering restlessly, like a lost spirit, while his arms and legs execute cheery, jumping movements. If we could only have told him that this is what all lovers do ... pine and fret and agitate. That it is all a part of this wretched thing called love. That, without that compulsory element in the business of love, we would never have had symphonies and poetry and art. Would he have felt comforted? 'Not bloody likely,' would not have been an unreasonable reply.

∎

But all is not lost. With as determined a Cupid as Neena on his side, Tarun's looming black cloud is still edged with the thinnest of silver linings. Neena, who has been quietly observing the shenanigans, decides to get to work later that evening.

'Rohit, I was thinking ...'

'Mmmm ...' Rohit's eyes are fixed on the television screen. It is obvious he is not listening.

Neena jiggles his arm. 'Listen!' she says.

Rohit, accustomed to the sound of his wife's voice as a constant backdrop to his nights of quiet television watching, grunts, still only half-listening. He has never worked out how it is that a few well-timed grunts can appear to satisfy her as she chunters on. He doesn't know, of course, that Neena too has wondered how a similar series of grunts manages to convince him of her satisfaction when they make love. But we digress.

'Rohit, sweetie, you know this Tarun-Gayatri thing? (Rohit's cue for a grunt) It's all going so badly. Did I tell you about the last aerobics session we had? (grunt) I wish we could do something to help,' she trails off as she thinks. Rohit settles back into enjoying *Top Gear* again. But just as that infuriatingly lucky Jeremy chappie gets into a bright yellow Lotus Elise and starts to rev it up, Neena starts off once more. 'Why don't we organize an outing, just the four of us! Before you leave for London. Isn't that a good idea? Somewhere really romantic, so Tarun gets a proper chance to tell her again how wonderful he thinks she is. And, of course, you, my sweet, could use the opportunity similarly to tell me how wonderful I am too (grunt).'

This last grunt of Rohit's is an ill-timed one. What he really should have said was this: 'What a clever idea, darling! And of course I think you're wonderful. You are, in fact, the best.' Instead he is still slavering over the Lotus Elise, while Neena's angry glare bores a little smoking hole into the side of his head. 'Oh, I give up!' she says, getting up and stamping off. 'I'm just going to go and organize it, and you'll just have to fall in line.' As Rohit grunts again, pleased to be finally left alone to watch the last few minutes of his favourite programme at last, a patter of small feet announces the arrival of little Rinku.

'Papa,' she opens, perching herself without preamble on his knee. Rohit cranes his neck looking over the top of her curly head so as not to miss the leather interior of the Lotus. Rinku, having found a comfortable spot and settled herself, shrilly starts off, 'Papa, you know, in my school there is a girl called Arushi who has a fringe on her forehead, Papa. (Rohit grunts.) Papa can I have a fringe too? Please? Here?' She taps the top of her head looking around at her father beseechingly. (Rohit grunts once more, he has never seen a car as sexy as this one, beats the BMW hollow.) His grunting has quite the opposite effect on his daughter as it did on his wife. Rinku leaps off his lap and runs off screaming delightedly, 'Papa says I can have a fringe, Mummy. I asked him!'

■

Neena, an efficient Cupid to say the least, has booked a table for four at Larry's China and is now trying to get passes to Some Kind of Place. She has it on good authority (from her old schoolmate Shonali, who graduated quickly from school tart to Delhi's best nightclub crooner) that this is the best discotheque for playing slow dance numbers.

'Really slow romantic numbers?' Neena double-checks on the telephone, just to be sure.

'Really slow, yaar,' Shonali drawls, 'but go after 11 to be on the safe side.'

'Oh, that's useful to know. Thanks for all that, Shonali. Listen, we must have that coffee sometime.'

But Shonali is not about to let Neena off the hook that easily. 'Wait a bit, yaar,' she says. 'All these questions about slow numbers and late-night romance! You don't think I'm going to hang up until you tell me who the lucky chap is, honey!'

Neena is covered in confusion, 'What! You didn't think? Oh, Shonali, you idiot, I'm a respectably married woman, you know!'

'Married! What the hell, yaar, as if that's ever stopped anybody!' Shonali retorts scornfully. 'Which era have you been living in, honey? Every married person I know is having an affair.'

Neena is instantly interested. 'Really? Who, who?'

'Well, that would be telling,' Shonali drawls mysteriously. 'First you tell me who you're planning to go slow dancing with, you crafty little thing. Not your husband, surely.' The determinedly single Shonali utters the word *husband* as though it burns her tongue to say it.

'Of course I am!' Neena defends her virtue hotly. 'I love my husband, you idiot, however crazy that may seem to you.'

'Nobody loves her husband, yaar. Well, at least not after the first three days. After that, it's called *putting up with*.'

Neena finds it difficult to argue with Shonali's air of authority on the subject. 'Oh, shut up, yaar,' she says. 'Leave me to deal with my marriage, and I'll next speak to you on the subject only after you've gone and fallen in love.'

'Never!' declares Shonali.

'Oh, and don't forget to invite me for your wedding!' Neena cries cheerily before Shonali hangs up.

■

'Oh, not a disco, darling! You know how I hate discos,' Rohit wails piteously.

Neena glares at him. 'You used to love going dancing. Once. A long time ago, admittedly.'

'I know, but I was young then! And not the father of two.'

'You talk as if you're the one who's chasing after the kids all day. You just sit in the air-conditioned comfort of your office.' Rohit contemplates telling her that running a large textile factory involves marginally more than sitting in his cabin, but he decides that she is not likely to accept this piece of information with particular astonishment and wonder. Neena carries on talking, closing finally and unsympathetically, 'If I can find the energy to go dancing after a whole day with the kids, then so can you. So stop moaning!'

That evening, the younger Sachdevs set out for their planned destination. Tarun is nervous, but pleased that his thus-far shaky romance might be looking up again. He gives his sister-in-law's arm a grateful squeeze as she comes down the stairs, balancing herself precariously in her nightclub shoes. 'Thanks,' he whispers. 'Let's hope this works, huh?'

'Well, it had better work, sonny!' she replies. 'These shoes are killing me.'

Swarn, hovering at the vicinity of the front door, cannot resist a casual query. 'So! Everybody is all dressed up nicely and all, hanh? Going somewhere special?' She pretends to have suddenly spotted Tarun too. 'My wittle beta Tarun is going out too? With his big brother and sister-in-law! Oho, no girl to accompany you? Neena, why don't you find him someone nice, hanh?'

Neena, who has recently expended a great deal of energy trying to find her brother-in-law someone whom she thinks is nice, merely smiles murderously. Rohit hustles them all out of the house, throwing over his shoulder, 'Oh, I'm sure Tarun will have no trouble finding himself someone nice once we're there, Mamma.' They drive off in a roar of BMW power, leaving a very dissatisfied looking Swarn standing helplessly at the front door.

She is still there with a huge scowl on her face when, a few minutes later, Jagdish's car pulls into the drive. 'Where have they all gone?' he asks Swarn. 'I waved to them, but they didn't seem to see me.'

'Humph,' his wife retorts. There is no point telling him about this Gayatri business. What will he know about the kind of tensions she has to suffer, keeping track of all these girls who might be chasing their sons? 'Useless,' she mutters under her breath as she pushes past him and goes into her bedroom, slamming the door behind her.

Jagdish isn't sure if the adjective is meant for him or some distant person or maybe even her latest migraine. He merely hopes that Nek Singh the driver hasn't heard as he signals for his briefcase to be deposited in his study. He follows the driver into the small, dark room and nods absently as Nek Singh bids him a good night before closing the door behind him. Jagdish fiddles with the knob on the air conditioner, but the old machine seems to be completely dead. The night is muggy, and Jagdish takes off all his clothes until he is stark naked. 'Aaaaah . . . ,' he breathes loudly as he falls into his armchair. Another long day at the factory, another slog that no one will ever understand or want to hear about, not his sons, intent only on enjoying their night out in town, not his wife, intent on her latest migraine. He curls up his large frame until he looks like a large, hairy foetus resting in a black leather womb. The darkness is soothing. The silence is good.

■

Over at Saket, Gayatri is pacing up and down her living room, waiting to be picked up by the Sachdevs. She knows

Tarun has put Neena and Rohit up to this outing and is not pleased to be a part of such machinations. But Neena was insistent, and Gayatri thought it would be churlish to refuse to go. Keshava, sitting on the sofa, looks at her anxiously. 'Going out tonight?' He asks.

'Yes,' she replies, chewing her lip.

'With that Tarun fellow again?' After a moment's pause, he adds in what he imagines is a subtle but significant way, 'The one we haven't met yet.'

'Yes.'

'Well?'

'Well, what?'

'Well, will we meet him today or not?'

Gayatri glares at him. 'I don't know why you're so keen to meet him, Appa. To hear you talk, one would think he were my potential husband, you know.'

'So you keep telling us, but we like meeting all your friends too. Not unreasonable, is it?'

'No, but I'm not even sure he's my friend.'

'But he must be your friend if you keep going out with him.'

'Keep going out with him!' Gayatri is astounded at the cheek of her father's inaccuracy. 'I don't keep going out with him, I'd have you know! Once, just once.'

'Twice,' Keshava corrects her.

'Oh, come, Appa! I haven't gone out with him yet tonight. So it's still once.'

'But you are still going, aren't you? Or have you cancelled?' he asks hopefully.

'No, I have not cancelled!' Gayatri suddenly feels very confused.

'Well, whether once or twice, you have to admit that, in the space of a week, it is quite frequent. So you must be friends at the very least.'

'Oh, so now you're keeping tabs on the frequency too, are you?'

'Well, one can hardly fail to notice.'

'Notice what?'

It is at this inopportune moment that the doorbell rings, announcing the arrival of the Sachdevs. This time, before Gayatri can get to the door, Neena comes rushing right in. 'Hello, Uncle! Hi, Gayatri!' she bellows cheerfully. She is followed closely by Rohit and, much to Gayatri's discomfiture, a beaming Tarun.

Gayatri smiles back at them weakly and rather inhospitably waves half-heartedly at the sofa, 'Would you like to sit, or shall we just leave straightaway?'

'Oh, please could I have a drink of water before we go, Gayatri my sweet,' Neena says, plopping herself down on the sofa. Gayatri glares at her as though it is a most unreasonable request, but the signal is wasted on her as Neena is engrossed in kicking off her shoes and rubbing her sore feet with loud groans. Now, examining the underside of her feet, she orders her husband and brother-in-law to sit down too, informing them for the tenth time of how badly her feet are killing her.

Gayatri, aware that she ought to be returning the customary hospitality of the Sachdevs, looks at Rohit, and adds slightly less feebly, 'Yes, do sit down, everybody. Can I get anyone else some water too?'

Keshava, in the meantime, is rushing around the room, clearing away books and papers from chairs and sofa, 'Sit, sit. Do sit down all of you! Why water only? Let me get you some tea, coffee, something? Eh, Neena, what would you like? Some of your favourite south Indian coffee, eh?'

Gayatri glares at the back of her father's head on her way to the kitchen. She knows she has lost this particular battle as she sees Keshava virtually push Tarun down on to one of the Menon household's many tin trunks converted to divans. It cracks loudly with the sudden weight of a human body, but, to his credit, Tarun merely starts slightly before quickly regaining his cheery equanimity. Keshava is now grabbing his hand and asking in his jolliest voice, 'So you must be Tarun?' To Gayatri's horror, she next hears her father's voice say, 'I'm so pleased to finally meet you, Tarun. My Gayatri has told me so much about you.' She catches a glimpse of the huge happy smile this brings to Tarun's lips, before she vanishes into the kitchen to shudder privately over the water tap.

As she returns to the drawing room, bearing a tray with three glasses of water, she sees the unbearable sight of Keshava and Tarun deep in conversation. 'What on earth are they talking about? They haven't got a thing in common,' she thinks angrily to herself as she passes the glasses of water around. She can only hear snatches. 'Yes . . . textile mills' 'of course, Ph.D.' 'I know, lovely girl.' They are both looking up at her now, smiling, as she proffers the last glass on the tray to Tarun. She glowers at him, but he does not seem to notice. Whatever Keshava has been saying has made him a very happy man indeed. Gayatri puts the tray down on the table and drops herself resignedly into a chair. She feels all the forces are against her and blinks away an angry, self-pitying prickle behind her lashes as she pulls out a file on top of which she has sat, hurling it on to the floor.

A few minutes later, Raji enters the scene as well, and Gayatri slumps even lower into her chair, a pretty bundle of unaccountable misery. Raji too goes through the motions of offering teas and coffees, but the Sachdevs cry off, stating their prospective meal as the reason. 'Why bother,' Gayatri thinks miserably. 'No one seems in any hurry at all to go for that bloody meal any more.' The conversation swirls around her, and she notices that Keshava and Tarun seem to have, in some odd sort of way, actually hit it off. They are laughing and nodding at each other. At one stage, Keshava even has his hand on Tarun's arm, Gayatri notices with alarm.

After what seems like an eternity to Gayatri, she sees Rohit looking at his watch before cocking an eyebrow at Neena. Everyone gets up, Tarun with marked reluctance, Gayatri thinks, as the tin trunk cracks loudly again as though bidding Tarun's charming posterior a reluctant farewell. Keshava and Raji follow them out as they leave the house and get into the car. 'Nice car!' Keshava cries admiringly. 'It's a BMW, isn't it?' he asks, wandering around to the front to get a better look. Gayatri takes advantage of the dark to cringe openly this time. Details about the car are discussed, and Keshava clucks some more over it before they finally get in. After they have driven off, Keshava turns to his wife. His face is shining elatedly in the dim light of a nearby spluttering street light as, in a voice filled with delight, he says, 'Nice chap, that Tarun fellow, eh Raji? And what a nice car. I knew we could rely on our Gayatrimole to choose sensibly.'

And as they go indoors, you can just about catch his words, as he puts his arm around his wife and closes the door behind them. 'Oh, my little Rajikutty, isn't young love just the most wondrous thing?'

9

No more nakhras, please!

It is hard for Gayatri to continue sulking in the cheery presence of Neena who is in her element tonight. 'Let me tell you my latest Malayali joke,' Neena says to general groans after they have placed their orders for the food. 'No, no, it's a sweet joke!' she insists, launching into it without further ado. 'Gayatri, listen, you'll like this.' Turning on a heavy south Indian accent and waggling her head from side to side, she continues, 'I met this Mallu chap who was going from Kerala to Manchester on holiday, and he said to me, "I'm taking my mother-in-lah, my father-in-lah ... and ..."' Neena pauses here for effect, ' "my umbrellah!" ' She is convulsed in laughter. 'It's so sweet, isn't it?'

Gayatri puts up a spirited defence of her kinsmen. 'Oh, come now, how many Mallus do you know personally who say *mother-in-lah*, *father-in-lah* and so on? Be fair!'

Neena doesn't give in. 'But in Kerala there must be! You are only a half-baked Mallu, having been brought up here in Delhi.' She smiles at her friend and then adds generously, 'You're really one of us. I'm sure people in Kerala don't speak like you at all.'

'I'm not one of you at all. How dare you! I'm Malayali

and proud to be so,' Gayatri expostulates.

Tarun cuts in, 'How do you know how people in Kerala speak anyway, Neena? You've never even been there!'

Neena tries not to mind Tarun's unashamed leap over to Gayatri's side. She knows it is only because of his very vested interest, although inwardly she has a little message for him. 'I'll deal with you later, bachoo!' she thinks menacingly, looking at him under her lashes. But to Gayatri she says cheerfully, 'But so what if people do speak in a certain way. It's harmless jesting to poke fun at people's accents, isn't it?'

'Oh, but these are fine lines, darling, and then how can one tell when exactly one may be crossing over into being malicious, hanh?' Rohit cuts in.

'Precisely,' says Gayatri, 'it's merely racism of another kind, isn't it? And it can get quite pernicious because it's more difficult to confront without seeming like a bad sport.'

'You're not accusing me of racism, are you?' the irrepressible Neena says with a pout, pretending to be hurt. 'Me, who loves dosas and idlis for breakfast.'

'Well, I could accuse you of being no better than the skinhead who yells, "Oi, Paki" from across the road, while hurrying home for his customary curry and chips every night. But, I think I'm going to let you off the hook because I know your best friend is Mallu, and that must water your racist tendencies down ever so slightly,' Gayatri smiles at her friend.

'We might also forgive you your pernicious, racist attitude, seeing what a nice table you've got for us tonight,' Rohit says. 'Oh, and for agreeing to pay the bill!'

Neena kicks him affectionately and then yelps again before groaning, 'Damn! I forgot again about these goddamn shoes. They're killing me, and now I think I've fractured my toe trying to kick you!'

The food is served, and all arguments and awkwardnesses are temporarily suspended as the foursome pass dishes to each other, commenting on how wonderful the food smells, how this place has kept up its standards over the years, how Indian-Chinese food is so much tastier than the Chinese-Chinese food available in Chinatown in London.

Tarun's hand brushes Gayatri's as he passes her the salt-and-pepper pork. He feels a frisson and darts a glance at her. She is looking down at her plate but smiles and says, 'Thank you'. He likes to think she is thanking him, not just for the salt-and-pepper pork, but also for his earlier spirited and heroic defence of Malayalis against Neena's ridiculous, racist assertions. 'I *like* Malayalis,' he thinks fervently, quite forgetting that he knows only about two. He is feeling particularly pleased at the warmth of the reception he has received from Keshava tonight. 'That father of Gayatri's, Mr Menon, what a very nice man he turned out to be!' Encouraged by this heart-warming thought, Tarun asks Gayatri if she would like the honey-chilli chicken passed to her as well. She nods and smiles slightly. Tarun virtually snatches the chicken dish out of his brother's hands just as Rohit is about to serve himself a generous portion of his favourite dish. Tarun ladles out a solicitously large portion on to her plate. She smiles at him again, while Rohit looks balefully at the back of his brother's head, but Tarun is feeling too blissful to care that he might have permanently alienated his brother's feelings. The only thing that counts at the moment is that Gayatri is smiling at him again!

After dinner, the small group makes a beautifully timed entrance at the nightclub. The Filipino band has started playing soft music, as promised by the knowledgeable Shonali, and the lights are so dim that the foursome has to feel their way gingerly across the smoky darkness to an empty table. Perfect, Tarun thinks. It has already been planned in advance that Rohit will take Neena on to the floor for a dance, leaving Tarun and Gayatri alone at the table. This small and rather obvious contrivance doesn't seem to work very well as Gayatri scowls at the receding backs of Neena and Rohit making their way to the dance floor. She picks up a cardboard coaster and plays with it, reading the print on it with great seriousness. When it becomes impossible to read it any more, her gaze wanders around the nightclub, looking everywhere but in Tarun's direction. He remembers having read in one of his school books, a long time ago, that discretion is generally considered to be the better part of valour, but such aphorisms are meaningless to a desperate man. Tarun takes a deep breath and plunges in.

'Gayatri,' he says grabbing her hand and, with it, the cardboard coaster she has been fidgeting with. He clutches both ardently to his chest. 'Gayatri, my darling girl, what is wrong? Have I said anything to upset you? If I have, you just have to say the word, and I will correct all past wrongs, make up for every little mistake, make everything right again. Just tell me, what is it?'

Now, the offer of correcting all past wrongs and making everything right again is an uncommonly generous one and very hard to resist, even when, like Gayatri, you have made so many resolutions in the area of self-control. She still has the awful, rankling, heart-chilling memory of the coldness in Michael's grey eyes lurking inside her somewhere. It was not so long ago that she was made to feel as though she was the most worthless, unwanted human being alive, despite her brains and charm. It was not so long ago she was fleeing, on board a silver British Airways 747, desperately trying to get away from love and all the fear and pain it can bring.

And now, here she is, faced by an earnest, eager, handsome young man with a forelock quivering with passion. He is clutching her hand to her chest. He has no wife he has neglected to tell her about so far. His eyes are filled with the sort of hope and adoration akin to a soothing balm. He is saying something rash and wonderful about making everything all right again. Would you blame Gayatri for forgetting earlier resolutions? Would you have it in your heart to mind that she wants to be loved properly this time? By someone who will really adore her—and not just for a few months until his wife finds out about her. So what of the fact that she has already travelled through this whole Tarunloop, managing to come out of it only last week, only to be thoughtlessly re-entering it again?

If it is all too much for us, imagine the swirling mass of confusion raging inside Gayatri's head. She is normally an intelligent sort of girl, as we know, but now she does not want to talk or think. With her hand beginning to feel as though it is getting gangrenous against Tarun's chest, she can only bring herself to whisper weakly, 'Let's not talk, let's just dance, shall we.'

Tarun leaps to his feet, takes her hand again and leads her to the dance floor. Neena gives him a broad, encouraging wink as they approach, but he is too elated to return her puerile gesture. Turning to Gayatri, he takes her in his arms, wrapping them around her tenderly. Tilting his head, he can smell the shampoo in her hair. If he were to bend his neck another few inches, he would be able to plant a light kiss on the curve of that lovely neck, but this he reserves for later in the evening. For now, he is content to be holding this lithe, lovely body against his own, feeling it move as he does. He has danced like this before, many times, and with many a lithe and lovely body, but he has never felt moved virtually to tears by this activity on previous occasions. He cannot understand it but is not about to question it. He is concentrating on ascending his personal stairway to heaven.

Back at the table, Neena is craning her neck, trying to glimpse Tarun and Gayatri through the shadowy crowd on the darkened dance floor. 'Oh, I think they're kissing!' she yelps delightedly to Rohit.

Rohit, who desperately wants his bed after all the unaccustomed graceful hip-swinging of the evening, yawns openly. 'Offo, Neena, we really should have come in two cars and left them to it.'

'What! And gone home early without checking this out? No way!'

But, in another few minutes, and much to Rohit's relief, Tarun and Gayatri appear at the table. Gayatri takes her seat, bashfully avoiding eye contact with Neena and Rohit. Tarun orders a large bottle of Bisleri and, when it arrives, pours out a glass for Gayatri. Neena, who thinks Tarun should not be forgetting who was responsible for getting Gayatri out in the first place, plonks her empty glass loudly down in front of him. Sheepishly, he fills her glass too.

'It must be something about being single that gives people more energy than married people,' Rohit says.

'We aren't keeping you up, I hope?' Gayatri says apologetically.

'Well, normally I'd have been happy to party on but, as you know, tomorrow night I leave for my trip to London. I haven't even begun my packing!'

'God, I'd forgotten, it's tomorrow night, isn't it?' Neena pipes up. She turns to Gayatri. 'I'm thinking of moving back home for the week he's going to be away. I'll be able to see a lot more of you then, being so near. Tell you what, come and spend the night! It'll be like old times.'

Tarun, who has not said very much so far, looks somewhere into he middle distance with a kind of longing in his eyes at the mention of Gayatri spending the night. Even though it is not to be with him. And not even in his house. He merely likes the sound of it, he decides—Gayatri, spending the night.

His reverie is broken by his sister-in-law's insistent voice. 'Tarun! Have you got a pen?' she repeats loudly. He finds one in his pocket and hands it over. Gayatri takes the pen and writes something on a cardboard coaster before handing it over to his brother. Rohit slips it into his pocket, nodding as Gayatri says, 'Make sure you do give him a call if you need anything. He's really awfully nice.'

'Who is very nice?' Tarun queries, trying to sound casual. The pronoun has him worried.

Neena guesses what is on his mind and pats his arm reassuringly. 'Gayatri's old GP in Oxford. Seventy years old. Because Rohit hasn't taken out medical insurance. Where were you? Weren't you listening?'

Tarun looks only faintly reassured. He can only barely

cope with Gayatri referring to some man of seventy as *awfully nice*. Anything less than sixty-eight would have had him very worried. But there is no time now for wider concerns. His evening with Gayatri is all too quickly drawing to a close. The Filipino band is packing up, the girl singer is stretching her arms above her head and yawning, the happy, tired crowd is drifting out. Tarun turns to Gayatri and says, with a note of desperation creeping into his voice, 'Look, I've got to meet you again. Soon. Can I come and pick you up tomorrow? At about seven? Dinner. I'll buy us dinner somewhere.'

Gayatri looks at him, suddenly feeling very sad all over again. He seems truly nice, but she knows he is the sort she will never be able to fall for. However, in the illogical and often inconsiderate way in which we deal with these things (and who has never been prey to such quandaries?), she looks up at him and nods. 'I'd like that very much,' she says softly.

■

Keshava Menon wakes up that morning a happier man than he has been in a long time. He has it all worked out. Gayatri will marry that nice young man, Tarun, and live on LM Road, a mere seven miles away from the Menons. Not that he knows much about these Sachdevs, having only a very vague memory of a seemingly wealthy family at Neena's wedding. But Gayatri will have the fine advantage of having her good old friend Neena as her sister-in-law (or co-sister, as Keshava terms the relationship). Most convenient and suitable, avoiding all jealousies and rivalries with the co-sister who is often the bigger enemy than the mother-in-law. Even though Keshava has never lived in a joint family system, he knows that happiness in such familial set-ups comes only if the women get along. And, although Keshava does not particularly like the thought of Gayatri living in a joint family, the prospect is not so worrying because Neena will be there to see his daughter through.

Lovely girl, that Neena. Keshava always knew she would be a good friend for Gayatri to have—even all those years ago when the girls had first met as undergraduates and Raji had thought Neena might be too wealthy to be appropriate company for Gayatri. Neena's husband looked like a most agreeable young fellow too. And they were definitely well off—one could not ignore things like that. And what a very nice car! Then, of course, the textile business was thriving these days. Keshava was sure he had read somewhere recently that garment export was, contrary to all expectations, still one of the most booming businesses in the country. And the most important, the most crucial and deeply glowing thought now floated in among Keshava's more temporal reckonings: there was no doubt at all that Tarun himself was deeply enamoured of Gayatri. One might even say, the fellow was quite obviously completely crazy about her! Without being sure of that, Keshava would never ever nudge his beloved daughter, however gently, into anything she did not want.

Now all that was required was to meet Tarun's parents and put the proposal to them. Why postpone auspicious matters like marriage talks? And it had been playing on both his mind and Raji's for a while that Gayatri would soon be twenty-six—not too early to be starting to think about marriage and future prospects. With a beatific smile on his face, Keshava throws off his sheet and, humming along with radio, swings his feet off the bed and on to the floor.

He makes three steaming mugs of coffee, stirring sugar generously into all of them. As he knocks on Gayatri's door and peers around the door, she opens one sleep-encrusted eye and grumbles something unintelligible aloud. It sounds indistinctly like 'Go away please, Appa. I'm not awake yet,' but Keshava ignores her completely, shouting a cheery 'Good morning, good morning!' He makes loud clattering sounds putting the coffees down and noisily pulls open the curtains. Delhi's bright summer sunshine comes pouring in, bringing with it the early morning din of the milkman's aluminium can and the street sweeper's cane broom on the road surface outside.

Gayatri turns over with an irritated thump, opening her eye again to see if, by some chance, Keshava might have left the room. She sees that he has settled himself companionably on her fake divan. It is impossible to carry on sleeping in the face of such unabashed sociability. Clearly Keshava wants to talk. As he starts to hum his favourite bhajan loudly, she drags herself up, plumps her pillows behind her huffily and asks blearily, 'Wha'time is it?'

'Good morning, Gayatrikutty!' Keshava beams from over his glasses, moving the coffee across to her bedside table.

'G'morning, Appa,' she mumbles, taking the mug in both hands and sniffing its aroma appreciatively.

'So, my little Gayatrimolu, had a nice time yesterday?'

Gayatri nods, keeping her face embedded in the steaming coffee vapours. Keshava sweeps on, his eyes twinkling happily behind thick glasses. 'After you all left, we were saying, Raji and I, how nice a fellow your Tarun seems to be. So pleasant, so agreeable! Don't you agree?'

'Oh, Appa! He's not my Tarun at all!' Gayatri groans in despair.

'Well then, why not? Perfectly nice fellow. Well-mannered, good job, good family. Moley, these days one meets such riff-raff in Delhi, one has to be so careful.' Keshava cannot fathom Gayatri's thoughts as she continues to sip her coffee silently. He continues, speaking now with passion, 'Even arranged alliances don't work out well these days. Only the other day we were hearing about your cousin Geetanjali in Madras. You remember how Gopu Uncle and Maloo Aunty had got her married with such pomp and style last year to some fellow living in America. After that, they waited one full year for him to send a ticket for her to join him, which he never did. So, finally, they booked her on a flight to America, and the poor girl gets there only to find out that the rascal is already married! Can you believe it— even his own parents in Madras did not know. Turns out that he not only already has a wife (an American wife), but also three children! Three! Can you beat it! I heard that those children were even calling her Geetli-Geetli, running around her.' He breaks off with a shudder.

The story has woken Gayatri up, she remembers having met cousin Geetanjali at a family wedding many years ago, plump and pleasant, with a shy smile. 'Gosh, how terrible for her, poor thing!' she says with feeling. 'Where is she now?'

'Oh, she came back, of course, but now everybody is saying she should be sent back to take the scoundrel to court. In America she might at least be able to get some compensation for his cheating her like that. Here who will bother about her plight?'

Gayatri is horrified. 'Oh, but surely they can't be contemplating sending her alone to face all that! Hasn't she been through enough?'

'But, you see, unless she gets a proper divorce, or at least some money, no one else will come forward to marry her here. As it is, they will somehow come to the conclusion that it was all her fault.'

'I'll bet she isn't too keen on another marriage after all that!' Gayatri exclaims.

'What to do, moley. This country of ours is no place for a single girl. People won't let you live in peace, even if you have a good career and house and all.' Keshava is back to talking, subtly, about Gayatri's prospects and not Geetanjali's. 'People will always harass a woman who lives on her own,' he predicts gloomily. 'The world is no place for a single woman.'

'Oh, come now, Appa, there must be hundreds of single women living perfectly reasonable lives, even in a city like this.'

'You find me one who is happy!' Keshava retorts. 'Really happy!'

Gayatri falls silent again, draining the last of her coffee. Keshava rises and takes her mug from her. 'That's why I say,' he declares making his way to the door, 'if you meet someone nice, and someone who seems to love you, then you should not hesitate. After all, we all need a life-long companion, do we not? Otherwise, what fun is there in life, eh?'

He leaves the room, but not before firing a final Parthian shot in the direction of his still bleary daughter. Smiling broadly now and in a generous tone of voice, he says, 'As Raji and I were saying, these days one should not even worry about Malayali, Punjabi, Hindu, Muslim and all that. What is important is the person, and that he really loves you, don't you agree?' Having delivered this final piece of advice and feeling exceedingly pleased at having got such important paternal messages across so early in the morning, Keshava vanishes from sight without waiting for a reply.

■

When Tarun arrives at the Menon household later that night, he is given a hero's welcome by Keshava. Mrs Menon seems pleasant enough, but it doesn't take long for Tarun to work out that Gayatri's mother occupies some sort of other world filled with such large books that there is space for little else. At least, he knows he will probably not have an adversary in her. The love of his life is still circumspect, but Tarun can see that Gayatri's coolness has come down a notch or two. That is good enough progress for him at the moment.

Despite his protestations, he is treated to Keshava's best decoction coffee and a plate of some wiggly south Indian delicacy. 'Murukku. It is called murukku,' Keshava explains as Tarun crunches gingerly into a small piece.

'Hmm, they're nice!' Tarun observes with some surprise, helping himself to a couple more.

'Sent by my sister in Bhilai,' Keshava says proudly. Gayatri is shocked at her father's blatant lie about the origin of the snack that has only travelled down the road from a shop in R.K. Puram. It takes her a couple of seconds to work out that the reason for Keshava's falsehood is that he can now slip important details of the extended family into the conversation. She listens in growing horror as Keshava continues unabashedly, 'You see, I have only one sister, married to an engineer in the steelworks there. They also have only one child, Arun, studying for medicine in Vellore. Raji, now Raji has three brothers and one sister. All very well settled, all over India. They . . .'

Gayatri hastily cuts in, 'I'm sure Tarun doesn't need to know all their details, Appa!'

'Yes yes, I am boring you now, am I not?' Keshava laughs apologetically.

'No, no, of course not, it is most interesting,' says Tarun earnestly.

Keshava does not need more licence to proceed. 'You see, Gayatri is the only girl among all her cousins, the only girl! So she has always been very special. To all of her uncles and aunties also. We all try very hard to protect her, you see.' Tarun cannot tell if the hitherto pleasant Mr Menon is issuing some sort of a veiled threat and smiles nervously. Much to Gayati's discomfiture, Keshava gaily carries on talking in his high-pitched voice, 'We are basically a very traditional family, but we also know how to move with the times. These days, one has to be broad-minded about things like caste and community. After all, of what significance are all those things for you young people, no?'

Tarun nods. This sounds a lot more promising. Caste and community have never meant anything to him, especially in the pursuit of pretty young things. What a good egg Gayatri's father is turning out to be! But, before Tarun and Keshava can get further entrenched in detailed discussions of her future plans, Gayatri smiles sweetly at Tarun. 'Do you think we could leave now? I'm starving,' she says.

Tarun springs to his feet, 'Whatever you say, yes, you're right, I'm pretty hungry too.' They get up, and Keshava watches in delight through the curtains as they leave the house and walk to the car. It is not the BMW today, but a Tata Safari (loaned by Neena as a celebratory gesture of Tarun's second date alone with Gayatri). Keshava sighs as he sees Tarun hold the door open for Gayatri before going around to climb into the driver's seat. As they drive off, Keshava turns back to look at his wife who is still sitting at her desk. 'Nice boy, Raji. How I hope Gayatri has the sense to see that such nice boys are hard to find these days. And isn't it wonderful that they have such excellent cars.'

Raji looks faintly troubled behind her gleaming glasses, 'I know material wealth counts for something,' she says slowly, 'but I don't think I ever wanted a very well-off family for Gayatri. Sounds silly, doesn't it?'

'Why, what's wrong with a wealthy family? One has to be practical these days, Raji.'

'Well, it's about keeping up, or not being able to keep up, which is what will happen to us because we don't have much money.'

'Don't be stupid, Raji. Our Gayatri is such a lovely catch for any boy, and now she's a Ph.D. too. Why should our not rolling in money be the cause for too much concern?'

'I know, but you know these Delhi types. However wealthy, they must get their dowry and cars and all that.'

Keshava slumps down in his chair, looking mildly worried. He knows Raji has a point, but he soon sits up again, saying briskly, 'Well, we haven't touched my Provident Fund and we've got our State Bank savings. And half your mother's jewellery. We'll be able to do quite well by our Gayatri. You just stop worrying and get back to your writing.'

■

Unaware that her parents are worrying their heads over how exactly they will prepare for her trousseau and dowry, Gayatri is finishing off the last of her club sandwich at the Machan, wondering how she can get Tarun to stop taking her out for meals. It is not that she isn't enjoying herself, but she is now starting to feel slightly embarrassed that this is the third or fourth time she is eating a rather grand meal, without having to pay for it.

'In England this wouldn't happen at all,' she protests to Tarun. 'We'd either go halves or take turns to pay!'

He snatches the bill back from her. 'There's no way I'm letting you pay.'

'Why not?'

'Because the business has been keeping me so busy, I haven't had too many opportunities to spend my money. This is my chance.'

Gayatri laughs, 'Yes, but what's that got to do with me? I haven't done anything to deserve all these treats!'

Tarun looks at her. Gayatri knows she has inadvertently set him off again and tries to backtrack, but it is too late. Tarun is looking deep into her eyes, as though searching for some indication that there might be a little room in there for him. Please let there be a sign that Gayatri will say yes. Tarun spots a waiter at the next table nodding his head . . . Yes sir . . . yes sir . . . yes sir . . . That is as good a sign as any. He takes a deep breath and an enormous plunge.

'I . . . I . . . it's like this . . . you . . . Gayatri . . .' he says.

More or less aware of what is to come, Gayatri darts an alarmed look around the room. Diners are dining calmly, waiters waiting . . . all around is the steady clink of expensive cutlery cushioned by the low buzz of civilized conversation. No one seems especially perturbed that a declaration of love is about to be made at table number seven. Of course, if people knew this was the case, it would have been near impossible to keep all heads from turning to look at them. This smart young couple who seemed, at first glance, to be intent only on demolishing the club sandwiches placed in front of them. Waiters and diners, if they could have seen the hidden hand of love hover portentously over table number seven, would certainly have gathered around to get a better look. To raucously cheer Tarun on from the stalls as though he might be their favourite footballer, to chew their nails fervently until Gayatri responded. To slump back in disappointment if she didn't, to rise in one clamouring mass of bodies if she did. And, of course, roar their applause if the lovers actually got up, throwing all caution to the winds, scattering bits of bread and bacon and tomatoes, to grab each other and exchange a deep mustard-flavoured kiss. But none of this happens, of course, and diners merely carry on dining and waiters continue to wearily wait their tables. Tarun is left to his own devices, unbearably alone in a crowded room, to clear his throat and try again. He takes a deep breath, hoping a lungful of oxygen will rid him of the trouble starting that he seems to be encountering.

'Gayatri, my d ... darling,' he says, 'for long I have wanted to tell you ... ask you ... how do I put it? Please understand you do not have to tell me straightaway. In fact, take as much time as you like ... but what you need to know is. That I really. Think. I loveyou. Yes, I do, I know I loveyou. And ...' This bit of it has not been rehearsed. It is as if his tongue has taken off completely unbidden like a joyous, terrified, runaway horse. 'And, my dearest Gayatri, I also think ... no, I do not think, I know ... I know ... I just ... wanttomarryyou.'

Gayatri grabs the damask napkin off her lap and presses it to her mouth, eyes widening. Her shoulders start to shake, her eyes begin to water. All these could have been signs of either suppressed happiness or deepest sorrow. Tarun cannot tell, for a few seconds, which it might be. Tears are issuing forth from those lovely eyes as though from a spring. They are rolling out of brown depths, mingling with a touch of Max Factor mascara, before meandering down fair cheeks. Tarun looks on anxiously as Gayatri appears to crack up. Until finally the napkin slips from her mouth, showing the pretty flash of teeth, and he can hear her gurgling low laughter. She bends her head over until it is resting, forehead down, on the edge of the table. It takes a few minutes for Tarun to realize, much to his dismay, that Gayatri is convulsed in helpless laughter. She has grabbed the edge of the table, laughter turning to coughing and wheezing now.

'I haven't said anything funny, have I?' he asks piteously.

'Oh, Tarun! Gosh, you are a sweetie! Of course it's funny!' Gayatri looks up, trying to compose herself now, dabbing at her eyes with the damask napkin.

'But it's not funny. I meant every word of it,' Tarun whines peevishly.

'You can't mean you want to marry me. You don't even know me!'

'I know you enough to know I want to marry you,' Tarun maintains illogically. His chin sticks out stubbornly as he repeats, 'I already know all that I need to know.'

Gayatri's voice softens. 'Tarun, you are lovely,' she says, 'very marry-able. I'm just not sure we know each other enough to make as big a decision as that right now.'

'Oh, but we don't have to decide right now. I did say you didn't have to tell me straightaway.'

'But it could be a long time before we are really sure about our feelings.' A time as long as five years, she thinks suddenly, before she can stop herself.

'So, I'm willing to wait,' Tarun says, brushing his unruly lock back angrily again. In all moments of crisis, this feature of Tarun's has been known to take on a life of its own.

'Wait for how long, Tarun? I'm not really as sure about things as I might seem to be. Sometimes I take a very long time before I feel sure about things, and I still go and get it wrong too.' Gayatri surprises herself with her little admission, one she has hardly been able to make to herself until now. Suddenly, amidst the debris of club sandwiches, she feels unutterably sad. She cannot seem to stop those annoying stray thoughts from popping up inside her, even though she is trying as hard as she can to mentally stamp them down. Annoying stray thoughts that seem to be taking on lives of their own inside her somewhere, raising their little heads, swaying about, cocking snooks at her and grinning as they speak all at once.

'Remember Michael?' asks one stray thought, smirking shamelessly.

'Didn't take you long then, did it?' says the other.

'Oh, and exactly how much thought went into that then?' asks the first, elbowing its way forward again.

'Oh, about five short years,' giggles the other.

Now they are all shouting in a disorganized chorus, those horrid nasty little stray thoughts, creating a noisy inner bedlam that is making the room swim around her, tears (of a different sort) rushing to the space behind her eyes again.

'Five years and see what she got, tee hee!'

'But she thought she knew what she was doing.'

'She also thought she knew him so well!'

'Well, you'd think five years was enough time to get to know someone inside out.'

'Or should you be able to find out all there is to know about someone in just a few hours?'

Wasn't that what Tarun had just said? That he had recognized the love of his life (in fact, his future wife) the minute he had laid eyes on her. What had his words been . . . that he already knew as much as he needed to know. The rest was chance, the rest was destiny. All else would follow, taking its own path, with a little tweak here, a subtle nudge there. Why was it taking so long for Gayatri Menon (Ph.D. Oxon) to see that love and other similar phenomena (why, one might even say life itself!) were random, haphazard things? One might even think of them as accidents, some turning out fortuitous, some not. But certainly events that could be neither planned nor controlled. The combined force of a doctorate, a fine brain and a broken heart had not enabled Gayatri to see this great indubitable truth. How was it that Tarun, who had just about scraped through his BCom seven years ago, frittered away the major part of his adult life (save for the last two months as fledgling managing partner, Sachdev Textiles) and who could, it was generally accepted, see no further than his nose, comprehend this philosophy as easily as that? How did it come to be that he was to teach the proud and haughty Gayatri her most important lesson in life?

Don't let's question it, but merely accept, with joy and with satisfaction, that Gayatri will begin to see (in roughly the next five minutes) that lurking just inches beneath Tarun's designer clothes and air of frivolity is a certain enviable wisdom. A certain genius for the really important things in life. Gayatri might well be able to speak eloquently about existentialism and the poetry of exile. She knows who Proust and Nietzsche and Sartre are (names that would have Tarun furrow his forehead and rack his brains really hard before offering tentatively, 'Mmm ... architects?'). So, will it fall upon Tarun the Wise to finally bring Gayatri comfort? Will he make her humble, will he, best of all (and without ever knowing it), help her pull the curtain down on that ghastly Michael episode, almost as if he had been sent in to personally tug the cord?

10

A Madrasi!

There might have been many an admiring gaze following the young couple as they left the Machan, holding hands, that day. Many a hoary head would have nodded approvingly and muttered, 'Hai, ji, what a handsome, well-matched couple.'

But the view the world takes of events is never the same as that of the people to whom they are happening. And so, at the Sachdev household, on the unveiling of the news that Tarun not only had a girlfriend but intended marrying her, complete and utter pandemonium broke out.

Reasons having already been listed elsewhere, suffice it to say for now that Swarn took to her bed with one of her prize migraines, but not before she had had the chance to rant and to rave, to storm up and down the living room (if indeed it is possible to storm when lugging a full 80 kilos of flesh), weeping and wailing things that took even those who knew her well a certain amount of deciphering. Among the things she said were

1. 'Ai-hai! As if there are no decent Punjabi girls around! Delhi is full, full. Why not Punjabi, just North Indian, even Maharashtrian!' (Geographically speaking, this was the

furthest Swarn was willing to go.)

2. 'Madrasi! I have no time for Madrasis! Funny blacky people who say aiyyo-aiyyo and make a mess eating sambar idlis!'

3. 'All this Ph.D. and rubbish. She will think she can come in here and act like a queen, just because I am a college dropout. Not that I was not a good student, but I had to please my parents and marry your father! Those days we married whomever our parents chose, and when they said, whether we even liked them or not!'

4. 'Neena's friend! You wait and see how those two girls will gang up on me and drive me out of my own house!'

Tarun had taken it all in his stride, mainly because he had more or less anticipated some trouble with his mother and knew it was a phase that had to be passed through. Jagdish had briefly attempted to calm his raging wife down, but had then spotted The Migraine brewing on the horizon and, without waiting for the tears and the cold compresses and the dramatic downing of double doses of Calmpose, had quickly organized some extra work at the factory before quietly slipping out. Moolchand, with an excellent instinct for self-preservation, simply stayed cowering in the servants' quarters. Neena was completely unaware of the crisis, having moved to her parents' house for a week. Rohit was even less aware of it, already miles away, making a nervous, excited (and rather bumpy) descent into London.

■

Rohit looks around Heathrow Airport, wondering where to get himself a cab. He had been promised by Miss Seema at Flyfar Travel Agency in Delhi that he could book a prepaid taxi at the Terminal Three departure lounge. But it is all calm and orderly confusion here, quite unlike the proper confusion Rohit is used to at Indira Gandhi International Airport. England, so far, has been full of people wearing white mask-like faces that seem to say, 'I'm busy go away.' And there is certainly no sign at all of a desk touting anything resembling taxis, unless it is very well hidden. At Indian airports finding a taxi is the easiest thing in the world. Finding anything, for that matter. Even if you don't want anything, they come clamouring towards you, touts with their taxis and tours and hotel rooms, selling their wares, offering multifarious services, hissing the more dubious of their promises.

Here no one seems to care very much if you have a hotel room for the night or a taxi to get you to it, Rohit thinks distractedly. Hertz, Avis, Abbey National, Costa Coffee, McDonald's ... Rohit pushes his trolley past them all, still scanning a board for taxis, until he finds himself in front of an exit. There are bound to be taxis outside, he thinks, starting to feel slightly desperate. He begins to practice the English accent he will need if he is to ask for help, getting ready to roll his tongue around his mouth and say, 'Excuse me, could you help me please.'

Outside, a blast of cold air hits him by surprise. This is meant to be summertime, but the BBC world weather report back in Delhi had warned him of unseasonal gales. That always sounded rather dramatic and glamorous when you were sitting in air-conditioned comfort and Delhi roasted outside in forty-plus temperatures, but it feels as though the top of his head could be torn off.

He scurries back in through the revolving door but suddenly finds himself stuck. Jerking his trolley, he realizes that he has managed to jam it against the side of the door. He starts to jerk it more furiously, upset that he is probably going to make a spectacle of himself within his first five minutes in England, but he cannot seem to dislodge it. Hearing a shrill voice warble through the glass, he looks up to see the figure of a woman stuck similarly to him in the space across the door. She is waving her arms and trying to shout instructions that he cannot hear very well. He nods his head and tries to move his trolley again, to no avail. Helplessly he looks across at the woman again, hoping she isn't really furious with him. She is going red in the face under her spectacles and is now waving her arm and pointing at his feet screaming something that sounds like 'trapped'.

He begins to apologize through the glass, agreeing that they are indeed trapped, but tries to reassure her that it will not be for long. Her shout becomes louder. Bloody hell, this is all I need, Rohit thinks to himself, an angry Englishwoman who thinks I am trying to trap her. 'Madam, I am trying to extricate both yourself and myself from the confines of this door!' he shouts, trying to sound calm.

'Strap! It's the strap of your bag, you dork!' Her voice is clearer this time.

Peering over the side of the trolley, Rohit spots the cause of the trouble. The strap of his bag is trailing under the door, and the buckle is wedged under it. 'Oh, I do beg your pardon, madam. It is indeed the strap on my bag, as you say.' Rohit tugs on it unsuccessfully. There is some more shouting and banging from the other side of the door.

'The other way!' she is shouting, exaggeratedly mouthing the words and miming an action that denotes her desire to reverse the direction in which they are pushing.

'Ah, yes!' Rohit responds feebly. The door moves, and they tumble out. Mindful of the manners he does not want any English person to think he lacks, he bows deeply to the English lady and starts to apologize, but she has already gone, muttering something that sounds suspiciously like 'fuckin' tourists'.

Rohit picks up his errant bag and reattaches the strap. The back of his neck goes hot, even though he is still cold and wet from his foray outdoors. He bends down, ostensibly to examine his shoes, but he is trying in fact not to notice all the faces that have probably noticed him and his bungling. His best shoes and jacket (worn in an unsuccessful bid to be bumped up to business class) are soaked too. Rohit's feeling of excitement to be finally travelling abroad, and all on his own, is definitely fading. He is brushing himself down, vigorously rubbing the drops of water into the fabric of his trousers and jacket as though it matters terribly that he should look less damp. He hears a voice. A female voice. An

English female voice. Oh, no, it's not that angry woman again, he thinks as he straightens up reluctantly. Instead he sees a red lipsticked smile, a mass of bright blonde curls. (Rohit, of course, knows nothing yet of the kind of blondes that emerge from bottles.) And, at approximately nose-level (because he is still bending) is a pair of tanned legs, unstockinged, shapely.

Rohit straightens up. 'Hanh?' he asks. 'I . . . I mean . . . I do beg your pardon'.

She is smiling sympathetically. 'I saw that. Some people can be so awfully rude, can't they?'

Embarrassed, Rohit shakes his head. 'She . . . no, no, it was nothing.'

'You ought to go after 'er and report 'er for racialism, I think.'

'No, no, she was just slightly upset, that's all.'

'Fuckin' Paki, I heard her say. That sorta thing just shouldn't be allowed, you know.' There is an indignant toss of the blonde curls.

'I'm . . . I'm sure she didn't mean it. And she got it wrong anyway, I'm not from Pakistan. Could have done without such trouble on my first visit here, though.'

'First time here?'

'Yeah, and nothing seems to be going the way it should. I just went outside for a minute to look for a taxi.' Rohit runs a hand through his wet hair.

She looks at the sad, rumpled figure before her. First time in England, no wonder he gave the impression of needing looking after, she thinks. Expensive suit. Quite cute too. A bit like that Paki cricket player who married the Goldsmith girl . . . Imran Khan, was it?

'Yes, I was waiting for a taxi meself actually. There's not one to be 'ad for love nor money on a night like this,' she says chattily, brushing raindrops off her own hair.

'I must have stepped out for a minute, but now I'm completely soaked. It's blowing like crazy out there. Isn't there a desk or something in here where one can book a taxi?'

'Not 'arf a chance. I've bin 'ere an hour already, waiting for the rain to stop so I can try my luck again.'

'But my travel agent back in Delhi had told me there would be a prepaid taxi stand at the terminal,' Rohit complains peevishly.

'Prepaid taxis—never 'eard of such a fing,' she laughs a tinkly laugh.

Rohit is embarrassed by this gaffe. 'Bloody Flyfar Travels!' he mutters.

'Is that really their name?' she smiles, 'Flyfar?' Rohit nods. 'Fly-by-night, more like!' she says giggling (in a terribly charming manner, Rohit thinks).

He is smiling back at her rather dimwittedly when she asks, 'Where are you from then?' She looks so interested, Rohit thinks in surprise, as though it really matters to her where he has come from.

'Delhi,' he says.

'Oooo, Delly!' she squeals. 'That's in Indya, innit? I've always wanted to go to Indya. I just love 'ot places.'

'Where have you come from tonight?' Rohit asks.

'Miami. My sister lives there, you know. With Chuck, 'er American 'usband, and their two kids. I visit them every year. Do my shopping 'n fings there. It's so much cheaper,' she nods ruefully at two enormous suitcases nearby. 'But this is where I live. London . . .'ammersmith,' she trails off before asking. 'So what are you doin' 'ere? Your first time in England, imagine that!'

Rohit laughs, 'Yes, I was really excited actually, until . . .' he jerks his head in the direction in which the angry woman has vanished, feeling himself flush again at the memory. 'I've come on business.'

'Ooo biznis!' she squeals again, blue eyes shining encouragingly at him.

Rohit is starting to feel like a very important person indeed. A feeling he hasn't enjoyed in a very long time. In fact, not since the children arrived and Neena took to wearing them as constant appendages. If her attention wasn't focussed on one of the children, it was focussed fiercely her own bum or its reflection in the mirror, Rohit thinks suddenly, inconsequentially. Now why did that thought pop into his head? Why did his wife's face (wearing, conveniently, a nasty frown on her face as she examines the shape of her bum) appear out of the mists of his subconscious, a thing Rohit has so far been completely unaware of possessing? The reason is simple: Rohit wants to make sure he doesn't feel like a complete cad when he says the next thing he says to the woman. Something he knows he will never tell Neena about. He takes a deep breath and plunges forth.

'Look, why don't we share a taxi into London when we get one? I can drop you off at . . .'

"ammersmith,' she says helpfully, quickly assessing the situation.

'Yes . . . H . . . ammersmith,' Rohit says, unsure now of sounding too pukka.

'Where're you staying then?' she asks.

'I've been booked by the travel ag . . .'

'Fly-by-Night Travels,' she pipes up, giggling charmingly some more. Rohit laughs too, feeling a certain inexplicable kindred spiritedness with this blonde, blue-eyed stunner.

'Yes, Fly-by-Night,' he waggles his head to look funny and Indian as she squeals her delight again, 'has booked me into a serviced apartment somewhere in . . .' He looks blankly at her before scrabbling frantically in his shirt pocket and producing a tiny scrap of paper. 'Gosh, nearly thought I'd forgotten it behind.' She takes a step closer to Rohit as she peers with him into the bit of paper, and Rohit feels his head swim as a whiff of strong perfume assails his nostrils.

'Edgware Road,' they say in unison, raising their heads. Rohit finds himself inches away from a pair of very bright eyes. Having only ever seen blue eyes in films and in the pile of dusty, dog-eared *Playboy* magazines that were hastily transferred from his room to Tarun's just before he got married, he feels immensely moved. Moved in all sorts of places that have lain dormant for far too long now, in his opinion. It is a moment he will relive over and over again for a long time to come. It is, one might even say, the only moment of epiphany Rohit has ever had.

If one cannot help the sharp intake of horrified breath at the thought of what is to come, remember only this: Rohit has entered his thirties with terrifying, unstoppable velocity. For all that, he is still reasonably fresh-faced but tending to podginess and baldness and, if he examines himself very carefully in the mirror, to losing completely and inexorably that certain something that had made a few college girls swoon so helplessly once. He has been slightly overworked of late, his father makes a pretty demanding boss, and the unions have been giving him all sorts of problems. To add to all that, his wife has been awfully preoccupied; in fact, Rohit will tell himself testily afterwards, it has been months since she has even had a proper conversation with him, leave alone sex! Moreover, this is Rohit's first trip abroad. In fact, it is the only time he has been genuinely unsupervised for the first time in his life. If he wants, just this once, to attempt to soar, however briefly, into some long forgotten sky even if he then falters and plummets towards the ground as sweetly smiling eyes peer into his, who are we to judge, who are we to condemn?

And, as for the pretty woman with the eyes, she is kind hearted, which is what made her strike up conversation with the poor Paki who'd just been so badly insulted by one of her own kind. But she's no fool. Would she have normally accepted the offer of a lift from a strange man? Not 'arf likely, but this one here has already said it's his first time in England, and he's hardly likely to turn out to be an axe murderer. Especially so nicely dressed an' all and so confused looking and wet and really rather sweet.

'Taxi,' Rohit reminds her in a whispered croak. 'Let's get that taxi, shall we?'

Together they leave the terminal building, pushing their trollies—Rohit chivalrously exchanging his, bearing its solitary suitcase, with the woman's, which is weighed down with a very large Samsonite, a smaller one, a handbag and a package wrapped in paper. The rain is now hanging in the air, as though waiting for some celestial signal to drop. Taxis are starting to appear miraculously out of the misty night, like monsoon insects that arrive from nowhere after a downpour. Airport lights are reflecting in dark, oily, rainbow puddles. Rohit takes in a deep, wobbly breath of air that feels wonderfully wet and fresh after the dusty heat of Delhi. London, he thinks to himself, deeply, dramatically, London— oh, how I think I'm going to love this city!

The woman keeps up a constant stream of chatter during the drive from Heathrow, so Rohit's mind doesn't wander into those dark territories of guilt and shame. Her name is Tracy (Tricey). She works as a photographer's assistant. She was the photographer's girlfriend once, but they split. And now, although he has another girlfriend, Mandy, they have stayed friends, like, because now they're nearly business partners, y'know, after like so many years.

Rohit is not sure he quite gets that, but he is no social anthropologist attempting to question strange Western practices. Then she had Tim the plumber, who moved out last month, and so now she's single again and lovin' every minute of it, mind! Who needs men, she asks, with an engaging toss of her head. Now she's thinking of taking in lodgers, she confesses, talking to Rohit as though he might already have become her best friend. Even as her curls are still tumbling, glinting in the light of passing street lights, blue eyes widen as a thought strikes her.

'Hey!' she says. 'Look, if you 'aven't already paid for that place you got booked, why doncha live in my flat? There's plenny a room! You can pay me 'arf of whatever you'da paid there! I'll be away at work mosta the time anyway! And you'll save yourself 'arf your cab fare too!'

'No, really, I can't,' Rohit protests.

'It's like any business arrangement, love. You need a place to stay in London, and I could do with the extra money. It'll pay for all this shoppin' I've just done,' she says, kicking the suitcase on the floor of the cab with a white stiletto-heeled strappy sandal. She is wearing a tight white blouse with the top three buttons undone. Her upthrust breasts are just visible, like a pair of half-hidden cream jellies. A tight red miniskirt is hopelessly trying to cover the rest of her. Seated opposite Rohit, who is perched nervously on the foldaway seat in the cab, she has had to bend her legs (at what would be an impossible angle for Indian women, Rohit thinks) to keep from getting entangled with his own trousered pair.

'Well, why not,' he replies weakly, hunting in his pockets for a handkerchief with which to mop his brow.

'That's settled then,' she says brightly, 'twenny-five quid per day, with breakfast, no dinner. Cash only.'

As they approach Hammersmith, Tracy pulls back the window to give directions to the cabby. 'Next exit, love, right at the lights, third exit on the roundabout, right again at the T, slowly now, pink 'ouse up there on the left. Ta! How much is it, love? Nineteen seventy?' She turns to Rohit, who is already valiantly fishing out brand new notes and handfuls of change. 'Nineteen pounds and seventy pence,' she says. ''Ere, let me 'elp you count that, love. I'll settle up with you once we're indoors.'

Having paid the fare, Rohit staggers out of the cab lugging his suitcase and Tracy's smaller Samsonite after him. The driver pulls out the bigger one and places it, with the paper package balanced on top, on the pavement. Tracy is already bounding up a set of cracked cement steps to a bright yellow door, her red miniskirted derrière waggling in a most beguiling manner at the luckless Rohit, who is by now perilously close to a seizure as he staggers up after her bearing a suitcase in each hand.

'Unfit ... terribly unfit ...' he puffs at Tracy with an embarrassed grin as he deposits the suitcases and totters back down the steps to get the remaining things. Returning, now purple-faced, this time with Tracy's very large and extremely heavy suitcase, he can only just manage a brief nod as she bats her lashes at him and thanks him very sweetly. By the time he returns, for the third time, carrying just the paper package, he has recovered slightly and gasps, 'Just don't get the time to work out, you know, always business, business, business.'

As he hears himself using this favourite Swarn phrase, he has a sudden flash of his parents' faces, watching with horrified expressions as he simperingly hands the package over to the Englishwoman who pulls her disobedient skirt down over her hips for the tenth time before taking the package from him. Their collective (still horrified) gaze now shifts to the woman who is tottering around the room in her very high heels, turning on switches and lamps. They are still watching, open-mouthed, as she closes the front door with a resolute click, imprisoning their older son (scion and successor of the Sachdev business empire) in her house for God knows what sort of hanky-panky thing. Rohit manages to bundle them away hurriedly and out of his mind as he too looks around the room in awe and amazement.

It is not a room but a boudoir. There is only one piece of furniture in the room, which is a long, low-curved sofa in black leather. It sweeps from one end of the room in an enormous gleaming crescent to the other. Underfoot is a fluffy white carpet, resembling an enormous flattened cat. Rohit gingerly places one nervous foot on its edge, half expecting it to emit a miaow. The walls have been painted a deep vermilion, a colour Rohit has only ever seen on Indian wedding saris before this. A few black-and-white framed photographs with different views of the Eiffel Tower break the crimson intensity. Two enormous lamp-like contraptions sit on either side of the sofa, filled with some sort of red gloopy stuff that, at the turn of the switches, has started to bubble solemnly up and down.

'Larvely, innit?' Tracy breathes next to him. 'Did it all by meself last year. Set me back a few quid, I can tell you.'

'Yes, yes, it's ... quite lovely.'

'Well, lemme show you your room. I'll dust it and put on some fresh sheets when you go get your shower.'

Rohit follows her meekly into an adjoining room. There is more of an air of normalcy about this room as all it contains is a single bed and a mirrored wardrobe.

'I used to take in lodgers once, long ago, until one of them tried to get fresh with me.' She kicks off her strappy heels before starting to vigorously strip the bed. 'Showed him the door, I did, but not before I got Steve to rough him up a bit.' She giggles at the memory as Rohit winces. 'No, you don't need to help me, love,' she says as Rohit attempts to grab one end of a flying sheet that she has plucked out of the wardrobe and is now flinging over the side of the bed. He watches while she makes the bed expertly, throwing over it a duvet covered in pink and purple flowers. That done, she dives into the wardrobe again, emerging this time with a couple of towels. She hands these over to him and says, 'You need to get out of those wet clothes, love. Let me run you a nice hot bath.'

Rohit takes the towels off her and smiles weakly as she vanishes down a narrow corridor. In a few seconds he can hear the sound of a tub filling up. The aroma of roses comes drifting down the corridor in a cloud of steam. He is starting to relax. In fact, he is starting to enjoy himself hugely. The flat in Edgware Road would have been cold and businesslike, with probably just a bed and a kettle. That was the best Miss Seema at Flyfar Travels had said she could do for forty pounds a day. This, by comparison, was luxury. Rohit mentally pats himself on the back as he sits down on the edge of the bed to pull off his shoes and socks. He is not Jagdish Sachdev's son for nothing; he knows that for twenty-five pounds per day he has probably got himself a bloody good bargain—not just room and bathroom but also a miniskirt-wearing woman to run a bath for him! Something even his wife or mother would merely click their fingers to get Moolchand to do for him if necessary. His only regret at the moment is that he will not be able to brag to his father about this rather clever deal when he returns home next week.

∎

Back in Delhi, Neena and Gayatri are lying on Neena's bed, in the Sainik Farms house of her parents, talking to each other while gazing up in the dark at the lazily swirling ceiling fan. It is this horizontal position they were wont to take, even as teenagers, whenever they had really serious things to talk about.

'Look, I'm biased,' Neena is saying earnestly up at the ceiling. 'I'd just love it if you and Tarun got married. Imagine getting my best friend as a sister-in-law!'

Gayatri laughs, 'Well, that will be a great starting point for me as well, but unfortunately, it's not you I'd be marrying but Tarun. And that, Neens, is the bit I'm still not sure about at all. Tarun.'

'Oh, yes, of course, Tarun,' Neena says contemplatively, as though suddenly remembering the part he will play in this. 'Tarun,' she repeats, trying to think of a reasonably honest character analysis for her irrepressible, irresponsible brother-in-law that will not frighten Gayatri off for good. 'He's very caring,' she says brightly, 'a right old sweetie, really.'

'I feel a *but* hovering at the end of that sentence,' Gayatri says, laughing.

'Well, I'll give you the *but*, but only because you're my best friend and because I probably care more for you than I do for any of my in-laws, even Tarun.'

'Well, what is it?' Gayatri asks, intrigued.

'The only problem really with Tarun is that he's a bit of a (Neena whispers this next word) womaniser, Gayatri. Not in any terrible way, mind,' she adds hastily, 'but he's so far not been able to stick with any one girl for more than two months. No, let me think, three months was his record, I think. Sometimes I really wonder how it is that he is so different from my Rohit.'

(At the precise moment that Neena is making this naive and rather trusting assessment of her husband, he is lowering himself, butt naked, into a bath run just five minutes ago by a miniskirt-wearing woman. She has left him to it, thankfully, telling him to take as long as he likes before shutting the door behind her. But, as he takes off his clothes and gets gingerly into the bath, feeling the soapy rose-scented suds titillatingly enter every cranny of his body, it is the woman in the miniskirt, and not Neena, who is occupying his thoughts. Entirely. Nakedly. Wantonly. Really quite shamelessly.)

'But,' Neena says to Gayatri, 'I can't help thinking that you could be the one to change Tarun forever.'

Gayatri laughs again. 'I don't think I want to play nanny and help to bring him up, Neens!'

'No, I don't mean that. But it feels as though he's a changed man already. I suppose it's partly having met you and partly the fact that he's now quite involved in the business, thanks to some timely scheming from his dad.'

'And them? Your in-laws, how do you think they'll take it? I mean, forget marriage to a Mallu. Because that even I can't really consider with any seriousness at the moment, whatever Tarun may say. But even just the idea of their son going out with a Mallu girl might be bad enough.'

'Oh, be prepared for some fireworks. Papa'll probably eventually take it in his stride. I think the kind of dreams he used to have of his sons marrying into big business families to create some sort of empire died a death with Rohit's marriage to me. And because he's probably learnt that things don't just fall into place as easily as that, he might not mind too badly if Tarun turns up with someone who doesn't come from a business family. But Mamma, you want to watch out for Mamma. Definitely.'

Neena's voice sounds grim. As if on cue, a distant dog howls ominously in the stillness of the night.

'But, don't worry, sweetie,' she adds more cheerfully, 'you'll have the rest of us on your side, and she'll soon have to give in—ungracefully, no doubt.'

Gayatri sighs deeply. 'I'm not sure, Neens. I just don't have the energy to go through that sort of angst again—explaining myself, trying to make myself more acceptable, more likeable.'

Neena is surprised. 'Again?' she asks, turning to look at Gayatri's profile in surprise.

'Well, I just never got the chance to tell you, Neena . . . Gayatri's voice trails off into the darkness. Taking a deep breath, she starts again. 'In England, the year that I got there actually, I met this guy. Michael. He was everything I knew I'd always wanted in a man. Clever, articulate, terribly well-read—you know, all the really important things,' she laughs bitterly. 'Anyway, after I was really hook, line and sinker, I discovered he was married. Now, looking back, I know I should've dropped him then, but what did clever Gayatri go and do?' Neena is silent, and Gayatri continues, her voice turning harsh, 'Clever Gayatri, who imagined she could hack anything, decided not to drop him, of course. I gave it the briefest of thought and decided it wasn't important. The important thing, I decided, was that I was the one Michael loved and enjoyed being with. Which is why he was with me. Whereas the times that he was with his wife were only because he was married to her. You see?'

Neena doesn't see, but she nods vigorously in the dark, taking her friend's hand as she hears her start to cry. 'But why didn't he divorce her, if he wanted to be with you?'

'Aha,' Gayatri says, her voice now filled with tears, 'because that was only what he had said to me. And, idiot that I was, I chose to believe it. Because I so wanted to believe it. But what he really wanted, of course, was to have his cake and eat it too. Which he did. And when that was done, he had to get rid of the wrapper. Which he did. So easily, just like that.'

'God, you poor thing,' Neena says, slipping her arm under Gayatri's shoulders. 'So what did you do?'

'Do?' Gayatri's voice is bleak and faraway with the memory. 'I just left. And came back here.'

'God! And to think I never knew! How many things we just assume when we see people looking happy on the outside. Oh, Gayatri, I wish I'd known earlier!'

'But what could you have done? There's no point passing

on your pain when there's nothing people can do to help,
is there?'

'Well, I suppose you're right.'

'I haven't mentioned it to Tarun yet,' Gayatri says.

'If you ask me, it's best to never mention it, Gayatri. I
think it's just sensible not to go into all that at all.'

'I don't know,' Gayatri replies doubtfully. 'Shouldn't
relationships be based on trust? Doesn't seem too propitious
to start things off with secrets and enigmas.'

'Honey, the success of marriages sometimes lie in their
secrets and enigmas,' replies Neena sagaciously. 'Tell me
what the bloody point would be in telling him all your
secrets, huh? Particularly things from your past. He'll just
stop trusting you, I think.'

'Seems odd to me, though, that trust should actually
develop better out of reticence than honesty and candour.'

'Gayatri, darling, sometimes it's just kinder to be
economical with the truth. I should know. I've been married
five years now and probably know a bit more than you do
about love and marriage. Take it from me—what one doesn't
know can't hurt one, can it?'

■

Although two days have passed since Tarun broke the news,
Swarn is still raging. Swarn's rages usually follow a marked
pattern—starting off like a terrifying storm, filled with fire
and brimstone, before trailing off into a more silent, simmering
thing. Not that this version of it is any less terrifying, for
those who know her. This version of it waits like a stalking
pantheress, waiting to spring: it is quiet, it is deadly, it can
kill. It has another peculiar feature, however. It replaces its
subject, every so often and without wasting time with
rambling explanations.

And so Kammy, who has been its favourite subject for
the past few years has just been toppled in favour of Gayatri.
Now, suddenly, Kammy (despite all her stupid social work
talk and funny tribal jewellery) seems much the lesser evil in

the face of some Madrasi types with no sense of style at all. And no money, almost certainly ji. Swarn has already, exactly two days ago, mentally waved the white flag at her social worker samdhin, mouthing the Hindi equivalent of a magnanimous, 'Come back Kammyji. All is forgiven'.

In her erstwhile place is now the slim figure of Gayatri, whose features Swarn now only has a fuzzy memory of from their only meeting. Alongside Gayatri, occupying Swarn's hate category, is a large and motley collection of people, wearing the kind of clothes Swarn imagines Madrasis prefer. Some of the men are wearing lungis, some dhotis folded up to their knees exposing thin dark legs, covered in wiry hair. The women are all in tasteless saris, wound between their legs, and all have scraped their hair back into tight joodies. In their noses are large, three-pronged diamonds which (according to Swarn) is the only thing Madrasis will spend their meagre money on. For good measure, and to complete the picture, Swarn has thrown in a younger woman in full Bharatanatyam dance regalia. She is cocking her head and rolling her eyes from side to side, just about ready to spring into her dance routine. All the figures, male and female, are uniformly dark-skinned with wiry black hair reeking of coconut oil. This is the imaginary family Swarn has conjured up inside her fevered head as the money-grabbing Madrasis who are presently doing their best to steal her moneyed, handsome Punjabi son away from her. This is the family Swarn is determined to treat with such scorn and disdain, confident they will retreat after their first unsuspecting foray into the Sachdev domain, with frightened aiyyo-aiyyos.

■

'Look, I want you to come home again. Meet the folks properly. This time as my lovely, beautiful girlfriend, not just an old classmate of Neena's. And bring your parents too. Your dad keeps asking me when he can meet mine. We can't really put it off any more, can we?'

Gayatri shifts her head against Tarun's shoulder to look

up at him in surprise. They are sitting on a patch of grass, leaning on a tree in the vast, sprawling campus of Jawaharlal Nehru University where Gayatri has just interviewed for a job.

'Oh, no, I'm not sure I'm ready for that,' Gayatri says, passing the bottle of Pepsi back to Tarun.

Tarun takes a deep swig before saying, 'Look, babes, Mum's already thrown her blue fit,' he wipes his mouth with the back of his hand. 'Now it's safe to move on to the next step.'

'I'm quite content just to float around like this for a while. Please?' Gayatri's voice is imploring.

'It's your folks I'm thinking of, actually. I feel so terribly rude putting them off every time they ask if they can visit my parents.'

'Well, my parents will probably view such a meeting as the stage just preceding a wedding. There's no half-measures for them, as you've probably gathered. Think of the shock when they realize that your folks have no such plans at all!'

'The important thing, my darling girl, is that I have plans, very firm plans, to marry you. As soon as I can get around my folks. All else and everybody else is secondary.'

'And what if your family disowns you?' Gayatri teases.

Tarun considers this for a moment. The loss of the BMW, his little pad above the garage, the factory in Noida. 'Then you'll just have to get this job and support me,' he says, chortling at the heart-warming prospect.

Gayatri gets up and dusts herself down. She smiles down at Tarun as she says cheerily, 'Well then, it might be an idea to wait until next week to see if I do have this job before you go and get yourself disowned.' As she pulls Tarun up, she gives him a kiss square on his lips before saying, 'Oh, and another thing . . . apart from the view your parents might have on the subject, I can't help thinking it's just a little too premature to be talking marriage at the moment, Tarun.'

'Why?' Tarun demands.

'Well, it just is, my sweet.'

'Why, don't you love me enough?' Tarun sounds deeply hurt.

'Oh, of course, I do, silly!' Gayatri laughs, even though both Tarun and she realize that this is something she has not been able to say to him yet. Love. Gayatri has asked herself many times over the past few days whether this is something she is ever likely to feel for Tarun. Like—this is something she knows she already feels for this eager, sweet young man. But she cannot bring herself to tell him that and watch the hurt spring into his soft brown eyes. And, the truth is that it just feels so wonderful at the moment to have him so clearly and unashamedly in love with her, she doesn't really want to ruin that warm glowing feeling that he seems to have lit inside her somewhere. But all this talk about marriage, now that was genuinely alarming. 'I love the idea of being with you, Tarun, but I do have to say, the idea of marriage has always been anathema to me,' Gayatri trails off with an expressive shudder.

Tarun looks more than a little perplexed. His frown at the moment is not so much that he is pained at Gayatri's views on the institution of marriage, but because he cannot for the life of him remember what *anathema* means. He racks his brains, with erroneous images of anacondas and anaesthetics flying through his head. But he has learnt, in the past few days, to side-step Gayatri's fondness for polysyllabic words quite deftly and has also, to his credit, more or less mastered the art of inference by context.

'Look, I'm going to marry you, Gayatri. Whether my parents like it or not, whether you like it or not, whether the whole goddamned world likes it or not!'

And, with this declaration (which warms the cockles of even Gayatri's cynical heart, even though she would probably rather die than admit it), they get into Tarun's car and drive out of the car park. Tarun is silent as he makes his way out of the JNU campus and on to the crowded road outside. It is not the traffic occupying his mind. An idea is brewing in his head. His head is not usually an area abundant with too many ideas, so Tarun needs to think about this one quite carefully. He has, somehow, to edge Gayatri closer to the idea of marriage to him. He has to gather all his meagre resources together on this one. And his unwitting ally, of course, will be the artless Keshava. By the time they are pulling up outside the Menon gate, Tarun's plan has been hatched.

Keshava is pottering in the front yard with a trowel in his hand. He beams at the pair disembarking from the car, pushing his spectacles up his nose, blinking to see past the smear of mud this leaves on his left lens. 'Aha! I was just telling Raji that you would have gone to pick up Gayatri,' he says to Tarun.

'When I came out of the interview hall, he was there, even though I'd told him not to come.' Gayatri says this without sounding particularly irked.

'Oh, it was no problem,' Tarun says modestly, 'I'd stopped for lunch at the factory and thought it would be a good chance to pop across and see how Gayatri had got on at the interview.'

'One doesn't just pop across a distance of about fifteen miles through lunchtime traffic,' Gayatri demurs.

'He just wanted to see you, moley,' Keshava says, looking very pleased at the idea.

'But now I have to be off,' Tarun says. 'Busy afternoon. But look, before I go, I just wanted to say, why don't the three of you come over to my place this Saturday? Meet the parents, you know. As you've so often said you'd like to do.' Tarun looks directly at Keshava as he says this, not daring to look Gayatri in the eye. He stops just short of throwing in a joke about making sure Keshava is wearing the Menon coat of mail when he meets the fearsome Swarn Sachdev. But better sense prevails, and he grins cheerfully as he gets back into the car. 'Six-ish should be good,' he says, starting the engine noisily.

Gayatri widens her eyes on hearing this blatantly

unilateral invitation, but she does not get a chance to protest as Tarun revs up the car engine and races back down the road at top speed.

'Oh, God, look at him go!' Gayatri protests as she and her father watch this unusual exit from the gate and the BMW vanishes backwards around the corner in a flurry of dust. 'Idiot's trying to impress us with his reversing skills now, I expect.'

There is affection, however, in her voice, and Keshava looks absolutely delighted. Rubbing his hands together, he chirrups gleefully, 'So nice it will be to meet his parents now. I wonder whether they will remember us from Neena's wedding? I remember Tarun's mother smiling at me as we went up to give Neena her gift. Nice lady.'

Gayatri is silent as they walk indoors together. She knows Tarun has trumped her once again. But, at the door, she places an affectionate hand on her father's arm. 'Appa, I'm so glad you and Amma like Tarun. It's really is great to see you so happy!'

'Moley, the biggest happiness for a girl's parents is to see her well-settled in a nice family with a good boy,' he says fervently.

'What! More than seeing her get a Ph.D. from Oxford followed by taking up the post of professor of English at JNU?'

'More than Ph.D.s. More than the best jobs in the world, moley!' he declares emphatically. 'Marriage—a good marriage—is the only key to true happiness in life!'

■

'Marriage! To that Madrasi girl? Over my dead body!' Swarn shouts hoarsely.

'Look, Mamma, I'm going to get married some day. Even you agree with that. Now why don't you just calm down and accept that this is the only girl I will marry. Ever!' He throws the last word in with admirable defiance, glaring at his irate mother who has been arrested in the demolition job she had only just started carrying out on a bowl of lychees at the dining table.

'He probably means that, Mamma,' Neena chips in tentatively. She has been brought in from Sainik Farms for the day to lend support to a desperate Tarun. Swarn simmers silently at her. Her daughter-in-law has never been a great favourite with Swarn, but she occupies her category of people not to be messed with.

Taking advantage of her mother-in-law's silence, Neena continues, 'It's not as if Gayatri isn't a very desirable girl— beautiful, brainy' (Neena doesn't know these are the very adjectives Swarn cannot bear to think about and rambles on) 'and the Menons! I've known them years, and a finer set of relations you cannot ask for, Mamma! Really! You might end up even liking them more than my folks eventually, who knows!'

Swarn's well-hidden dislike of Kammy and Manny has already edged into something else, however. Already they have taken up position, jostling for space, in Swarn's must-put-up-with box. Here, along with Jagdish, Moolchand, Mrs Mehta at the mah-jong club and a few others, they will stay for the rest of Swarn's life. But it has been imperative for them to vacate their previous category, the absolutely-in-the-pits one, because stuffed in here are the south Indian clan Swarn has mentally put together, willy-nilly, angrily throwing together the dhotis and the lungis and the inelegant three-pronged diamond nose pins. She shudders and mutters with feeling, under her breath, 'Madrasis! Never had any time for them!'

'Malayalis, not Madrasis,' Neena says earnestly, quite forgetting her own tranche of Madrasi jokes. 'Perhaps you should have found some time for them,' she adds rashly. 'They're lovely people, Mallus.' Neena is given to sweeping remarks (good and bad) based on racial background and would have been genuinely shocked if anyone had pointed out that this was merely another sort of racism.

'Come on, Mum,' Tarun pleads, 'rise above it all like you always do. Rise, like a helium balloon!'

Swarn glares at him again. Just because he has found some slimmy-trimmy type, he thinks it is now okay to make fun of his poor mother's weight ji, she thinks, now feeling herself begin to brim and overflow with resentful tears. But Swarn is a sensible woman. A pragmatist to the core. She does not want to lose her sons' affections, whatever happens. She will deal with the enemy, the whole caboodle, Madrasis, Malaya ... She has never been able to even pronounce the damn word without stumbling, but she knows she will have to deal with them in her own sweet and subtle way eventually. Hasn't she always done that, ji? Always, always, having to cope first with this and then with that. Never a moment's peace in this life. What to do, some people are brought into this world just to suffer silently, ji.

Tarun heaves a sigh of relief and exchanges a look with Neena as Swarn starts to blub loudly. He pulls up a chair and sits next to his mother, putting his arm around her vibrating fleshy shoulders. Neena pulls a pack of tissues out of her handbag and shoves one across to her mother-in-law with poorly masked irritation. After blowing her nose loudly and wiping away a few more furious tears, Swarn yanks the bowl of lychees closer to herself with a belligerent air that indicates there are still some few things in life whose pleasures no one can deny her, ji. She starts to absent-mindedly peel a large red lychee, her multiple chins still quivering sorrowfully. Popping its pale grey flesh into her mouth, she chews on it slowly, ruminatively, sadly. The crisis, for the moment, has passed.

11

Another accident of love

Through the shenanigans in Delhi, it is indeed tempting to allow Swarn a peek into goings-on in the life of her elder son in faraway London. Just to distract her for a moment, just to throw things into perspective a little. But we cannot have this luxury for now. Patience, patience, dear reader, for it will come.

But we, on the other hand, may take a mental leap into that other vast teeming capital city on the other side of the world. As we spot a serpentine grey river, we will travel due west, through the wet, misty air, ignoring the majestic splendours of Whitehall and Westminster. Descending into the less salubrious environs of Hammersmith, we sweep up a road flanked by tall town houses, sitting cheek by jowl. When we spot the number thirty-four in brass letters on a canary-yellow front door, we will walk up the flight of slightly cracked cement steps leading up to it. And then step in softly. Stop for a moment and hold your breath, listen to the silence, for the door will have creaked a bit. Although tempted, do not stay for long looking around the living room in open-mouthed horror; some people like kitsch. It is in one of the two bedrooms facing the living room that you want to be. Choose the one with the door that is slightly ajar, for that is where the remainder of our story lies.

■

It is still raining when Rohit's eyes open at about six that morning. Through his sleep-addled and slightly jet-lagged brain, he wonders why Neena has removed the terracotta Ganesh and replaced it with a print of violently pink blooms on the wall across from the bed. He then notices frills around his head, pink and purple, and ponders on the possibility that some new pillows have been bought to replace the white ones. He thinks he ought to inform Neena that he has noticed them, for one of her favourite grouses is that he never notices anything. He reaches out an arm to ruffle her hair and whisper a grateful thanks and finds his fingers sinking into a mop of stiffly lacquered curls. Those are not Neena's, he thinks, nor, for that matter, is that freckled white arm slung proprietarily over his chest. Very slowly he raises his head and peers over the frilled horizon until he spots her. Tracy. Tricey. From last night. A few bewildered random thoughts drift through his muddled mind. This house. That walk down the road, to the wine shop. A Chinese takeaway with greasy floors and greasy smells. Wine, lots and lots of it. And then, later. Oh, God. Hey Bhagwaan! Oh, crikey (Rohit's newly learnt English expression from the night before).

Rohit remembers a few other newly learnt things from the night before and shoots up to sitting position in bed with a stifled cry. He promptly falls right back into pink and purple flounce as something resembling a sledgehammer pounds him neatly between his eyebrows. He closes his eyes in agony as his hangover announces itself to the rest of his body and all the events from the night before come flooding back to him.

Through rising waves of nausea and a headache that splits his skull like Moolchand's cleaver slicing a watermelon in two, the images of the night float through Rohit's head. It was the wine, it was the bloody wine, he thinks in agony, still feeling some traces of its tannins on the sandpaper surface of his mouth. Of course, up to a point one could certainly hold the 12 per cent alcohol content of the Cabernet Sauvignon responsible for doing Rohit in. Later he will find a few other reasons too as he casts about in his sorry little head. (Neena's maternal and posterial preoccupations, pressures of work, his father's overbearing nature, etc.)

Tracy will have her own little theory too (which she occasionally giggles over with the odd girlfriend) of how no poor sod has ever been able to resist her charms when she has decided to hook him good 'n proper and so on. And charms she has in plenty, one does have to say, in the fullness of her cream pudding breasts and the long litheness of her newly tanned legs, which she certainly used on Rohit, for reasons that are not too complicated to explain. She is single (and has been for a while, since Tim the plumber, that is). She has just had a holiday with her younger, married sister who now lives in a large American house with her realtor husband who is crazy about her. She (Tracy, not the younger sister) had no sex at all while on holiday, and not for the want of trying. Besides, she has never had sex with a Paki before and was just a little curious. She had liked the look of Rohit (wet and confused) at the airport yesterday, and she had genuinely felt for him when that racist woman had shouted her abuse. It was obvious, when he said it was his very first time in England, that he was unlikely to be dangerous and turn out to be a rabid, psychotic rapist. Did Rohit have half a chance in the face of such a catalogue of reasons? Oh, poor Rohit.

But back to him now as he lies among the flouncy pillows. He is attempting to lift his head again, this time more gingerly, so as not to wake Tracy and to make sure he does not risk cracking his head open in halves with any sharp and jerky movements. He succeeds and sits on the side of the bed for a few fuzzy minutes, before attempting to stand and stagger towards the bathroom. Once standing he looks down at Tracy, still only half believing the events of the night, but she is still fast asleep, her curls rampantly spread across polyester flowers, one pink nipple peering shyly over the edge of the duvet.

God, she was just too too beautiful to resist, he thinks angrily, once he is in the bathroom holding his penis over the toilet bowl. To Rohit, the fault at the moment lies, naturally, everywhere else but with Rohit himself. But he studiously avoids looking into the bathroom mirror that seems to be staring accusingly at him from the opposite wall, keeping his eyes on his now shrivelled penis, both villain and hero in last night's performance. It seems less prepared for action this morning, lying tamely between his fingers awaiting orders. 'Not quite the beast you were last night, eh?' Rohit mutters testily, giving it an annoyed shake. Slowly it progresses into unwilling action, emitting some of the night's excesses in a pale yellow stream.

Rohit contemplates going back into the bedroom but, squinting down the darkened corridor, decides it is too long a distance to negotiate. Instead he shuffles the shorter distance into the living room, clutching his head, and collapses on to the leather sofa. It is here, three hours later, that he wakes to the smell of frying eggs.

'Hi! I thought you was dead!' says a cheery voice.

Rohit looks around blearily and sees Tracy wearing an apron and wielding a yellow spatula in the tiny kitchenette off the living room. He grabs a nearby cushion, hastily placing it over his privates. 'Aaaah, I feel as if I'm dying,' he croaks.

'I've made you some coffee, real strong, that'll help,' she responds knowledgeably.

'Thanks,' he replies as he takes the steaming mug off her, still holding the cushion to his midriff. As she returns to the kitchen, he notices that she is wearing nothing under the apron, and her retreating bottom, wobbling ever so slightly, seems to be giving him a cheeky sideways smile. Putting the coffee down on a side table, he collapses back on to the sofa with a silent groan. He puts the pillow across his burning eyes, wondering desperately if preventing them from seeing more traces of his shame from the night before will somehow help to make it vanish in a puff of nothingness.

'Ooooer, wot's 'appened to 'im then? 'E seemed a bit perkier than tha' yesterdi !' Tracy's voice floats across from the kitchen.

Rohit guesses she is referring to his sadly depleted penis and slaps the cushion back down to cover it again. He opens one faded eye and rasps, 'I'm so very sorry. But you see there's been a horrible mistake.'

'My life, darlin', has been a series of mistakes. Now which one was you referrin' to, eh?'

Oh, crikey! How can she be so bloody cheerful, Rohit thinks, and able to stand before a bloody frying egg so bloody early in the morning. 'I ... I need to call myself a taxi,' he says.

'Yes, of course, love. Aunty Tricey'll get you a taxi. But first come 'n 'ave some heggs. You can't leave without breakfast!'

'I'm so sorry, but I don't think I can face the idea of breakfast. I just need a taxi. Please.' Rohit stands up and, as the room begins to swim around him, hopes frantically that it is on to the sofa that he will descend, as descend he knows he must. Before this happens, however, Tracy comes running out of the kitchen in alarm. She places her shoulder under his arm, and they stagger together to the bathroom. They just make it in time for Rohit to shove his head over the toilet bowl and heave into it the entire contents of numbers sixty-two, twenty-seven and thirty-five from the greasy laminated menu card of Lee Wang's Takeaway.

'Oh, dearie me, you poor thing!' Tracy says, yanking off a length of pink toilet roll and mopping Rohit's sweating brow with it. 'No heggs for you then.' She helps him to his feet again, and they perform the same three-legged stagger, this time with her steering him expertly back into the bedroom. 'You just lie there for a while, love,' she says solicitously, maternally almost, Rohit thinks gratefully as he feels himself gently lowered into a soft mattress. He can't seem to help the fact that his eyes are closing again. He is distantly aware of her covering him gently with the duvet and drawing the curtains to shut the grey morning light out.

'Thank you,' he says, remembering to use his posh voice, 'I'm ever so grateful to you for your kind hospitality, so kind, but I really do need to get myself a taxi, you know. I have a flat waiting for me at Edgware Road, and, oh, by the way, I also happen to have a wife waiting for me . . . and two kids too—Rinti and Riku—oh sorry, make that Rinku and Ritik . . . waiting for me . . . at Edgware . . . oh, I do beg your pardon . . . I really mean in Delhi . . . yes, if you could please tell the taxi I need to get to Delhi.' He is still mumbling in his best English as she closes the door behind her and returns to the kitchen.

■

Tracy returns to the eggs, now cold and congealed and stuck unappetizingly to the frying pan. She moves one to a plate and scrapes the other into the bin under the sink. Pulling out a stool, she perches herself at her tiny breakfast bar, feeling the cold metal of the bar stool penetrate her warm, bare bottom. 'Damn fool idea,' she thinks to herself. 'Thought I'd look irresistible to 'im like this, but I'll probably catch me death of cold now. And what would the bloody point 'ave been, eh?' She waggles her fork and starts to speak aloud to herself, 'Eh Trice? Another lovely man down the chute? You sure know 'ow to choose 'em, doncha?'

She puts down the slice of cold toast she is tearing into angrily and uses her fingers to count, 'Stan went off with Mandy, din 'e? Stevie ran off with Paul, Rob went back to his wife, Andy, bastard Andy, beat me black and blue, Tim just went, no particular reason.' She tears off another piece of cold toast and, dipping it into the yolk, starts to munch again resolutely. As a small tear rolls down one cheek, she starts speaking through a mouthful of soggy toast, 'And now 'im,

Imran Kaan.' She chucks her head towards the closed bedroom door, curls tossing indignantly. ' 'E seemed nice enough. Kind and gentle. I needed that kinda thing. I coulda done, really, with that kinda break, a man with a bit of money too, for a change.'

She is no longer addressing her fast depleting fried egg but is speaking directly to the small fridge magnet of the Madonna her friend Julie brought back for her from Lourdes last year. 'You knew that! You knew what a rough time I've been 'avin,' she says accusingly to it. The Madonna continues to smile implacably while Tracy gets up to tear a piece of kitchen paper off its rack and blow her nose with a wet, shrill sound. 'Now 'e turns out to be married too, dun 'e? Oh, why can't I hever, hever, hever get it right, eh? Eh?' The Madonna, who looks as though she knows little about these accidents of love, gazes impassively on while Tracy, now weeping copiously in the middle of her tiny kitchenette, feels her bottom freezing in earnest as the clock jumps to 9.00 and the heating system turns itself off.

By the time Rohit is properly awake, Tracy has regained her composure and her sartorial sense. She is clad demurely in blue jeans and a white shirt, which shows only a fetching hint of cleavage. She is leafing through a magazine with her feet up on the sofa, as Rohit emerges from the bedroom, looking like a big, shambling embarrassed bear. He has pulled a pair of trousers on and has a towel slung across his shoulders.

'Thought I'd take a bath,' he mumbles sheepishly, 'if you don't mind that is.'

''Course I don't mind, love! You jus' go ahead 'n pretty yourself up. Would you like some coffee or summink?'

'Er . . . oh . . . yes, please.'

Tracy busies herself in the kitchen again while Rohit goes for a bath. He emerges in a few minutes, dressed and towelling his wet hair vigorously. 'I tried to clean up in there after me,' he says. 'You keep everything so neat and clean, I must say.'

'Oh, ta, love!' Tracy seems surprised that he has noticed. 'I do try, you know. But it's not often that people notice.'

'Yes, I've been accused of that as well,' Rohit says ruefully, 'but you could say I'm better trained now.'

'By your wife,' Tracy states. There follow a few minutes of awkward silence until Tracy adds piously, 'Abou' last night ... I wouldn't 'ave, you know, if I'd known you was married and all.'

'Yes, I know,' Rohit replies. 'I don't know what came over me either.' He takes the mug of coffee and stares into its black depths as though willing it to reveal a logical reason or two.

'It 'appens sometimes.'

'Yes, I know.'

'It doesn't 'ave to mean anything, though, does it? You could be back in Delly and've completely forgotten about me in a month's time. P'raps even a week, say!'

Rohit nods again, doubting this very much. He has never had his left ear nibbled until he was almost in agony. Nor has he had vast experience in blow jobs but has decided that he likes them very much indeed. But he nods again, more resolutely, trying to sound cheerful as he declares, 'Yes we'll have forgotten about it in a week. In a matter of days, even.' He looks at her, trying to smile, and notices that there are streaks of black coursing down her face as her mascara starts to run.

Alarmed he asks, 'What, what is it? Why are you crying? I haven't said anything, to upset you, have I?'

She dabs at her eyes, smudging them even further, looking now like a small, blonde panda in jeans. ''S not you, love,' she says, ''S not you at all. 'Sme.'

'Smee?' Rohit queries, genuinely baffled.

'Yeah, 'sme. Me. I'm the problem. Can't blame anyone else, really. I dunno why, but I just can't seem to hever get it right. H ... e ... ever.' Her voice breaks on a sob as Rohit gets up and puts his arms around her. She breaks out into loud heart-rending wails as he rocks her back and forth, murmuring soothing noises. Through her wails, she starts to enumerate once again all the occasions on which she has got it wrong—Stan, Stevie and so on—in a rambling, tearful monologue that makes no sense at all to Rohit. But he continues to stroke her hair and her back until she gradually calms down to stand silently in the circle of his arms with her nose pressed against curly black chest hair. After a while, and rather reluctantly, she pulls away to look up at him, 'You're nice, y'know. I 'ope your wife knows wot a catch she's got.'

Rohit contemplates this possibility. Does Neena know what a catch she's got? She knew it once, he recalls, but had it become something she had sort of come to forget over the years? Or, on the other hand, had he, perhaps, just become a little less of a catch over the years? The inside of Rohit's head is still feeling far too mushy to work any of it out. All he knows, at the moment, is that he likes (very much) the sound of the words *you're a catch, Rohit*. It feels to him like a bloody long time since anyone (Neena, most of all) has told him this. It is, he thinks, the kind of thing that people should remember to tell each other once in a while. It prevents one from doing silly things. Like taking Tracy's tear-smudged chin in his hands and looking into her now reddish-blue eyes to throw all remaining caution to the winds.

And as Rohit does precisely that, Caution flies cheerily out of Tracy's first-floor window, catching the tail end of a breeze blowing down the street to head off in an easterly direction. It is carrying with it the first ripples of genuine doom that will invade the closed shutters of the Sachdev household on LM Road, New Delhi, India. Things like dust and summer heat and the noise of ceaseless traffic can be kept out very effectively by shuttered windows. But there are those other things that can fly in unannounced, from faraway places, turning everything, even seemingly happy families, upside down.

Blissfully unaware of this rapidly travelling thing, hurtling at great speed towards his faraway family, Rohit takes Tracy in his arms again. Burying his nose in lacquered curls, he says, 'Look, don't cry please. I can imagine, I really can, how lonely you must sometimes get, living on your own like this. I wish I could help.'

Tracy pulls away and, looking up at him, says wistfully, 'Look, don' get me wrong, but why doncha spend the week, as planned. I promise I'll stay away from you now that I know you're married and all. It'll be lovely just to 'ave some company.'

How can Rohit jump at the chance and convey to her, somehow, that he'd really rather she didn't keep away from him? How, also, can he silence that nagging voice in his head that's squawking things at him about deceit and desire and pretence and the horribly tangled web that he is starting to weave?

It is achieved, after about a nanosecond's hesitation, with one easy sentence. 'Yes,' he hears himself say. 'It is a good idea, I suppose. My wife won't know I'm here. She'll only call on my mobile phone anyway.'

'And wot one doesn't know can never 'urt, can it?'

'Never,' Rohit agrees optimistically.

■

And that is how it came to be that Rohit Sachdev, Delhiwallah, family man, ex-half-baked-Casanova, scion of the prospering Sachdev Textiles and Exports, came to love (there's that word again) Ms Tracy Budd, born in London's East End, school dropout, photographer's assistant, die-hard romantic, avid reader of lonely hearts columns. What do we call that sort of thing? A miracle, a misadventure, a mishap? Something akin to two cars that head inexorably towards each other only to meet in a headlong crash, splintering and wrenching each other with no warning and no mercy? It is in the looking back that all wisdoms lie. Only days, months, even years later is it possible to see the route one could have taken, the turning one ought to have missed.

■

If Rohit, aboard the descending Flight AI 002, could have seen Tracy at Heathrow airport, with her two and a half suitcases, looking out at the dark night, anxiously waiting for the rain to stop ... if he had known, as he had queued up at immigration and walked through the green channel, wheeling his baggage, of the kind of things he was headed towards so unstoppably ... if he had even the tiniest of insights into where that short taxi journey with a garrulous, pretty young blonde would finally take him ... what are the chances that he would have gone down that road anyway? And, having gone down that road, either wilfully choosing that path or having it thrust on him, should we be expecting him to undo his error now? Maybe, on the other hand, having found himself neck-deep in the mire of his mistake, already surrounded by the gathering flotsam of its consequences, should we hope (as he is doing) that he will somehow be spared the penalty? Accidents could technically happen to anyone, at any time. Oughtn't we, then, to merely shrug and say, 'Poor sod, there, but for God's grace, go you or I.'

But, while we stand around, in various states of consternation and apprehension, asking each other these questions, pondering and cogitating on all these different possibilities, there is Rohit, doing very little to make up for his mistake. In fact, what he does seem to be doing is nurturing and fostering it, while strolling around Tracy's flat in a happy daze. First he takes a phone call from Neena and tells her that his flat on Edgware Road is very comfortable indeed, thank you, even with coffee making facilities, darling! (His saving grace being that he studiously avoids Tracy's eye while having this conversation and even feels a certain queasiness in the pit of his stomach.) Then he calls up his father and discusses his impending meeting with the A&G Group while watching Tracy walk around the flat flapping a big pink feather duster. She dabbles it playfully into his free ear as she walks past, while his father's voice echoes tinnily into the other. Finally, he sets out to explore London with

Tracy tripping along beside him, hanging on to his arm, so as not to lose a stiletto heel to the vagaries of London's pavements. Rohit is aware that the possibility of being spotted with Tracy (by some old gossip who knows his family or Neena's) is very remote in this vast, busy city. The knowledge is bringing an enormous smile to his lips. On the other hand, he can certainly think of a few people (mainly old college mates and a few old windbags at the Rotary Club) by whom it would have been quite desirable to have been spotted with this beauty on his arm.

12

A meeting of unlike minds

Back on the wings of Caution (still travelling those winds), let us return to Delhi with no further delay, because this is where storm clouds are gathering, despite the summer heat. Descend through the smog-laden air until you hear the tootling of cycles, the cry of street vendors in the marketplaces and the angry blasting of horns. Circling the city like a highly-stretched belt is a six-lane ring road that seems to be doing its best to contain its extended, overblown girth. Cars are darting everywhere, ignoring lanes but seeming to keep to wherever shade covers the road. Towards the southern sweep of this ring road, getting on for the more salubrious estates of the city, you will spot another long, less wide road going by the impressive but long-forgotten name of Lakshmanrao Mindaspuria Road, LM to all trendy Delhiwallahs.

■

Jagdish Sachdev's nose for lucrative deals had always been legend and, within ten years of buying his property, LM Road had metamorphosed from a sleepy leafy avenue to a main thoroughfare down which traffic roared at all hours.

People who valued the state of their inner ears had long since moved out. The Guptas three years ago, building themselves a gaudy farmhouse in Gurgaon, having sold out to Kids Wearhouse for a never-disclosed sum. More recently, and on the other side of the road, what had once been the Kapur residence, had recently been converted into the office-cum-studios of Chic TV after the death of old Mr Kapur. 'Those useless sons are not bothered about what happens to the old man's house!' Jagdish had lamented. 'One in Washington, the other in New York, they can't even be bothered to see what goes on here. Why should they care that the old man must be turning in his grave?' That old Mr Kapur had no grave because he had been cremated and floated in the Ganges and that his sons actually lived in Cleveland and Phoenix were inaccuracies that Jagdish would only dismiss irritably, as he did any suggestions that Sachdev Mansion might not be located in Delhi's best residential area any more.

We approach it now, Sachdev Mansion, tucked between Kids Wearhouse and Chic TV, unmistakable with its pink turrets, granite walls and tightly shuttered windows. But not shuttered tightly enough, alas, for foreign troubles to somehow seep through. But what is this? An argument raging in the dining room?

'I refuse to make anything special for them. Just tell that Moolchand to buy some chanas or something from the shop down the road,' Swarn is saying.

'Muuum!' Tarun responds helplessly. 'Come on, Mamma, what's happened to your usual ability to rise to occasions, huh? Just like . . .'

'I know, I know, just like a helium balloon,' she mimics him sarcastically. 'Well, I just don't feeling like rising to anything this time. If you want special snacks made for them, you organize it with Moolchand. If you are wanting somebody to sit and chit-chat with them, then please go and call your father.'

Tarun throws his arms into the air in a despairing

gesture and stalks angrily out of the room. He finds his father in his panelled study examining swatches of cloth at his desk. His clothes have been flung over the back of his leather chair. Tarun notices with some surprise that Jagdish is sitting in his air-conditioned study wearing nothing but his spectacles and a pair of white leather slippers. He is too caught up in his own angst, however, to give this a second thought until later. 'Papa, are you busy?' Tarun asks as his father cheerily waves him in.

'Aha, just the fellow I need,' Jagdish says, rolling up a swivel chair beside him. 'Tell me what you think of this material, eh?'

Tarun takes the swatch into his hands, feeling it with his fingers but not looking at it. 'Papa, please, I need to talk to you.'

Jagdish takes off his glasses and looks at his younger son with concern. He notices an unfamiliar look in his eyes and asks gently, 'So what is making you look so rootha-rootha, eh?' Lately he has been very pleased with this younger son of his. Ever since their pact was made, he has not been able to find fault with the way he has, in the space of a couple of months, learnt the ropes of the business. Even with this new girlfriend on the scene, Tarun has missed no important meetings or deadlines. In fact, Jagdish cannot be too sure, but it even seems to him that Tarun's whole attitude might have improved even more with the arrival of this girl, Gayatri. There is, he thinks, a new seriousness about Tarun, a new sense of purpose.

Yes, the crusty old man is feeling kindly to his younger son. Tonight he is in a particularly good mood because he has also just heard from Rohit in London who has had a most successful meeting with Mr Attwood of A&G Group. In fact, he might even have to stay an extra week to make sure he can really convince him of the tie-up. Jagdish absent-mindedly looks for something to polish his glasses on but can find no convenient sleeve or shirt edge. He puts them back on and peers at Tarun through dusty lenses. 'Kya hua, what is the matter, beta?' he asks again.

Tarun sighs, 'Mummy. She just won't accept that Gayatri is the girl I want to marry.'

'Naturally,' Jagdish chips in, 'you have to see it from her point of view. She is upset because Gayatri is not from a Punjabi family.'

'Yes, yes, I know,' Tarun picks up the newspaper and turns to the matrimonial column. 'Beautiful, fair, homely, convented girl from a good well-settled Punjabi family, preferably holding green card.' Putting the paper down, he looks at his father with exasperation. 'We don't need any of that green card rubbish, do we?' he asks.

Jagdish looks at him and smiles. 'Show me one parent who does not want the best of everything for their children, hanh?'

'But what's wrong with Gayatri? I think she's the best. Isn't it rather arrogant of us to imagine that being Punjabi is the best?'

'Oho, beta, not that Punjabi is best, but what is best is to have things in common, like for you both to be Punjabi or both to be Madra ...' he trails off as he sees the look in Tarun's eyes and hastily modifies his last word, '*Mayalami* ... *Malayali*. Beta, these things all matter, whether you want to believe it or not, to have same-same background, financial standing, caste, community.'

'I don't see why,' Tarun mutters.

'Why? Why, because marriage is not such an easy-peasy thing. It is all about adjusting and accommodating. When you start off, it is better to have not too many altu-faltu differences, you see?'

'So how particularly has it helped that you and Mummy are both Punjabis and Khatris or whatever?' Tarun, though still annoyed, sounds genuinely curious.

Jagdish, who in a million years will not find an answer to this question, furrows his brow and thinks deeply. He has never had any illusions about his own marriage, or marriages in general for that matter. It is true he fell deeply in love with the sepia photograph of a young Swarn Malhotra that was shown to him before his marriage to her was fixed. Those arched nostrils decorated with a tiny sparkling diamond, that lustrous pair of eyes that had looked dreamily into the camera's lens, withholding serenely any lurking signs of a temper and the predilection for migraines. Who would have thought that the demure figure, clad in a red sari woven with gold, waiting so sweetly perched on the flower-bedecked bridal bed, would turn out to be such a terror, eh?

Jagdish chuckles briefly at the memory and then remembers, in an unexpected wave of sadness, how he had gradually come to spend longer and longer hours at the factory. Just to stay away from the house and Swarn. 'Well, it helped to build up my business very quickly, sitting there till midnight, just waiting for her to be asleep by the time I got back,' he thinks wryly before heaving a deep shuddering sigh.

He smiles with a rare look of wistfulness at his son who is still sitting before him waiting for his explanation. 'Beta,' he whispers, ruefully running his hand through a small clump of greying chest hair, 'if only, if only she had been less pretty.'

'Who, Gayatri?' queries a baffled Tarun.

'No, no, beta, your mother. She was so pretty, you know, half of Delhi was in love with her. I used to feel so proud to be going out with her, knowing that all heads would be turning to look at us.'

Tarun tries to remember the last time his parents have gone out together and can only remember cousin Shefali's wedding at the Maurya two years ago. His parents' obviously empty marriage has never mattered to him before. In some ways, it has even worked to his and Rohit's advantage, the lack of direct communication between their parents, by allowing the two boys to easily and often hilariously play one off against the other. Now, inexplicably, he feels sorry for his father, the nemesis of his youth comically transformed into a big, lumbering greying man forced into lurking nudity in his study room to escape the heat—not just of the Delhi summer but also of his wife's rages outside.

'Papa, why are you not wearing any clothes?' he asks, suddenly aware of Jagdish's new vulnerability.

'Air conditioner not working,' Jagdish mumbles in reply, only half telling the truth and hardly able to explain, even to himself, why this small and secret act of rebellion should recently have been bringing him such immeasurable comfort.

'I'll get Nek Singh to look at the air conditioner,' Tarun says, even though it is a promise that he will forget as soon as he leaves his father's study. His own problems are far greater than his father's have ever been he reckons. 'Papa, you must understand that I'm not doing this to hurt either you or Mamma. But Gayatri really is the girl I want to marry.'

'You love her,' Jagdish is making a statement. This is no time for asking questions whose answers are clearly written all over his younger son's handsome, unhappy face. Tarun nods miserably.

'Then at least try and look happy about it, bewakuf,' he chides, switching over to a jolly voice again. Bonhomie, particularly with his sons, does not come easy to him, but he makes a huge effort now. 'This is maybe the happiest time of your life and look at your face, all rootha-rootha. Don't worry about your mother. She will carry on like this for a few days. Let me see what I can do.'

'You'll speak to her? Manao her?' Tarun asks, sitting up.

Jagdish nods, not looking terribly convinced himself. 'Your mother is a sensible woman. If I explain things, I think she will understand. You go and arrange for Gayatri's family to visit us here. I will handle your mother.'

Tarun leans over to give his father's shoulders a hug. If he were to look back, he would realize that it is the first hug he has given his father since he was about six. But today he is a man on a mission of love. He rushes out of the room. Jagdish picks up his swatch of samples again and looks at it sadly. Who would have thought anyone could make many bits of cloth such a passion, eh? He remembers that he hasn't always been like this, so single-minded, so unimaginative. He too felt the pangs of love stir madly at his insides once, albeit about thirty years ago for roughly ten or twelve days. What happens to love, he wonders, sorrowfully scratching the greying pubic hair in his crotch. From where does it come? And why does it come at all, if it is meant only to die?

He gets up and slowly starts putting on his clothes as though they are likely to be his armour and readies himself for his encounter with Swarn. He would really rather not be invoking the wrath of the gods to fall upon his head, but has no option. In return for Tarun becoming a businessman, it is really the least he can do.

∎

Kammy and Manny are having one of their famous rows. Neena, who is staying over for the duration of Rohit's London trip, is arbitrating unsuccessfully.

'Oho, come on Mamma, it's not worth fighting over,' Neena says beseechingly.

'No, no, beti, this is too much, too much, you know, one must have a sense of priorities in this world! That is, unfortunately something your father has never learnt. And now he is passing it on to his children too!' Kammy has gone a magnificent shade of purple, so great is her rage this time.

'Who are you, let me ask, to decide what the world's priorities should be, hanh?' Manny roars from the other room.

Staying where she is, seated in a wicker chair with cream-coloured raw-silk cushions, Kammy roars back, 'We were not brought into this world to accept everything unquestioningly. It is our job as human beings to question the world, Manny Singh!' She breaks out into a fit of coughing, sending old Sultan whimpering to his retreat under the coffee table.

'Why on earth are you two shouting at each other from different rooms anyway? You'll give yourself laryngitis, Mamma!'

'Let her bring on some laryngitis, beti. Maybe then I will get some peace and quiet in the house,' floats another loud salvo from the Manny camp.

'And you, Papa, you will give yourself a hernia if you keep shouting from there!'

'Even if I get hernia and die that woman will not remember me with any sorrow, beti. I hope at least my children will mourn my passing!'

'And that is your essential mistake, Manny Singh! You think you can buy your son's affections by showering him with money? Well, it doesn't work that way, let me tell you. If you die, it's your money your Danny will miss, not you, you fool!'

Manny appears in the door at this. 'Neena beti, see, see how she insults me! Is that any way for a woman to talk to her husband, I ask you?'

'How can I not call you a fool, Manny Singh? People are dying, in Gujarat! You have the cheek to grumble about my sending a lousy money order to the Prime Minister's Relief Fund while you want to send your son five thousand dollars!' Kammy's apoplectic coughing fit is starting to make Sultan shudder with real fright now. He rolls his eyes mournfully at Neena, who tickles him reassuringly under his ear with her big toe. But Kammy hasn't finished, she wipes her face with a tissue and takes up where she left off. 'And for what! We all know for what! Not to buy books, oh no, no, no. For tuition fees? Not a chance! I know Danny better than you, Manny Singh. Five thousand dollars ... five thousand dollars will go to get him some more beer, some more petrol for his damned car.' Kammy suddenly recalls Danny's car purchase, subject for the last Singh row. 'This car that he needed to get from his flat to his classes, two blocks away, two blocks, Neena!' She trails off. The memory of this last injustice has reduced even the stoic Kammy to tears.

'Oh, come on, Mamma,' Neena cries in alarm, putting her arms around her mother's ample shoulders, 'what are you crying for? It's only crazy old Danny. We all know what he's like.'

'But that's the point, beti,' Kammy wails, now seriously upset. 'All I wanted was for my children was to study and get educated and become good human beings.' She is flooded now in copious tears at the thought of how this dream has managed to elude her twice.

Neena squeezes her mother's shoulders again, although cut to the quick at the thought that she has now been included in her mother's list of woes. 'Look, Mamma, stop crying or you'll wake the children up. You know how cranky they get if they haven't had their afternoon nap. Why don't I do something? I'll call up Tarun and tell him I can't make it back for this Menon visit in the evening, and we can go and see a film or something. Just you and I, hanh? I heard this new *Charlie's Angels* thing is quite good.'

Kammy raises her head just enough to mumble scornfully, snivelling through her tissue, 'Not *Charlie's Angels*. Can't you think of something more edifying, Neena? Let's see *Life Is Beautiful* instead. That won an Oscar or something, I believe.'

■

Keshava Menon is concerned that he has nothing decent to wear on his visit to the Sachdev household. This is a feeling entirely new to him as he riffles through the meagre collection in his tiny wardrobe. White shirt with thin brown stripes, white shirt with thin grey stripes—his choice isn't endless. Things are so much easier for women, he thinks with surprise, never having given this fact very much thought before. Raji has, for years, managed with the collection of Kanjeevaram saris her parents gave her for their wedding. 'Such good silk, they never tear, never go out of fashion,' she often says, never agreeing to buy anything new. She has already chosen a blue and gold Kanjeevaram sari for herself, despite Gayatri's protestations that she will probably die of heat stroke by the time she gets to LM Road. 'This is the season for chiffons, Amma, not silks!' Gayatri expostulated on seeing her mother's choice. Which threw Raji into a state of utter confusion, surprised that Gayatri kept track of these things, that the

Sachdev visit meant so much to her and that her daughter had even imagined that her not too commodious wardrobe would contain anything even resembling a chiffon.

Raji is right, even Gayatri is unusually overwhelmed by the situation and has pulled out a modest salwar kameez suit to wear. Her usual trousers and T-shirts will not pass muster. Why push at those Sachdev boundaries so early on, she asks herself in a rare show of respect for other people's opinions. As she airs out the salwar kameez, getting ready to send it to the press-wallah down the road, Keshava wanders in holding an ancient pair of faded white seersucker trousers in his hands. 'What do you think of this one, moley?' he asks, smoothing the crumpled fabric with his palms. 'I bought it in Aden in 1963, while returning from England.'

'Oh, Appa! Are you saying you have nothing newer than that? Nineteen hundred and sixty-three, for heaven's sake!'

'Of course not, of course I have bought other clothes,' he replies, flustered. 'I just thought this would be nice, sort of dapper. This used to be the height of fashion then, you know.'

'Well, it isn't now, Appa,' Gayatri says more gently. 'Why don't you wear your brown trousers? Those are quite nice.'

'With what shirt?' asks Keshava, looking completely helpless.

'Oh, any of your shirts will go with that. They're all pretty neutral, aren't they? Just make sure that the collar and sleeves aren't frayed.' She gets up and puts her arms around him. 'You're really nervous about this visit, aren't you?'

'It's not every day one goes seeking a proposal of marriage for one's daughter.'

Gayatri clearly does not like the sound of this. She scowls fiercely at Keshava, 'You're not seeking anything, Appa,' she snaps. 'You're just going to meet them. To get to know them better. So that you're not complete strangers to each other if and when Tarun and I do agree to get married. . .'

'What do you mean, if?'

'If, because I haven't decided yet if Tarun's the right man for me, Appa.'

Keshava looks shocked. 'So you'll just keep him hanging till then? And how long will that take, I ask you?'

'Not hanging, as you put it. And I don't know how long these things take. We just need to get to know each other better, that's all.'

'Well, he thinks he's going to marry you,' Keshava points out.

'I've tried telling him, but he won't listen,' Gayatri says, sulkily pulling a stray strand of hair out of her mouth. She doesn't need this interrogation now, not just before this ghastly Sachdev visit. Whose rotten stupid idea was this anyway, bloody Tarun, she thinks, angrily banging the door of her cupboard shut. 'Oh, it's no big deal anyway, Appa. Let's just get ready and go, shall we?'

'You worry me, Gayatri,' Keshava replies. 'You would never have talked like this before going to England.' Gayatri does not respond but merely throws her eyes heavenwards. Her father pretends he hasn't noticed and carries on, 'How can you say marriage is not a big deal? It is such a big deal. The biggest deal you will ever make in some ways, moley.'

'Sure, I'm not denigrating its importance, Appa. But nor do I believe it's as important as you make it out to be.' Gayatri ignores Keshava's hurt expression that seems to suggest he has been personally insulted and continues talking, 'Let me put it this way, Appa, I believe it's important to keep working at a marriage if it is bringing one happiness. But it's not important enough to put up with if it turns out bad.'

'Bad. What is bad? These days, for you youngsters, it doesn't take much to decide things are bad. Unlike our generation that took the bad and did the best they could with it.'

They are interrupted by Raji, attempting to look dazzling in blue and gold, who comes scurrying in waving a bundle of brand new safety pins. 'Moley, help me put these pins in the sari. I haven't worn a Kanjeevaram for so long, I'm worried it'll slip. Why are you two sitting around and chit-chatting? Shouldn't you be getting ready? We'll be late!'

'Oh, Amma, how have you worn your sari? It's all askew! You look such a mess. Let me redo these pleats.' Gayatri springs up and begins to fuss over her mother.

Keshava gets up too, still holding his seersucker trousers. He wanders over to Raji and pats her cheek gently, 'Askew or not, I think that sari always makes you look like a real princess.' He cocks his eyebrow meaningfully at Gayatri in the mirror and gives her a look that he hopes will convey how effortlessly his generation always did the 'best they could'.

After he has left the room, Raji looks down at her daughter who is rearranging the pleats of the sari, strenuously pulling them closer to the floor. She sounds very confused as she asks, 'What's got into him, eh? That's the first compliment he's paid me in years.'

■

At the Sachdev household, Tarun is having a quick look around the drawing room to make sure everything is in order for the Menon visit. Apart from the fact that Gayatri will be gracefully occupying this room in a mere hour or so, Tarun realizes that he has never actually entertained a female friend in this manner. Of course, he has had female visitors in this house before, some of whom have arrived riding the pillion of his motorcycle, others in their own cars. But these visits have always been surreptitious, often nocturnal and designed to avoid his parents. Now, here he is preparing not only to so openly entertain a girlfriend but also her parents and his! It is all too amazing. There are moments when Tarun is as astonished as everyone else at the change in himself.

Is this true love, we could ask ourselves fervently, as we watch Tarun bend down to rearrange a couple of ceramic doves canoodling on a glass twig. He then wets his forefinger and carefully lifts a speck of dust from the coffee table. Is this the behaviour of all young men in love for the first time? Or is it all merely symptomatic of the nesting instincts that seem to overtake people as they finally turn that corner in life, acquiring jobs and the odd grey hair, needing soon enough to find that helpmeet to traverse the remaining path of life? Is it merely this that is making Tarun, for the first time in his young life, actually check the state of the teacups, startling old Moolchand in the kitchen just as he was contemplating sneaking a quick cup of sweet tea? If asked, Tarun would have none of that rites-of-passage theory. As far as he is concerned, Gayatri is a golden swan that has by some freak chance landed on the muddy pond of his life. He will be damned before he lets some blunder make her fly away.

■

Soon the Menons are piling into Keshava's battered old Standard Herald. Keshava takes up station behind the steering wheel, jauntily jingling the keys in his hand. Now that they are all ready and Gayatri is looking so demure in a salwar kameez, Keshava is back to being in a terribly good mood, his happiness shining out of his face and spectacles. Gayatri pats his shoulder as she gets into the passenger seat next to him, armed with the piece of paper on which Tarun has painstakingly drawn a map of Maharaja Colony and LM Road. Raji occupies the back seat, where she can cogitate contentedly on more mysteries of the marrow family until they reach the Sachdev residence and she is compelled to socialize. A little of Keshava's glow is dimmed as the car refuses to budge, needing its usual coaxing with the choke button. Small beads of perspiration appear on his well-scrubbed forehead, framing the top of his spectacles. Gayatri and Raji unhelpfully offer a few suggestions, which he generously ignores, even though he is tempted to remind them that neither of them knows how to drive a car. Finally, however, the small white car starts up, almost seeming to surprise itself, and lurches out of the front gate carrying its three anxious occupants. It clearly does not share their anxiety as it trundles down the road showing no desire to hurry to its assignation on the other side of town, coughing and spluttering like an indignant old pensioner complaining feebly that he simply cannot see why he should be dragged to the party when all he wants to do is sleep.

The face of Keshava's car certainly does not fit in the party of cars currently occupying the Sachdev front drive: the BMW, bought by Jagdish from a returning NRI four years ago; Neena's Safari, a smart silver grey, with a shiny chrome bull bar around its front end; and Tarun's Maruti Esteem, souped up with leather bucket seats and, inexplicably, a flashing yellow light on its bonnet. Keshava pulls his car in behind this motley, fashionable collection and steps out, locking it carefully and walking around it to make sure the other three doors are locked as well.

He follows Gayatri up the drive and to the front door as Raji, still fussing with her pleats, brings up the rear. They wait nervously as the doorbell rings somewhere in a distant part of the house. A lined old face, resembling a piece of brown leather shaped vaguely into human features, peers out at them and nods dourly. More bloody visitors, the expression on his face seems to be saying as Moolchand steps aside and allows them in. The Menons follow his stooped figure into the plush living room, and Keshava tries not to gasp in surprise at the sight of the dripping chandeliers, false Rubens and acres of brown velvet. Keshava and Raji take up tense positions on the edge of one of the sofas, sitting side by side as though hoping to pass some element of moral support to each other over the undulations of the velvet. Gayatri, for whom nervousness is an alien sensation, can feel it emanate from her parents and enter her own body, which is now starting to feel both hot and cold.

'Hello! Hi! Welcome, welcome! So pleased to see you here.' Tarun comes rushing into the room, rubbing his hands together. He is dressed in a crisp cotton kurta and sits down next to Gayatri. She smiles at him gratefully, pleased to see him looking his usual buoyant self. Tarun thinks she looks lovelier than ever, but he turns his attention to Keshava who is still looking around the room, awestruck.

'No problem finding the house, I hope,' Tarun inquires.

'No, no,' Keshava mumbles, looking at a plump woman frolicking in a fake Rubens forest.

'This used to be a really quiet area when we first moved in, but you wouldn't think that the way it is now,' Tarun says chattily.

'Yes, yes, very quiet,' Keshava says, noticing the split-level air-conditioning unit, taking pride of place on the opposite wall. Swarn hasn't bothered to turn it on today. Why should she do it for any old anybody, ji?

These uncommonly brief responses from Keshava are beginning to disconcert Tarun as well. 'Moolchand, paani lao,' he calls out. In a few seconds, Moolchand shuffles in with the water, and everyone silently welcomes the temporary break in trying to think of something to say as it is served. Keshava takes the last of the three glasses with an elaborate thank you to Moolchand, who eyes him with disdain.

Like his mistress, Moolchand has an unerring knack for assessing visitors based on an elaborate system of appraisal involving cars, clothes and impolite behaviour to the domestic staff. According to Moolchand's snob scale, cars have to be big, clothes new and brightly coloured, and sahibs and memsahibs have to behave as rudely as possible to the likes of him. This new sahib has already managed to irritate him. First, there was the small battered Standard Herald, clearly visible to all from LM Road and which will no doubt make people wonder what this piece of wreckage is doing cluttering the drive of such a fine mansion. Now, at close hand, Moolchand can see the unfashionable clothes too—all greys and browns, servants colours. The worst transgression of all, something Moolchand absolutely cannot cope with, so lightly practised by these trying-to-be-fashionable types: the mixing up of the social classes, the wilful breakdown of carefully preserved norms and customs that exist precisely to remind everybody of who is who and what is what—things that this so-called sahib obviously has no respect for. Look at him now, Moolchand thinks scornfully, grinning and smiling as though he were my oldest friend! Even making eye contact, something Moolchand's sulky, pouting Swarn memsahib hasn't ever done, except maybe purely by accident.

Moolchand waits until Keshava has drained his glass and shudders slightly as he is thanked elaborately. It doesn't take much for him to guess that what this sahib's obsequiousness means. It is clearly marriage of his daughter to Tarun Sahib that he is after, such cheek! Pretending not to have heard Keshava's grateful, 'Thank you, thank you, shukriya, ji', Moolchand loftily accepts the glass on his tray, barely bending down, before returning to his place in the kitchen.

'Let me get my parents for you,' Tarun says, getting up and leaving the Menons looking uneasily at each other and completely out of place in the gaudy drawing room. In a few minutes he is back, accompanied by a sheepish-looking Jagdish. These are the kinds of encounters Jagdish wishes his life could have been spared. The travails of Rohit's wedding had been alleviated by the exciting potential for future joint ventures. That had made some of the helloji-how-are-you stuff almost bearable. Now, quickly scanning the drawing room and seeing a rather awkward, clearly nervous south Indian couple perched on the sofas, Jagdish can feel his heart sink. What common ground can he find? Particularly given that Swarn is likely to be cool and aloof and silent when she does deign to appear. Business? No, Tarun has already told him they are teachers or something like that. Textiles? Probably not, even Jagdish knows that not everybody shares his passion for weft and weave. Fashion trends? Definitely not, going by the look of the clothes these people are wearing. Jagdish, having been introduced around and done his namastes, sinks into the sofa feeling weary before he has even started.

'So!' he declares loudly, making Raji seated next to him jump. 'So, congratulations . . . um . . . um . . .'

'Gayatri,' Gayatri says, while Tarun closes his eyes.

'Yes, yes, congratulations, beti, Tarun tells me you are

taking up a teaching post at the Indira Gandhi University.' Jagdish tries to make this sound like a celebratory event vaguely equivalent to finding a Swiss or French buyer.

'Yes, at the Jawaharlal Nehru University, actually,' Gayatri says, smiling, as Tarun dares to open his eyes again.

'So!' Jagdish declares again, this time generously taking in the two senior Menons in the sweep of his gaze and still sounding overly impressed. 'Following in the footsteps of both the parents, hanh? Tarun tells me that both of you are teachers.' Tarun closes his eyes again as three pairs of Menon eyes turn to him in surprise.

'No, no, slight misunderstanding,' Keshava chips in hastily. 'Raji, my good wife, is a professor of botany at the Indian Institute of Science. M.S., M.Phil., Annamalai University. I am employed by ISI, I am sure you know, Indian Standards Institute, for the last thirty years. Technical director.' He beams at Jagdish, pleased to have got the chance to present the Menon credentials so early on in the visit. Jagdish nods disconcertedly, absorbing only about half of this neatly packaged piece of information.

Instead he says, as though offering the Menons a prize treat, 'My wife, Swarn, will join us in a few minutes.'

Tarun feels a shiver travel down his spine at these words. He is not terribly sure what exactly transpired between his parents after Jagdish promised to talk to Swarn, but he saw his father emerge from their bedroom earlier in the evening looking drained but signalling a weary thumbs up from across the corridor.

After his initial panic at the news that Neena was not coming to support him through this Menon visit, Tarun cheered up at the idea that this was going to be his show altogether. He is, of course, grateful to Neena for her help, for having so fortuitously chosen to have such a lovely friend in her college years and for having first sent Cupid's dart flying across the aerobics room and so on and so forth. But it was very important that this first Menon visit go off without a hitch, and he was not really sure that Neena's presence would ensure sane and decent conversation. Now he can't help wondering if he might have made a terrible error. Her garrulousness, why, even her endless supply of Mallu jokes, might have been far preferable to these ghastly silences. 'Please tell me who would like tea and who would like coffee,' he asks, his voice rising in a piteous bleat.

It is at this point that Swarn makes her entry into the drawing room. She is clad in white, the colour of mourning. There are dark hollows around her eyes, visible today only because she has not bothered to hide them with her usual foundation make-up. Her eyes are focussed somewhere beyond the walls of her drawing room, in search of some distant place where there is only peace. ('Peace of mind is all I want from this life, ji, is that too much to ask?' she had inquired earlier of Jagdish.) She wears about her a general air of tragedy and only whispers an indistinct helloji to the assembled gathering. As she tearfully informed Jagdish, she has come down to meet these people only because she has been brought up by her parents to always be gracious and polite to people who came to her house. ('Even if they are paupers, ji.') This is, of course, perfectly untrue as it is Swarn's own snob scale on which Moolchand has based his own, but she is determined to martyr herself today. And so, aided by a little curiosity, she has made it a point to come downstairs, even though it pains her greatly. Let her husband see how much she agrees to put up with, let her foolish son see what a long-suffering mother he has. Let the whole world see how poor Swarn Sachdev has such a thankless life, hai bechari.

Keshava scrambles to his feet at the entrance of this white spectre, spilling some water down the front of his shirt. Raji scrambles up too, even though Gayatri is trying to signal from across the room that she does not have to. Swarn nods vaguely at them, noticing through her misty faraway look that the woman, the mother (Tarun's potential mother-in-law, hai Ram!), is wearing a ghastly blue and gold thing. (It looks like a Kanjeevaram, madwoman, in this heat!) And a red stick-on bindi that is just about to fall off and (oh, God!) white sandals! This is much, much worse than Swarn had expected. She sinks into the sofa in a half swoon.

'So pleased to meet you, madam,' Keshava squeaks excitedly, while it is Gayatri's turn to close her eyes. Swarn nods absently, her head still reeling from the visual onslaught of the blue and gold apparition across from her. Now it is saying something too. Swarn looks at her, trying to hear her words even though she is captivated by the quivering bindi that she is very tempted to slap back on to the forehead from which it is escaping so indubitably.

'You have a very beautiful house, Mrs Sachdev,' Raji says. Even Raji is awed enough by the occasion to sink to untruths and flattery. Then her normal self surfaces as she adds brightly, 'Your drawing room alone is about the size of our drawing, dining and kitchen.'

Swarn nods again. It is just as she had thought—another impoverished Madrasi.

Jagdish chips in again to compensate for his wife's continuing silence, 'Mrs ... Mrs ... umm ...'

'Menon,' says Raji helpfully.

'Yes, yes, Mrs Menon is a professor of botany, Swarn, at ... at ...'

'Indian Institute of Science,' Keshava says.

'Ah yes, yes ...' Jagdish trails off.

'Tea, coffee?' Swarn rouses herself finally to speak. She is addressing no one in particular.

'I've asked for it,' Tarun growls.

As if on cue, Moolchand reappears, bearing a large tray with the tea things. He was instructed by Tarun Sahib to make cheese pakoras and to get some burfis from the nearby halvai. But he had heard the argument between mother and son earlier and was sure that the memsahib had been telling Tarun that even Moolchand would support her. He had heard her say his name a couple of times and then something in English: 'Moolchand git-pit, git-pit, Moolchand, git-pit, git-pit.' Moolchand has no doubt at all in his mind whose

side he is on anyway. After all, it is the memsahib who pays
his salary every month. It is also the memsahib whose face
appears so sweetly as his right hand winds around his penis
every night. It is to her salt that he is indebted, he often likes
to say. And so, there are no pakoras and no burfis on the
tray. Only a plateful of Brittania orange cream biscuits,
crumbling slightly at their edges.

Tarun notices the omission as soon as the tray is placed
on the table. 'Are the pakoras coming?' he asks Moolchand,
hissing threateningly in Hindi. Moolchand looks down and
shuffles his feet to indicate a negative. He tries to slip back
to the kitchen, but another sibilant whisper arrests his
progress. 'And where are the burfis?' Tarun asks, his face
turning dark with anger as he realizes there are none.
Moolchand attempts a quick backward shuffle out of the
drawing room, but Tarun is too swift for him. Before the
astounded collective gaze of the small gathering, Tarun gets
to his feet, not even noticing that he has knocked into a small
teapoy that keels over on to the marble floor with a crash. All
eyes turn first to Tarun and then to the little rosewood
teapoy on the floor, as though it were, in some strange way,
responsible for this sudden spectacle.

Later Moolchand will tell his mate, Nek Singh the driver,
that he was just about to explain to Tarun Sahib that it would
only take him five minutes to fetch some burfis, nice and
fresh, from Haldirams down the road. But the speed with
which Tarun Sahib had leapt up left him with no chance to
explain. Particularly as the next thing Tarun did was leap
over the teapoy to grab the old cook by his kurta collar,
shouting unrepeatable things. It is almost as if the whole
thing happened in slow motion, when the scene is recalled
later. Everyone has his or her own version, of course,
Moolchand's being the most exaggerated.

'Just imazine, Nek Singh,' he will say later over a couple
of beedis and many cups of sweet tea. 'I don't know what
tensun was going on between Tarun Sahib and the sahib and
memsahib and why I, of all people, had to be dragged into

it. But there he was, our Tarun Sahib, suddenly shouting and swearing at me! And what language, baaprey, haraamzaada this and bhainchute that, ohoho ... and then the poor memsahib burst out crying and had to be taken indoors. And those guests of Tarun Sahib's, who must, if you ask me, have been responsible for all the tensun in the first place (I did not like the look of them at all, low-class people) they all just got up and had to leave. No, no Tarun Sahib did not go with them. Only up to the gate. Then he was back in here, in his mother's bedroom, shouting and swearing while his poor mother was wailing and crying. I could not hear very much because the door was closed, even though I started to quickly do the dusting in the corridor to see if I could make out what was going on. Not that I need to know what these people want to talk about or shout about, after all they are our owners, our maliks. No, no. I just wanted to know if I was going to lose my job, you know. We are only poor people, working hard to fill our stomachs, we just keep ourselves busy doing that. Not like these moneyed people, nothing better to do, just shouting at each other ... what a kalyug it is we live in, Nek Singh ... believe me, if I had money and lived in a big house like this one ...'

Keshava Menon's version would be markedly toned down by comparison, dismissive, good humoured even. 'It was all some silly misunderstanding,' he would say, patting Raji reassuringly on one silken knee during their drive back to Saket. 'That's all. I still think that Tarun's a good fellow, in fact a very fine fellow. He was just worried about something. Maybe that cook has been giving them problems for a long time before this. I certainly don't think it had anything at all to do with us, did it, moley?'

Gayatri does not reply as she avoids her father's questioning gaze in the rear-view mirror and continues to stare out at the rush-hour traffic. Something inside her is constricting her stomach muscles, and the ache is spreading to every part of her. Her head hurts, her forehead and her temples and even the space behind her eyes. She does not have the heart to point out to her parents that they have just received one of the biggest insults of their lives and that she has been responsible for it. That, it seems to her, is the bit that hurts the most. 'Tarun, Michael, what a bloody waste of time,' she thinks angrily. 'What a bloody, foolish, ghastly waste of everything. Love! Ha! It's a mug's game, nothing else! Why did I ever go to those stupid aerobics sessions?' she wonders, leaning her head back on the car seat and closing her eyes. 'Why did I agree to go for that meal? Why, oh why, did I let Neena talk me into it?' A tiny tear appears amongst her lashes, trembling there for a while before trickling down her right cheek. 'Oh, why, why, why did I ever go to work in that pub back in England? Why did I get talking to Michael that night? Why am I such a fool when it comes to love?'

■

How can one tell Gayatri that you can't blame yourself for accidents? They happen. They happen to the best of us. And, having let them happen, we seem to grow no wiser to them. We merely let them happen again.

13

Love in London

And while his younger brother informs his parents that he is choosing to move out of their house, Rohit, far away in London, comes close to doing exactly the same, only minus the honesty.

He has spent a wonderful morning with Tracy and has learnt many new things. English ways, fine English expressions. Like *luvverly jubbly* and *cor blimey* and *Gordon Bennett!* So sweet, so utterly charming, he thinks, licking an ice cream cone while watching a street performance at Leicester Square. Or rather while watching Tracy watch the street performance, clapping her hands in glee. He thinks briefly of Rinku, who would probably have done the same, and then wonders what that constricting feeling is somewhere in the region of his chest. Guilt is not an emotion he has dallied with for too long whenever it has accosted him in the past, though the past has presented him with a few opportunities.

To be fair, the faces of his wife and children have floated in and out of his head a few times during the course of the day. And he hasn't particularly enjoyed the sensation, but to deal with his unnameable feelings, he has bundled them as hastily as possible out of his head into some unreachable mental top shelf and has concentrated instead on the pretty curly-haired girl at his side, the meal they will have at a good Indian restaurant later in the evening, the bottle of Pernod that she says she has back at her flat, and ... and ... the things she will do for him afterwards, as she did last night ... dear God ... Rohit has to stop licking his cone and cling briefly to a lamp post as this blissful thought floats through his head.

'Oooo, jus' lookit 'im!' Tracy cries, jiggling Rohit's arm, as the street performer swallows a small ball of fire, gulping and smiling as though it were a merely an extralarge pork won ton.

Rohit nods and smiles, popping the last inch of ice cream cone into his mouth before joining the crowd in its applause. As the performance finishes, they wander off, attempting to get away from the crowd. It is a balmy summer afternoon, and it feels to Rohit as though all of London has decided to step out and head for Leicester Square. The steps coming up from the tube station are disgorging people in droves. He allows Tracy to lead the way, happy to follow her as she determinedly takes him by the hand, pushing past shiny-faced tourists and Chinese women shrilly calling out the wonders of head-and-neck massages.

Rohit tries to remember when he has last gone on a wander like this, an aimless stroll, just enjoying the feel of the sun on his face and the breeze in his hair. His sudden wistfulness is not without a touch of self-pity. This train of thought makes him feel a bit more cheerful for some reason, so he pursues it for a while longer, warming to it as he goes along. 'Why is it that I have spent my entire youth, the best years of my life, in fact, chasing after business deals and my father's dreams of goddamned foreign buyers?' he asks himself sourly. 'Always rushing here and rushing there, never a moment to myself. If I do get a moment, it is Neena needing something, or the children wanting this and that or mother asking to be taken somewhere. Tarun has never bothered with any of that. It's always been me, hasn't it? Rohit the dependable, Rohit the good guy. Well, I've had enough of being the good guy. Enough! It's my turn now. Everybody please step aside. Now, before I've lost it completely, this is my turn for some fun. Let's see if anyone will dare stop me. Ha! Having never done anything wrong, ever' (at this point, of course, Rohit has lapsed into total amnesia, forgetting just a few stray incidents) 'having always done what everybody else has always wanted me to do for them. Now I'm entitled!'

And so, suitably buoyed up by the conviction of being entitled, Rohit spends his six remaining days with Tracy in her tiny, kitschy Hammersmith flat. For six heavenly days, he lives a life so far removed from his own it is almost as though he is temporarily someone else. Someone called Steve or Vince, living a Steve or Vince type of life. He gets up next to Tracy Budd (not Neena Sachdev) and, after a bit of what Tracy refers to as rumpy pumpy, he washes and gets himself ready. He has to iron his own shirt, which is a new experience for him, as ironed shirts in Delhi have always appeared on a dhobi's cycle every morning. He then sits down to a bowl of All Bran ('It's good for you, love. Watch it make you go') followed by an egg placed lovingly on a slice of toast by Tracy (and not a surly Moolchand).

After helping Tracy with the washing up (another unfamiliar exercise), he leaves the house, not in a BMW or a Tata Safari, but on his own two legs, trotting down the road with Tracy to Hammersmith tube station. He packs himself into a crowded tube along with several thousand others, not listening idly to the film music favoured by Times FM on his car radio, but with his nose pressed up against some news-hungry commuter's tabloid paper instead. At Green Park he bids a long farewell to Tracy, who has to change to the Victoria Line for her studios near Euston, and he proceeds to Holborn. They exchange a long kiss, tongues and all, while commuters look on with bored, blank indifference. For the rest of the day, Rohit is on his own and, apart from a few business meetings at the offices of A&G Group behind Holborn station, he can wander as much as he likes, feeling the sun on his face, the wind in his hair—all the things he has never, ever been given a chance to do so far. He has, as far as he can tell, truly reached heaven.

But, three business meetings, six sessions of rumpy pumpy, twelve French kisses and about seven glorious blow jobs later, it is time unfortunately for Rohit to leave London and Tracy.

Later he will recall waking up very early on the morning of his departure for Delhi feeling as though a cannonball had lodged itself squarely in his stomach. It hangs there, heavy, dull and unmoving all through the morning as he starts gathering his things from the bedroom and the bathroom. He had not realized how much he had spread himself out in the week he has been in Tracy's flat. His things seem to be everywhere—his portable iron in the kitchen, his clothes in the airing cupboard, his razor by the washbasin, his soap dish by the bathtub, a pair of trousers flung over a bar stool (although he cannot remember the deft-though-drunken manoeuvre that got them there in the first place). Tracy too has woken up with two small purple shadows under her eyes, although she says they are because of the wine she downed at night. She announces that she feels funny, like, and does not want to go into work.

Rohit's flight is very early in the morning and, as he makes a call to remind the taxi of the address, Tracy starts to cry. She has not changed out of her nightshirt and is sitting curled up in her armchair, still wearing her ridiculous rabbit slippers with pink ears that quiver when she walks. Rohit can feel a squeezing pain in his chest that he assumes is his heart breaking. He sits at Tracy's feet, looking miserably at her rabbits, wondering what he can say to comfort her.

'It's nearly time for me to get ready, Trace,' he says finally, looking up at her. She blows her nose on a piece of tissue, pulling it out of the pocket of her dressing gown, into which she appears to have perspicaciously stuffed a whole wad in advance.

'Yeah,' she sniffles, her voice muffled by damp tissue, 'you'd better get yourself ready, lovey.'

'Look, I'll probably be back in a couple of months,' he trails off as he remembers having promised Neena in a rash moment that he would be taking her along for his next trip to England.

'Will you call me from Delly—jus' once in a while?'

'Yeah, sure love. I'll call. I'll call every day if I can. Somehow.'

Tracy smiles at him through her tears. 'I'm sorry, I don't mean to be a pain. I dunno . . . jus' can't explain why I feel so miserable.'

'I know, me too. Who'd have thought that in just a week . . .'

■

If only we had the capacity to see some of life's accidents come hurtling towards us, if we were occasionally given some sort of foreknowledge, some kindly warning, how much pain and suffering would we save ourselves and everybody else? But life, as your mother has told you on many an occasion, Rohit, is not easy-peasy, ji. And, having taken that leap into the unknown, one just has to make what one can of it. There's nothing anyone else can do to help.

Can we feel sorry for Rohit, then, as he leaves Tracy's flat staggering down her cracked cement stairs to the taxi carrying a suitcase heavy with the toys he and Tracy bought for the children from Hamleys the previous evening? Especially as he misses a step because of his stupid, bloody blurring vision, nearly entering the taxi through the window, head first? Do we have it in our hearts to feel our own panic rise along with his as we think of how he will be able to face everyone back in Delhi?

And what of the poor, pink-faced, essentially kind-hearted Tracy, of whom our last glimpse is a small, forlorn figure in a nightshirt and dressing gown, standing at her window, a piece of tissue clamped to her quivering mouth? Wouldn't it be cruel not to spare her a kindly thought as she turns, sniffling, to face her empty little flat once the taxi has pulled away from her door? Her small flat, shorn once again of all its comforting manly clutter, suddenly seems very large indeed. With no razor on the washbasin, no Imperial Leather soap melting softly by the bathtub, no XL T-shirts hanging next to her minuscule ones in the cupboards, no one to yank his trousers off, throwing them willy-nilly on to the kitchen counter in his hurry to put his arms around her at night, in fact, no one, no one at all.

14

A Delhi-type denouement

Even as AI 002 has started its descent to Indira Gandhi International Airport, Rohit's strategy is not very well prepared. While other passengers leap up, pulling out large pieces of hand baggage from the overhead lockers and ignoring the air hostess's voice crackling dire warnings to people who do so, Rohit stares out of the window hoping desperately inspiration will strike. Outside, Delhi is approaching at a terrifying approximate speed of 200 miles per hour. Already he can see tiny cars and houses and the spaghetti system of roads. Above the aeroplane is a thick puffy layer of cloud that seems to be cheerily signalling to him that all escape routes are hereby closed. Around him, inside the aircraft, there is the excitement of homecoming, of gift-giving, the anticipation of rupee garlands and mouthfuls of laddu. The excitement is so great that the air hostess finally has to dispense with her crackly mike and emerge to roundly berate a few people intent on maiming their fellow-passengers with heavy pieces of hand luggage. She shakes her head apologetically at a few bemused white faces and smiles at Rohit as she passes him, clearly appreciating that at least some Indian passengers know how to behave properly, thank God!

As the aircraft lands, Rohit gets up along with everyone else and begins milling out of the aircraft wanting, for some inexplicable reason, to swat the back of the head of the man in front of him. Bloody talkative man, kept on about his new media company all through the bloody flight. Then there was the air hostess coming around with those chilled beers and then dinner. All through the bloody flight there was just too much happening around him for Rohit to be able to concentrate too hard on exactly how he will face Neena and what he will say. Or, for that matter, the children. Or even his parents. Rohit feels his knees buckles slightly at he imagines the expressions on all these faces if he makes a slip and mentions over the evening meal where he stayed while in London. 'Edgware Road, Edgware Road,' he practices, chanting softly to himself as he approaches the immigration desk. 'Edgware Road,' he says to the immigration officer who asks him, looking at his passport, where he normally resides. It takes another five minutes before he can convince the suspicious young man that he really meant to say LM Road, Delhi, but was thinking of something else altogether.

He feels faint again, five minutes later, as he leans on the steel trolley, dizzily watching the carousel move bulging suitcases around and around like some kind of mad, taunting playground dance. He imagines it written all over his face, for all to see. All the salacious little details of his guilt that Neena, and possibly his mother, and maybe even Rinku will probably spot straightaway. The only people who will probably miss it completely are the baby, Tarun and Jagdish. Tarun and the baby, because they are always completely concerned with their own affairs and Jagdish because he lives and breathes business. Rohit suddenly remembers that he will soon have to think up some convincing reasons to present to Jagdish if he wants to go back to London again before too long. He looks at the customs officers standing in a huddle at the entrance of the green channel, inwardly begging them to stop him so that he can spend a little more time in the safety of the terminal, but they carry on with their banter, barely aware of all these suitcases they really should be checking. Rohit considers taking down their names and reporting them for shamelessly shirking their duty, but he walks on, half-heartedly wheeling his trolley. Feeling ready to vomit, he finally walks down the corridor and into the waiting area.

'Pappaaa!' He hears them before he sees them, squinting as he scans the sea of faces in the swirling evening darkness. The crowd seems to be swaying as one body, held away from him by the cordon that keeps, for some mysterious reason, the travelled and the untravelled apart. Suddenly he spots Neena's smiling face in the crowd. She is holding Ritik up, pointing out his papa out to him while he dribbles blankly, looking more Mannyish than ever. Rinku, below and getting a better view through trouser legs and salwar bottoms, slips under the cordon and heads determinedly for her father, throwing herself headlong into his stomach in a rush of curls and frills and flashing pink pants. Momentarily winded, Rohit picks her up and buries his face in her dark, sweet-smelling curls, wanting to burst into loud, wailing tears. He is still carrying a chattering Rinku as Neena approaches. As she gives him a huge hug with a loud whoop, he is careful to keep Rinku's small person between them. It makes him feel less crummy, somehow, that their two children are squashed and wriggling in between them as they embrace.

'Hello, baba!' Neena cries, using an old endearment. 'Good trip?'

'Yeah, great,' he mumbles in reply.

'We all missed you here,' she continues to chirrup happily, 'didn't we, babloo?' She gives a little shake to Ritik, who has only just worked out who this vaguely familiar looking man is and is now giving Rohit the full benefit of his toothless smile.

Rohit puts Rinku down to take the baby off Neena and, as he does so, it comes to him in a flash. The question he had been asking himself intermittently and half-heartedly through the flight. The question of whether to bare his breast and tell all or play it safe. The question of whether a wrong can be righted by a shamefaced confession. For some reason, what had appeared so fuzzy on board the flight is now crystal clear. As Rohit follows Neena to the car, with his baby son in his arms and his small daughter skipping happily alongside, it is suddenly as clear as a bell. There is nothing to be gained by trying to be bloody honest now, is there? What has happened has happened. Neena obviously hasn't spotted any giveaway traces on his face. It is all in the past now. What is to be gained by bloody upsetting everybody, hanh? As Tracy so judiciously declared, 'Wot one doesn't know can never 'urt, can it?'

■

Rohit congratulates himself for making his very wise decision when Neena tells him in the car about the events in the Sachdev household while he was away. She is filled with breathless excitement, telling him all the gory details, even though she was not present to see most of them. 'And then Ma just hit the roof! . . . then Tarun gave her as good as he got, for a change . . . somebody has to tell her these things. Hats off to Tarun! . . . can you imagine, the poor Menons just got up and walked off—what an insult! . . . and Papa will not speak to anybody at all after that.'

By the time Rohit walks through the carved front door of Sachdev Mansion with his bags and suitcase, he has not only exonerated himself completely for his own crime, but has thumped himself a few times on the back in a silent, self-congratulatory exercise. He is starting to feel almost smug. At least he didn't descend to shouting matches with his mother. Nor storm out of the house, taking a car, threatening to return only for his clothes. He, Rohit, has always done his duty, no one can deny that. Tarun has always got away with this and that, just because he is three years younger. It's not fair, is it? Life's just not fair. Those who do their bloody duty are the ones who always suffer.

But Rohit is determined to continue doing his bloody duty by the looks of it. He walks into his mother's room and puts his arms around her weeping, heaving frame as she collapses into him. She is wailing and only a few words emerge coherently, distorted completely by long drawn out sobs. 'Beta . . . I said no-othing, really! . . . How can my bay-bay-baby . . . just go like that! . . . What a chudail she must be to have hi-i-im go running to her! . . . You are all I have left!' Rohit murmurs soothingly, stroking her back, while Neena scowls from the door.

Rohit lowers his mother gently down on to her bed and covers her with a sheet. He tells Neena to put a few drops of eau de cologne into chilled water, so that she can dab her mother-in-law's forehead with a handkerchief dipped in it. Neena scowls some more, and noisily thumps around Swarn's cupboards looking for a handkerchief with very poor grace. Leaving her to it, Rohit goes off to sort out his father. Where would his whole family be if it wasn't for his steadying influence, huh?

He finds Jagdish locked into his study. Jagdish is, as is now his wont, stark naked. It is as if he has gradually and with deep relief discovered a kind of womb-like comfort in this dark, airless room. Rohit follows his father into the study, too preoccupied with other things to question the nudity, only vaguely noticing his father's sagging brown bottom with some surprise. When did it age, he wonders distractedly, not remembering that he hasn't seen it for at least twenty-five years.

Jagdish sits heavily on his swivel chair behind his desk and lets out a long breath, heavy with sadness. 'Have you seen your mother?' he asks.

'Yes, she's okay. I've left Neena with her.'

'Neena told you everything?'

'Yes.'

Jagdish sighs again, remembering the look on his younger son's face as he left the house. 'Tarun has not come to the office either. I thought he might at least turn up there today.'

'Have you any idea at all where he might be?'

'I thought you might know. Is there any friend he might stay with?'

Rohit shakes his head. 'No, unlikely,' he says.

'Your mother thinks he might be with that girl, Gayatri.' After all his earlier struggles to remember her name it now seems to be etched in Jagdish's mind indelibly.

'No, according to Neena, Gayatri hasn't seen him since then either. And doesn't want to, by the sounds of it.'

Jagdish sighs again. Rohit is sure he is imagining it, but his father's eyes have a funny sheen to them, almost as though a stray tear might have emerged from some long forgotten duct. He feels strangely moved himself as he realizes that this is the first real crisis that has hit his small family. Whatever their inadequacies they are a nice family, he thinks to himself. Suddenly he wants to see his brother again and put his arm around his shoulder and play a game of squash with him. He feels strange waves of relief overcome him as he remembers London and Tracy. They seem so far away now, both that busy, unconcerned city and the girl with the bright golden curls and piercing East End voice. And no longer so desirable, funnily enough, with distance. Thank God he didn't make any commitments or give her the Delhi address and telephone number in some silly unguarded moment! In the distance he can hear a phone ring. As he gets up, he reaches out over the desk and puts his hand on his father's shoulder. He pats it, feeling the fluffy white hair that has sprouted there in recent years.

'Don't worry, Papa,' he says, 'I'm back now. I'll sort it all out. You can depend on me.' Feeling incredibly moved himself at these magnanimous words, Rohit turns to leave the room, wiping an eye with the back of his hand.

At the door he turns to nod reassuringly at his father again and see him casting about frantically for some piece of clothing on which to blow his nose. He finds nothing close at hand and grabs at a piece of blotting paper. As Jagdish trumpets loudly and tearfully into it, Rohit asks, 'Why, Papa, are you not wearing any clothes?'

Before Jagdish has time to find a reply, however, Neena enters the room, red faced. She is brandishing Rohit's mobile phone in her hand. 'For you,' she says icily. 'Some woman called Tracy. Says you stayed with her in London.'

■

When the world shatters, you cannot make sense of it unless you pick up the pieces individually to examine them. Later you may try placing them together in the way they were meant to be. Generally, of course, the exercise is hopeless. But look at them separately you must, if you want to make any heads or tails of it all.

■

In London, Tracy puts her phone down and gazes out of her window. 'Bastard,' she mutters, 'just like the rest of 'em. And that phone call musta cost a bomb too. "My wife never answers my mobile." Ha!' Tracy waggles her head in what she thinks is an Indian manner as she mimics Rohit's accent. She had thought he might have been different, like. He'd seemed nice, buying her that big bottle of expensive perfume, dinner at that lovely Indian restaurant, Delly Nights in Covent Garden. Course, she knew he was married and all, but, just for a moment there, she had wondered . . . ain't a girl allowed to some dreamin', eh? And she'd only called to make sure he'd got to Delly safely. She certainly meant no 'arm. And 'ow was she to know who the silly cow was that 'ad answered the phone? It wasn't even as if she'd said anything incriminitting, like, jus' that 'e'd stayed with 'er (which didn't 'ave to mean anything, did it?). And she's only said that because that silly cow'd been so bloody persistent, not because she'd wanted to get 'im into trouble or anything. There was no need for him to be so crabby, like. So snarly and nasty and 'orrid. Just like all the others, once they'd 'ad their fun—Brit, American, Paki—they were all the same, at the end of the day.

Poor Tracy wasn't to know, of course, that Rohit had taken the call with his wife glowering red faced and his father looking on, naked and open mouthed. In fact, so surprised had Jagdish been that he had not even thought of covering up his nether regions in the sudden and angry presence of his daughter-in-law. Her anger was fortuitous in that it had also prevented her from noticing her father-in-law's nakedness behind his desk, intent as she had been on hearing what exactly Rohit had to say to this woman with whom he had so clearly been shacking up in London. Hadn't taken him long, had it? To go and find himself some kind of English floozie to cook and clean for him. And God knows what else too! As this thought occurs to Neena (just as Rohit is clicking his phone off and wondering where to plant his gaze), she rushes out of the room, shouting more or less the same profanities that Tracy is using for him in faraway London.

Rohit dashes after her but makes it only to the top of the stairs when she slams the bedroom door shut, locking it with a firm click. 'I can explain!' he shouts hoarsely, as many a good man before him has unsuccessfully done. But the door remains resolutely closed, and Rohit can only hear a new muffled wailing emanate from the depths of his bedroom. He is losing track of exactly how many wailing women he has had to deal with in the course of the day so far.

Savvy old Jagdish, nobody's fool, doesn't take long to work out what has probably happened. He too can hear Neena's wails from where he is sitting, and, as they mingle together with Swarn's from down the corridor, it is as though a crazy caterwauling has been set off to drive him just stark staring paagal. Something has to be done. This is no time to be namby-pamby any more. He gets up and strides out of his room purposefully, still forgetting that he has no clothes on.

Swarn, blissfully unaware of this latest event, is still in a state of disbelief about her younger son's antics. She just cannot believe that her beloved little Tarunbeta can have walked out on her like that (especially to go to some awful girl). She continues to lie prone on her bed, wailing up at her ceiling whenever she remembers some of the terrible things that witch had made her darling beta say to her. Tarun would never have said any of those things without that chudail-girl telling him to say them—that she knows for sure. Periodically she wrings out the handkerchief and places its icy wetness over her forehead and her eyes. Tomorrow her best features (eyes and nose) will be all puffy, she thinks in alarm, but even that thought cannot stop big round tears from sliding down her cheeks. 'Where is that stupid girl, Neena?' she wonders, feeling her ire rise again. 'She was supposed to be here comforting me. Rohit had told her to do so. See, how disodedient these modern girls are, ji!'

The door is suddenly pushed open without ceremony. Swarn screams loudly as, in the doorway, is the figure of her husband, stark naked. 'Hai, what a time to want sex, silly man!' she thinks to herself furiously. Tucking the sheet under her chin in a determined effort to preserve her chastity, she hauls herself up and roars, 'What are you doing, ji! Here I am dying of sorrow, and all you can think of is this! Are all men jaanwars and animals, hey bhagwan, that the cure for all problems should lie in the sexual act!'

Jagdish does not have the faintest idea what she is talking about as he steps in and closes the door behind him. 'Stop shouting, you stupid woman!' he growls. Swarn blinks in alarm, lovely brown eyes round like saucers. Jagdish has never called her a stupid woman before. For that matter, he has never told her to stop shouting before either, his normal course of action at any crisis being a sensible and silent exit.

She decides she has probably misheard and reverts to her normal blasé self. 'Have you gone mad, ji?' she asks. There is no genuine concern for this possibility in her tone of voice, merely annoyance that, if indeed he has, he has chosen a most inopportune moment to do so.

Jagdish advances a few steps towards the bed, and Swarn cowers under her sheet, only her brown eyes showing,

more puffy than lovely today. Something is not right. She
has never seen that expression on Jagdish's face before, his
eyes so red, his big bulbous nose quivering, his *thing* (*baaprey!*)
now all erect and shiny. 'He has gone mad!' she decides,
feeling a tiny frisson of fear travel down her spine. 'He has
gone mad, and now he wants to rape me, hey bhagwaan!'
'Rohit!' she calls out weakly. 'Where has the boy gone? And
his stupid wife! Aren't they supposed to be somewhere here
looking after me?' Swarn wonders how quickly she will be
able to leap out of the other side of the bed if Jagdish
advances towards her any more. But Jagdish has stopped
advancing and is now standing at the foot of her bed,
swaying slightly. His voice is thick as he starts to speak.

'Rohit!' he says sneeringly, 'you are wanting Rohit to
come and rescue you! Fine one he is to try and help anyone
else now!'

'My son, Rohit, what have you done to him?' she screams,
recovering her earlier voice.

'It is not what I have done to him, you stupid, stupid
woman,' Jagdish cries, now openly weeping himself. 'It is
what he has done. No, but you . . . you . . .' Jagdish waggles
his hands, losing his flow for a few seconds before starting
up again, 'you cannot see how either of your sons is capable
of being bad. In your mind, it is only I who am like that. I
have never claimed to be perfect, ji, but there are things,
there are things, Swarn, that I have never done. Never. In all
my years with you, you stupid, ungrateful woman. Have I
ever received any thanks for that, have I? But your sons!
First, your Tarunbeta tells you what he thinks of you. That
was only the start, Swarn, Now just go upstairs and just take
a look at what your pyaara dulaara beta Rohit has done.'

'What . . . what . . . what has my Rohit done?' Swarn
squeaks, real fear gripping her for the first time. She knows
it must be pretty serious as she realizes, in a sudden rush of
terror, that she has never seen Jagdish cry before. Tears are
now coursing down his face. His nose (the one whose
bulbous-ness had almost ensured Swarn against becoming

Mrs Jagdish Sachdev) has turned a vile shade of maroon.

Before Swarn can repeat her question, Jagdish answers her, now wailing himself, his deep guttural bellows making a tragic parody of the earlier high-pitched female wails that had filled the house. 'I will tell you what he has done,' he says, 'I will tell you! Your darling son, you know, your wonderful, pyaara pyaara beta, Rohit . . .' Swarn nods rapidly, eyes still wide open, willing Jagdish, forcing Jagdish, begging Jagdish to get to the bloody point, ji!

And Jagdish does. 'Your son, ji,' he says, his voice lowering and becoming thick with sorrow, 'your bloody-fool son Rohit has gone and done,' he breaks off at this point while a hoarse sob escapes his throat, 'he has done some hanky-panky, ji. With a firangi! In London! So! Are you happy now?'

Swarn, whose expression can be described as anything but happy, falls back on to her pillows in a swoon. Jagdish, having delivered his announcement and with no thought for reviving his unconscious wife, turns and walks out of her room in search of a pair of underpants.

■

In the meantime, over at Saket, Tarun has just completed his seventh unsuccessful attempt at making contact with Gayatri. Since the Menon visit to Sachdev Mansion, he has only managed to speak to her once on the telephone, on which occasion she had clearly told him that she did not want to see him any more. As he has, in previous relationships, understood this to sometimes mean the complete opposite of what it states, he persists in trying to be seen. He has already run most of the normal gamut and is now running out of ideas. He has lurked behind trees, hoping to jump out at her as she leaves the house. He has stood forlornly in the pool of light under a lamp post, slapping away insects, hoping she will see him from her window and come flying out into his embrace. He has called her, using many different voices (even what he imagines is a British accent), but he has been found out each time.

On this latest occasion, he manfully marched up her path and rung the bell. Girls sometimes like the direct approach, he knows. But it was Keshava who opened the door and asked him to leave. Tarun could tell that he was unhappy, at least. That was faintly heartening, but he would really rather have seen that sorrowful expression on Gayatri's face instead. In fact he'd have quite liked just to see Gayatri's face. To find out exactly how much she must really be missing him. To exult in her pale and wan expression, to rejoice in the dark shadows under her eyes. On the telephone, unfortunately, she had sounded plain angry. Very angry. Then, she had started to explain that she really did not think they were meant for each other in the first place. What was the word she had used? Incompatible! Tarun, who has never liked words of more than three syllables anyway, finds this one particularly jarring. Later in the conversation, hope had quickened as she had started to sound tearful. But then she had started to warble on about some Michael person in England. Her voice had gone all funny, and the line had crackled as she said this, so he couldn't quite make out what she was saying. Who the hell was this Michael person now? It was all very worrying.

∎

Inside the Menon household, the argument is over. Keshava found himself lined up against wife and daughter in a last-ditch effort to save the Tarun-Gayatri relationship. But it hadn't lasted long. Even he knew, deep down, that it was a lost cause. In fact it was probably a very bad idea to proceed any further. 'What to do, eh Raji?' he had asked. 'Better to let it go,' she had replied philosophically. 'After all, Gayatri is still relatively young. Luckily she also has above-average good looks.' (This was about the furthest point Raji would allow herself to rise to with regard to complimenting her own daughter's looks.) 'She will find someone who will be more suitable, both for her and for us.'

Spoken with confidence, Raji, spoken with enviable confidence. How is it that even a woman of science, with a rational, intelligent mind, can make such sweeping pronouncements? Of course it is our hope that Gayatri will soon meet someone more compatible than our Tarun with the floppy lock. And that Tarun too will find someone who uses words less long to make his own life easier from now on. But we know that all it will take is another blind turning, another futile screeching of wheels, before the inevitable happens again. Before the bits, the smithereens of two lives, go flying up into the air, glinting and catching the light, only to descend again and lie as scattered fragments in the sand, until someone bothers to sweep them up. To attempt piecing them together, just to remember how it had all looked before.

But for now we shall have to leave the lovely Gayatri ruining her above-average good looks with floods of tears as she lies on her old bed. It is hard to tell who it is she is crying for—Tarun, Michael, the man she cannot seems to find, the general state of her love life—she barely knows which herself. All she does know is that despite a Ph.D. from Oxford and the job of professor of English, Department of Humanities, Jawaharlal Nehru University, it is still a bloomin' love life she seems to crave. She almost cannot believe her own stupidity, her own pusillanimity. She remembers how Tarun looked blankly at her once as she had used this word and the memory leads, mysteriously, to a fresh flood of tears.

■

A short distance away, Kammy and Manny are sitting down to dinner in their Sainik Farms dining room. It is a rare evening of calm, unheeding of distantly brewing storms.

'Aha! Dum aloo!' Manny sniffs appreciatively as he raises the lid of the casserole dish.

'Yes, I got it made because I thought Neena and Rohit might drop in tonight. It's Rohit's favourite dish,' Kammy replies, ladling out a portion on to Manny's plate.

'The flight must have been late,' Manny mumbles through a mouthful of steaming dum aloo.

'They'll come tomorrow I suppose,' Kammy says, 'Neena has her aerobics session too. Rohit will probably come and pick her up after her aerobics from here. Ooffo, keep some of the dum aloo for them, Manny. Don't guzzle it all.'

Vain guesses. Sad hopes. Neena will come, but without Rohit. Then Rohit will follow, but Neena will not go with him. But wait! Is it really that sad? If Neena can transform herself suddenly into the free-spirited, unafraid feminist Kammy has always wanted her daughter to be . . . if for once, just once, she is not led by one or the other of the men in her life into making major decisions . . . if she has finally woken up to the fact that her life has a potential all of its very own, not linked necessarily to husbands or fathers or children . . . and if she does with her marriage what her own mother (Kammy Singh, chairperson of Seva, general do-gooder, first-rate feminist) could never bring herself to do in her own very incompatible marriage, would that be such a bad thing? Would it, Kammy?

∎

For, if we were to return at this point in time to Sachdev Mansions, we would find a crimson-faced, weeping Neena, wiping tears and snot off her face with the back of her hand, throwing clothes willy-nilly into a suitcase. She is leaving. For good! This is it! Why does she have to put up with all this nonsense when her parents will have her back any time, hanh? In fact, her father will probably kill Rohit for doing this to her. And a jolly good thing that would be too. And maybe she can finally go off and do a Ph.D. or something. Something for herself for a change. 'Rohit—ace cad,' Neena mutters clicking one latch of the suitcase down furiously. 'Rohit—horny bastard,' she says, doing the other side and breaking a vermilion fingernail in the process. 'Horny, bloody, stupid bastard Rohit Sachdev!' she cries, sucking her finger and putting the nail carefully away in her pocket. 'If he thinks I'm leaving even my nail behind, the bloody, fucking bastard's mistaken!' With this she hauls the suitcase off the bed and staggers towards the door.

Rohit looks up in relief as the door swings open. He is still perched on the top step, head in his hands. 'Neena!' he cries joyously on finally seeing her.

There is no similarly ecstatic response. Instead, a stony-faced Neena staggers past him, knees buckling under the weight of the suitcase.

'Neena, darling, where do you think you are going?' Rohit asks even though it is eminently clear where she is headed.

'Home,' she says, not letting him overtake her on the steps.

'But this is your home, darling,' he says, attempting to grapple with the suitcase handle from behind.

'Fucking, bloody, stupid, get your hands off my suitcase,' is the unfriendly response. It has taken mere minutes for Neena to enter the realm of yours and mine so familiar to separating couples. Your house, my suitcase, your life, my life . . .

'My Safari!' she reminds him, picking up the keys to the car presented by her father with such fanfare at their wedding just a few years ago and jangling them under his nose. He tries to grab them back, but she dances out of his reach as she reaches the bottom of the steps and puts the suitcase down with an angry thud. 'Nek Singh!' she bellows for the driver.

■

Nek Singh and Moolchand have heard and seen the night's events through a chink in the kitchen door. They have put two and two together and reached the approximate figure of 400.

'It is those people who came to visit. It is their curse,' Moolchand pronounces morbidly, wishing now that he had not glared quite so sullenly at that sahib in the drab polyester shirt. You never knew who had the powers of witchcraft these days ...

'I think that they had something to do with Tarun Sahib's departure, yes,' Nek Singh replies, scowling with the effort involved in making this deduction. 'But what is all this between the sahib and memsahib, eh?'

Moolchand furrows his brow. All this thinking is giving him a headache. 'Give us a beedi, bhai,' he says. As Nek Singh passes him one reluctantly, he lights up and pulls deeply on it. Life's mysteries always seem a bit clearer when viewed through a cloud of acrid beedi smoke. 'The sahib and the memsahib—my feeling is that the poor memsahib has never had a good life with the sahib.'

Nek Singh contemplates the state of Swarn's life. It seems like a bloody good life as far as he can see. He has never liked the memsahib very much. Not since she publicly rebuked him once in the middle of a crowded Connaught Place car park for failing to notice that she had left the shop and neglecting to go darting across with the car to pick her up in three seconds flat. 'Do you think the sahib will leave her?' he asks hopefully. 'I saw the sahib pulling out a suitcase from the garage a while ago.'

Moolchand ponders this possibility. It is not a bad thought. It is, in fact, a most cheering thought. Maybe, just maybe, if the sahib were to leave, it might—just might—make the memsahib view him through new eyes. Moolchand has it on excellent authority that these rich memsahibs who live on their own sometimes turn to their drivers and cooks for companionship. You know, just friendship and things like that, nothing more than that. But Moolchand's thoughts are far from platonic as he feels a stirring in his pyjamas. Of course, he would then be in direct competition with Nek Singh for the memsahib's attentions. He looks at his old friend, who is grimacing while trying to suck on the last millimetre of his beedi. 'Monkey features,' Moolchand thinks with satisfaction. 'Arrey, no contest at all!'

Their camaraderie is broken by a loud bellow from within. 'Nek Singh!' Neena's voice flies into the kitchen with ear-splitting ferocity.

'Ji!' Nek Singh cries, leaping to his feet, quickly stubbing the glowing beedi in fright. He leaves the kitchen in an obedient trot, leaving Moolchand peering curiously into the darkness of the house after him.

■

Outside, in the lobby of Sachdev Mansion, all the lights are on and pandemonium reigns. Neena thrusts the suitcase at Nek Singh, ordering him to put it in her Safari. Rohit pushes him away, telling him he will be out of a job if he dares to do any such thing. As Rohit and Neena glare at each other like horn-locking rams separated only by the diminutive, trembling figure of Nek Singh, Jagdish emerges from his room, fully clothed and carrying his own, smaller suitcase. He is off to County Castle Motel near the factory. He needs a few days to clear his head, he has decided. To decide what to do next. For too long has he put up with things silently, ji. Now it is his turn.

As everyone breaks off to stare at him, a new figure appears at the front door, also carrying a suitcase. It is Tarun whose floppy lock looks like it is badly in need of a wash. His suitcase carries the label of the County Castle Motel from where he has only just checked out himself. They all break out into conversation.

Neena: 'I am leaving.'

Rohit: 'You are not leaving.'

Jagdish: 'Yes, you should not be leaving, beti. I'm leaving.'

Neena: 'Why should you be leaving, Papa? This has nothing to do with you.'

Tarun (plaintively): 'I don't understand it. I thought I was the one who had left.'

Jagdish (sarcastically): 'Yes, but now you're back.'

Rohit (angrily, because he has to take it out on someone):
'Yes, what a time to choose to come strolling back in, hanh?'
Neena: 'Well, I'm telling you now, I'm not coming back.'
Rohit (to Neena and not to Tarun): 'Darling, of course
you'll come back. How far can you go without me?'
Neena: 'Just you wait and see, sonny! Ha!'
And with that she pushes past him. Clambering into the
back seat of the Safari, she suddenly remembers something
she forgot in her agitation. 'The children,' she says, 'sleeping
with the maid downstairs!' For a moment she looks confusedly
out of the car window. She knows the effect of having just
stormed so dramatically into the car (her car) will be
diminished somewhat if she merely storms out again. She
makes a quick decision, regaining her composure to correct
herself. 'My children. Tell Lily to get my children ready in
the morning as usual. My mother will come and collect them
for me.' She taps Nek Singh on the shoulder. 'Chalo, Sainik
Farms,' she says, her snot-covered face looking almost
dignified in the darkness of the back seat.

As they watch the Safari disappear down a nearly empty
LM Road, Tarun turns to Rohit, a look of awe on his face.
Even he knows that what happened between him and Gayatri
has faded into nothingness by comparison to this.

'What on earth is going on, Rohit?' he asks. 'Why has she
gone? Haven't you only just come back?'

Rohit sinks on to the polished marble step of their foyer.
'Crumbs, crikey, Gordon Bennett!' he cries despairingly,
'Tarun, help me to sort this bloody mess out, please!'

'What is it, what has happened? And who the fuck is
Gordon Bennett?'

'Nothing happpened, Tarun, I swear! Well, nothing that
meant anything, anyway. It was just an accident, yaar, just a
bloody stupid accident!'

The sound of another car starting up reaches their ears.
They watch as their father sweeps out of the gates in his
grand old BMW.

'And what about him?' Tarun asks. 'What's he leaving
for? Is it a part of the same accident?'

Rohit's reply is drowned in the roar of the powerful car as Jagdish revs it up and takes off down LM Road in his first-ever bid for freedom. He cannot even remember when he last drove a car himself. Tonight he doesn't need Nek Singh. He doesn't need his good-for-nothing sons. Most of all, he doesn't need to put up with his sullen, sulky, unloving wife. He presses a button by his side and, as the window rolls down, he can feel Delhi's night breeze blow pleasantly through the scanty hair that is left on his head.

■

Moolchand has also watched the sahib drive off from the safety of the kitchen window. He cannot believe his luck. It has finally happened. Maybe now his fortunes will start looking up, hey bhagwaan! After all, every dog must have his day, he tells himself gleefully as he walks slowly up the backstairs that lead to his minuscule servant's quarters. Closing the door behind him and taking care to latch it, he lies down on his bed and takes a deep breath. What a day it has been, baaprey! And, now that it has ended the way it has, who knows what joys the morrow will bring. He imagines the memsahib waking up alone and then pouring out her woes to him when he takes in her morning tea. He will think up some wise and wonderful things to say to her by way of comfort. He will think them up tomorrow though. Right now, he is too tired to think. One needs to be fresh in body and armed with a beedi to think.

But now for his standard bedtime ritual, without which he has learnt that sleep simply will not come. Loosening the string of his pyjamas, he clamps his hand over his shrivelled penis and closes his eyes tightly, closing out the dirty walls and the lone curling calendar on the wall. He imagines himself in some silken boudoir instead. And conjures up those lovely features in his mind as he starts to move his wrist up and down. Those eyes . . . that nose . . . that lovely, sulky mouth . . . all that creamy flesh bursting out of her sari

... on top and below, this side and that, bouncing and jouncing, bobbing and throbbing, quivering and shivering ... hai, hai, hai ... it is too much, it is too much, it is too much ... Moolchand's bony frame judders in agony and in ecstasy before he falls back again.

He can feel the customary tears as he opens his eyes and finds himself back on his small, smelly bed. Love! What do all these rich people know of love? This is love, he wants to tell them, this silent, distant, devoted thing. For how many years now? Ten? Fifteen? What does it matter? The important thing is, he has loved too. Oh, yes, however mistakenly, however accidentally, Moolchand (of District Farookabad, sixty-seven last autumn, professional cook of average talent, never married and now never likely to) has, for nigh on fifteen years, loved (yes, loved) Swarn Sachdev (née Malhotra, of Civil Lines, Delhi, wife of Jagdish Sachdev, mother of two fine sons, mah-jong player, society lady, good wife). For fifteen years Moolchand's silent love has allowed him no peace, no sleep. Now, at the thought of what new promises tomorrow might bring, he can feel his poor old heart quicken and knows it will be yet another sleepless night.

■

For now, though, pull away from Moolchand, alone on his semen-stained sheet. Fly out of his window and into Delhi's dark, silent night. The city is trying to fall asleep below, lights are going out one by one. A million windows are darkening, melting into oneness with the night. Behind some are lovers, reaching out for each other in the dark; behind others are broken hearts (Neena's, Gayatri's, Rohit's, Tarun's and many, many more). Behind some lie people together but apart (Kammy, Manny, to name just two). Behind others are those who will lie alone but who could have never been happier for it (Jagdish Sachdev being a fine example of that tonight). Behind yet others are some people who are really quite alone but not even aware of it yet (spare a thought for poor swooning Swarn Sachdev who will rise in the morning to a brand new life).

■

As Jagdish's BMW approaches Country Castle Motel, his spirits are still high. He cannot believe he has finally found the courage to do exactly as he feels like doing, without worrying about his wife and children, without being concerned about what other people think. Wah ji, he congratulates himself, suddenly remembering with a chuckle all those things he said to Swarn earlier, things lain unsaid for so many years, cluttering up his head. He will get to this motel place, take off all these sweaty clothes, have a nice long bath and after many many months, have a really good night's sleep—not wearing any clothes, ji, not even underwear. Jagdish lets out a low, heaving sigh at the thought of this final treat.

He pays no heed to the music that is playing on the car radio—some English station that one of his useless sons must have tuned into earlier. The orchestra is now rising as one, soaring into the Delhi night as the voice of Luciano Pavarotti belts out its operatic warning to the world. Jagdish still does not hear it as the towering voice warns, sadly, wisely, 'Nessun dormah . . . nessun dorrrrmaaah'—none shall sleep, oh, none who loves shall sleep.